AT • POINT • BLANK

A SUSPENSE NOVEL

Virginia Stem Owens

BAKER BOOK HOUSE
Grand Rapids, Michigan 49516

Copyright © 1992 by Virginia Stem Owens

Published by Baker Book House

Second Printing, June 1992

Library of Congress Cataloging-in-Publication Data

Owens, Virginia Stem.
    At point blank : a suspense novel / Virginia Stem Owens.
        p.   cm.
    ISBN 0-8010-6752-9 (paper)
    ISBN 0-8010-6724-3 (cloth)
    PS3565.W576A94   1992
    813'.54—dc20   92-11716

Published in association with the literary agency of
Alive Communications
P.O. Box 49068
Colorado Springs, CO 80949

Scripture references are from the King James Version.

Acknowledgments

Special thanks go to my friend Doug Duncan for his technical instruction and equipment demonstration. I also thank Harold Fickett and the Milton Center for encouragement and the suggestions which have made this a better book than my efforts alone would have produced.

CHAPTER • ONE

I F YOU GROW UP IN WATSON COUNTY, you eventually see enough dead bodies to get used to them, at least the way they look after Holcombe's Funeral Home gets through with them. Open-casket funerals are what people expect here—except for Episcopalians and Catholics. But I had never seen a body actually loaded up and carried away in the hearse before. What surprised me most was how slight Miss Mineola seemed when the mortician and his assistant grabbed the body by the feet and armpits, lifted it from the bed, slipped it onto the gurney, and covered it with the sheet. Her diminished weight left hardly a print on the mattress, and the bedsprings barely creaked as they lifted her. A little shower of hairpins, used Kleenex, and other sickbed debris was all she left behind.

Mineola Magillberry was considered a woman of substance in our little community. She had outlived three husbands—a school superintendent, a musical instrument salesman, and a minor executive at Texaco. Before she married any of them, she'd put herself through the Somerville Normal School while serving as the only teacher at the Point Blank one-room schoolhouse. In between the salesman and the Texaco man, she had been a buyer for Neiman-Marcus, commuting between Dallas and New York. But most important, during her ninety-four years she had bought and sold the biggest part of Watson County. Nevertheless, her earthly remains were as light as a dried weed.

Miss Mineola's sixty-seven-year-old niece Cecelia, who lives in the little brick house across the road, had tried to make her aunt look presentable for the undertaker. The long, bony hands were folded over the shrunken stomach and her shell-pattern sweater was pulled neatly down under her back. Cecelia had closed Miss Mineola's eyes, but she couldn't get the mouth to shut all the way.

As the two attendants wheeled the body out through the door onto the east verandah, Cecelia pulled pale reddish hairs from the comb she'd just used on the dead woman, wadded them into a ball, and dropped them into the wastebasket beside the bed.

"You won't forget her teeth, will you?" she reminded the mortician. "She's always been particular about people seeing her without her teeth." She might have been getting the old lady ready for a social call instead of sending her off to the funeral parlor. But then Cecelia's taken care of Miss Mineola for years.

Cecelia Ramsey had been my mother's best friend in Point Blank, which is nothing more than a wide place in the road about fifteen miles east of Somerville, the county seat. A hundred years ago, Point Blank had been the most thriving town in Watson County, thanks to the railroad, but all that's left of it now, other than the post office, is a filling station with a faded Esso sign out front and the Point Blank Baptist Church. My mother didn't have much in common with the people in Point Blank, and I'd always been grateful to Cecelia for being her friend. I don't know how I'd have gotten through the long year of my mother's last illness without her, and since then Cecelia has treated me like a member of the family.

That's why she called me when she discovered Miss Mineola dead that afternoon. She said she'd already called the sheriff's office, but she couldn't find Lois anywhere.

"I thought you all might have gone somewhere together since Lois's car is in the driveway. Maybe she went for a walk."

Lois is Cecelia's daughter, and I've known her as long as I can remember, though we'd never been close friends. Lois didn't have close friends in Point Blank. She was valedictorian of our class in high school and left us all behind when she went away to college out of state. But when she came back to go to graduate school in Houston—Miss Mineola's stipulation for footing the bill—Lois started calling me up on those occasional weekends she came home. We'd go to the movies or out to eat at the Mexican restaurant in Somerville. Lois likes margaritas, even if she was raised a Baptist.

I told Cecelia I'd see if I could find her, and then I closed up the Water Board Office—which is really just what used to be our dining room. I checked the post office and the filling station first, then stopped by the church and let the preacher know about Miss Mineola's death. I hadn't really expected to find Lois at any of those places. When she goes for walks, it's not to Point Blank but across the pasture or along the back roads. I drove slowly on the way out to Miss Mineola's, thinking I might spot her. I figured the best way I could help Cecelia out was to be around to keep Lois company.

Not that Lois would need much consoling. There was no love lost between her and her Aunt Min—they were too much alike, both of them headstrong and obstinate. But she might want someone around she could talk to. Lois and her mother aren't that close either. Not that Cecelia doesn't try. Anyone in Point Blank will tell you Cecelia Ramsey is a saint.

When I came in through the back door of Miss

Mineola's big old ramshackle white house, I found Lois already there in the kitchen, talking on the telephone. She looked up and made a face which I took to mean something like "Isn't this the pits?" or "Can you believe this?" Then she turned back to the phone.

"Just let him know, that's all," she said. "His sister. That's right. There's no need for him to come at this time. We haven't even set the day for the funeral yet."

I could tell she was talking to Miss Mineola's sister-in-law out in San Antonio. Miss Mineola only had one surviving sibling, Larry Laudermilk, a ninety-year-old brother who had figured out early on that there wasn't enough room in the same county for him and his sister both, unless he wanted to end up one of her hired hands or dependents—like Cecelia's father.

"Here at home, yes. Died in her sleep. I know it's going to be a shock." She made another face and waved me on into the living room, where Archie, Lois's cousin, was sitting on the sofa, trading stories with the deputy sheriff who'd been sent to accompany the body to the morgue.

I slipped into the high-ceilinged front bedroom from which Miss Mineola had watched the world go by on the dirt road. From there she could also keep an eye on Cecelia's little house, sitting across the road like a five-acre island in the sea of Miss Mineola's pasture that stretched away to the woods on the horizon. As I came in, Cecelia was explaining how she'd found her aunt's body to the justice of the peace who'd come along with the deputy to certify the death.

She interrupted her recital as soon as she saw me, and held out her arms. I hugged her and kissed the top of her white cloud of hair. "I'm so sorry, Cecelia," I said.

"It was a blessing, Beth Marie," she said, squeezing my hand.

The j.p. nodded to me and then looked back at Cecelia, who continued her story.

"I'd just gotten back from town," she said, bobbing her head for emphasis the way she does when she's winding up for an unedited version. "I was bringing her groceries in the back door. I looked at the kitchen clock as I came in and saw it was one-thirty. She wanted me to go to three different stores, but I'd already gotten so flustered trying to redeem those coupons she saves from the Sunday paper—though half the time it's for things she doesn't even use, like that Weight Watchers yogurt. She doesn't even eat yogurt. Anyway, I decided to come on back home. I was supposed to go to the bank too, but I had the nursery to get cleaned up at the church before services tomorrow."

The j.p. frowned and cleared his throat noisily.

Cecelia broke off, fluttering her hands around her face. "I'm sorry. My mind seems all discombobulated. Anyhow, I came in the back door and was just putting two sacks down and getting ready to go back out to the car for the rest when I heard a noise. Sort of a bump. I stood there a second trying to decide whether to go get the ice cream or check on her first. She'd been by herself for over an hour while I was in town, although she would have sworn it had been all day. She just didn't seem to have any sense of time. She sometimes gets up in the middle of the night and wants her breakfast."

The j.p. tapped his pencil on his clipboard.

"I'm sorry," Cecelia said again. "Well, anyway, when I heard the noise I decided I better go check on her. I didn't want her falling out of bed, and I figured the ice cream would get hard again in the freezer by suppertime. It's about all she'll eat anymore. As soon as I came around the corner from the stairs, though, I knew something was wrong. I just had this feeling. You know how you get a feeling sometimes? Sure enough, there she was, all curled up in a little ball on the bed."

She paused, frowned, and tilted her head to one side as though she wasn't quite satisfied about something.

Then she shook her head and looked down at her hands. "I guess I shouldn't have left her alone at all. But she hadn't been feeling that bad. At least not any more than usual."

"Now, Cecelia," I put in. "She was very old. It could have happened at any time, whether you were here or not."

"I know. But for her to be by herself. That's what I hate. If I could just have been here with her. I always worried she'd be scared when the time came."

The j.p. made an indistinct murmuring noise and stuck his pencil back in his pocket. "Well, I put it down as around one o'clock. I guess that's as accurate as we can be, considering." He paused a moment, frowning at his clipboard. "One more question, ma'am. Did the deceased have any medical problems?"

"Congestive heart trouble. And emphysema. She had to take oxygen several times a day." Cecelia's face brightened momentarily. "I guess that explains the noise I heard. When I came in, the oxygen tank was laying over on its side." The frown returned. "Do you reckon she could have been struggling for breath and knocked it over, trying to turn it on? That's all I can figure. But she looked so peaceful when I came in here, all curled up in a ball."

The j.p. looked around. "Where is it now?"

"The oxygen tank? I moved it out onto the east porch so it would be out of the way when you all got here." Cecelia stopped and then added in a gently instructive tone, "She was ninety-four years old, you know."

"Yes, ma'am. It's just for the records." He stood up. "I thank you, ma'am. I know this is a real trial for you."

Cecelia looked up wide-eyed and shook her head. I knew she was going to say something about how death is just a highway to heaven, so I squeezed her hand hard and spoke up first. "She's going to be just fine. Thank you so much for your kindness."

The j.p. nodded and left through the living room,

tearing off a form from his clipboard to hand to the undertaker, who was anxious to get started on his job.

So Cecelia and I were the only ones to watch as Miss Mineola left her earthly home forever. I nudged her little dog Teensy out of the way—he'd taken up his position at the foot of the bed—and the mortician and his assistant, followed by the deputy, wheeled the body out the bedroom door onto the screened-in verandah, navigating between the old freezer and boxes of empty Mason jars, and lifted the gurney down the steps and into the waiting hearse. With no more ceremony than that.

Cecelia put her arm around me as we watched and said cheerfully, "All flesh is grass, Beth Marie." You never know with Cecelia whether she's actually aware of the seriousness of a situation or if her religious convictions, which are more thoroughgoing than most folks', give her a different perception of reality.

Not being able to come up with an appropriate biblical quotation myself, I started picking up the pins and tissues and cough drop wrappers Miss Mineola had left in her wake. A blue jar of Vicks salve tumbled from the bedspread as I flipped it back to cover the exposed mattress. Bending down to retrieve the jar, I saw something else caught between the springs and the bed frame, a long notebook or ledger. I pulled it loose.

"Look at this, Cecelia," I said, holding it out to her.

"Oh, my goodness!" she cried, taking it eagerly. "Can you beat that? I've been searching all over this house for that notebook. It disappeared a few days ago—was it last Wednesday?—and I haven't been able to find it since. Aunt Min kept everything in here, you know. She was getting so forgetful she had to write everything down."

Cecelia blew the dust off the ledger and started thumbing through the pages. "She all but accused me of hiding it, and here it was all the time. I'll be. She must have forgot where she put it."

Her exclamations had brought Archie to the door.

Archie is Miss Mineola's great-nephew who lives in a trailer house out behind the barn and works the night shift as a guard over at the state prison farm. All the Laudermilks aren't as brainy as Miss Mineola and Lois, but at least they're average. All except Archie. Some people in Point Blank think maybe as a teenager he burned out his brains with drugs. Cecelia says maybe he suffered brain damage at birth. But then that's Cecelia's standard excuse for everyone with what Lois calls "aberrant behavior." Cecelia had even thought Nixon was brain-damaged. But secretly, most people in Point Blank attribute Archie's denseness to his mother's people. They're Hawaiian.

Hattie Laudermilk, unlike her sister Mineola, only married once. But like her, she only had one child. However, it had the advantage of being a boy, while Mineola's was only a daughter. Hattie's son had been sent to the Pacific in World War II, and when the war was over, he decided to stay and settle down with a native woman. He must have known he could never bring her back to Point Blank, at least not in that day and age. Some people even speculated that's why he married her, so he wouldn't have to come back.

Anyway, as the years went by he had a whole string of what Hattie called "little half-breeds." After Hattie's husband died, she went to visit her son and his family for the first time. I suppose either her religion or her curiosity finally got the best of her. She brought back pictures of them, along with a collection of long muumuus that she took to wearing around the house. She wanted to wear one to the community Thanksgiving dinner at the church once, but Miss Mineola wouldn't hear of it.

The photographs Hattie brought back from her trip showed that her son had grown enormously fat and morose-looking. But his Hawaiian wife was smiling, surrounded by their five stair-stepped children, all with black hair and eyes.

"Are they just real dark?" Miss Mineola wanted to know.

"Sort of walnut-stained," said Hattie.

But the pictures Hattie saved for last were of her youngest grandson. He had big round dark eyes, and his hair curled all over his head like a dusky cherub. That was Archie.

Hattie was obviously much taken with the youngster and started a campaign to bring him to Point Blank. She tried everything, even appealing to Miss Mineola's missionary spirit, but it wasn't until 1960 that her sister finally relented.

Miss Mineola's change of heart has been attributed to various causes. For one thing, Hawaii had just become the fiftieth state, so the boy could no longer be considered, strictly speaking, a foreigner. Then, too, Kennedy had just been elected president, and Miss Mineola was convinced the Catholics would be taking over the entire country soon. Hattie assured her the boy was not being raised as a Southern Baptist over on that faraway and cosmopolitan island. If Miss Mineola could contribute only one more Baptist in the battle against the Pope, Hattie argued, it was her duty to do so.

Actually, though, I think the two old women were getting very lonely there in that big house, and the thought that they were the last of the Laudermilk line weighed heavy. One brother had produced only female progeny—Cecelia—and the other, Larry out in San Antonio, none at all. The Laudermilk name seemed destined for oblivion.

Then Miss Mineola's daughter Vivian died of breast cancer at forty. Her husband, a lawyer, was killed in an automobile accident two years later. Miss Mineola's two grandchildren—a teenage boy and girl—were left unconscionably well-provided for. The two old ladies hadn't enough leverage to get either of them to change their name to Laudermilk. Thus Archie seemed their only hope for carrying on the family name.

Not that his name was Laudermilk, of course. Hattie had married a man named Sherpanine during the Depression, a railroad conductor with a steady job. But the Sherpanine name was a mere technicality, easily remedied. What mattered was that Archie was a boy. So they wrote to Hattie's son and offered to bring Archie to Texas to go to high school and then to college. On the condition that he would change his name to Laudermilk.

What they didn't know was just how hard it would be for Archie to make it through high school, much less college. Nor how incredibly handsome he would turn out to be by the time he finally loped across the stage to receive his high school diploma. The dusky cherub became a full-grown seraphim, with dark liquid eyes and a strong olive brow framed in crisp tendrils. But Archie's beauty was, unfortunately, only skin deep.

Intellectually, he's a lost cause. Not that he's retarded or anything, despite Cecelia's fears. He's just plain dumb. Easily distracted. And, above all, lazy. What got him through, not only high school, but every other difficult situation, was his superb ability to mimic. If you were to meet Archie at a party or some social function, just casually, you'd think he was a stockbroker or a sociologist or something. He picks up people's intonations, phrases, whatever jargon is current, and repeats them flawlessly. And he has an uncanny way of knowing just who it would be profitable to imitate. He never imitates a service station attendant or a construction worker, for instance. Which makes you wonder if maybe he's not so dumb after all.

He managed to keep his grandmother fooled to the day she died. He had her convinced that it was only racial prejudice that kept him from doing well in school. At first Miss Mineola went along with that too. But after he'd gotten fired from three jobs in a row—jobs like delivering pizza and taking tickets at the movie theater and selling coupon books over the phone for the Somerville Jaycees—she began to wonder if she hadn't bought herself a pig in a poke. Still, he had the Laudermilk name by then, and there was nothing she could do but keep on being responsible for him.

Archie's also got a terrible temper. He's like an eternal three-year-old. If he doesn't get his way, he throws a tantrum. I've seen him break off the head of a water hydrant with a hammer when he couldn't get it to turn on. He only manages to keep his temper under control if there's someone around he wants to impress. Like Miss Mineola. She never would put up with any nonsense.

Archie went from job to job after high school till there was no place left for him to work except the prison farm. The prison system is Watson County's biggest employer. We've got six regular units of the state correctional system here, plus the farm. You see the gray and blue uniforms of the guards all over the county. Since the crime rate started going up in the sixties and the oil business bottomed out in the eighties, prisoners have been our only growth industry. Right now, if it weren't for prisoners, there'd be a lot of people going hungry in Watson County. And Archie would be one of them.

At the moment, however, he was shifting from foot to foot in the doorway of Miss Mineola's bedroom, looking considerably more somber than when he'd been joking with the deputy a few minutes ago.

"Oh, Archie, honey," Cecelia said, looking up from the ledger and smiling at him, "I know you must be grieving, but just remember Aunt Min's a lot better off now that she's gone to be with Jesus."

"She was always better off than me," Archie muttered under his breath.

"And look what Beth Marie found, Archie," Cecelia said, holding open the ledger. "Aunt Min's notebook. And here I thought it was lost."

Archie scowled at me and then nodded his head. The

discovery obviously meant less to him than to Cecelia.

Lois came in through the doorway to the verandah. "Hey. Who unstuck the door out here? Why'd you let them go out this way, Mother? Through all this junk. It's embarrassing." Then she saw the book Cecelia was holding. "What's that?"

"Aunt Min's notebook. You know how she kept account of everything in it."

"Let's see. I bet there's all kinds of juicy stuff here." Lois took the ledger from her mother's plump pink hands and flipped through several pages. "Can you believe it? She was only paying Loomis ten dollars a day. No wonder he never got anything done around here."

"Loomis is over eighty, Lois," Cecelia said. "Aunt Min thought she was doing him a favor."

"Aunt Min never did anyone a favor that she didn't expect a good return on," her daughter said. "Look at this—this was a week ago. 'Call Southwest Securities to confirm offer. Tell Loomis to fix leak.' That upstairs shower is still leaking. Loomis never even touched it."

Archie's scowl grew deeper as she continued to turn the pages. "I don't think we should be—" he said and then broke off.

Lois looked up at him sharply. "What's the matter, Archie? You afraid there might be something about you in here? Let's see." She flipped to the last page where an entry had been made.

Archie made a sudden lunge for the ledger, but Lois was prepared and held it just out of his reach. "Here we are." She looked at her cousin mockingly. "These are like Aunt Min's last words, Arch. Don't you want to hear her speaking to us from beyond the grave?"

"She ain't in the grave yet. Give me that book," he shouted and grabbed for the ledger again.

Cecelia's eyes grew wide and her mouth fell open. "Now let's not—"

"It says," Lois went on, ignoring them both, "and I

quote: 'August 25. Talk to A. Call in note. Call B. about changing will.'" She closed the ledger with a snap. "August 25. That is today, isn't it, Arch? The day they'll put on the brass plaque down at the Baptist church? But I guess she never got to have that last little talk with you, did she? How sad for you."

She handed the book back to her mother but kept her eyes on her cousin. "I'm sure Bartholomew will want to see this, Mother. In fact, I'll go look up his number for you right now. Meanwhile, I suggest you put it in a safe place." She pushed past Archie and went into the living room where she started rummaging through Miss Mineola's desk, looking for the lawyer's number.

Archie glared after her, then turned and lunged through the doorway to the verandah. The outside door slammed after him.

Cecelia sat down on Miss Mineola's bed, all the starch suddenly taken out of her. "This is no time for family...for us to be—" She stopped and shook her head, as though she didn't even want to put into words what she meant.

I lowered myself cautiously onto the bed beside her and put my arm around her stout shoulders. I knew it should have been Lois in there comforting her mother instead of me, but that wasn't likely to happen. After my mother died a few years ago, Cecelia took over as her surrogate. She never forgets my birthday, and she brings cough medicine over when I get a cold. My own mother was a tall, upright woman who wore nylon stockings and tailored skirts every day of her life, even here in Point Blank. Cecelia is round and soft and wears a lot of pink polyester she never worries about getting rumpled. Her solicitude has meant a lot to me. I couldn't let her down now.

"Beth Marie, honey," she finally said, "would you slip out to the kitchen and get something for me out of my purse there on the counter? I think that's where I left it when I came in. Don't bring the whole thing. There's a card in the side pocket where I keep my keys. It has the number for Bartholomew's office and home phone."

"But Lois is looking for—"

She closed her eyes and shook her head. "She's not going to find it there though. Not the home phone number, and he won't be at the office at this hour. I need to talk to him right away."

I hesitated a moment. "All right."

"And Beth Marie, honey," she said as I started from the room, "don't say anything about this to Lois, okay?"

"All right. But don't you think you ought to lie down and rest for a while, Cecelia? On your own bed?"

"No. Not right now. The sooner I get this off my chest, the better," she said with a heavy sigh.

"Get what off your chest, Cecelia? What are you talking about?"

"A confession, Beth Marie. I have a confession to make."

CHAPTER TWO

THE MORTUARY HEARSE HAD just left when people started arriving. Some brought food; others just brought their condolences and curiosity. I was kept busy making pitchers of iced tea to serve the guests. Lois made a couple of trips to Archie's trailer to get ice. He had taken off for town after the ledger incident, but he has the only refrigerator on the place with an ice-maker.

The passing of its leading citizen had Point Blank buzzing. None of us knew then, of course, that Miss Mineola's death would soon be eclipsed by the news that Finney Blalock had escaped from the state prison farm.

Since Archie works there, he might have known about the escape, but he had come off his shift around seven that morning, and Finney wasn't discovered missing until the noon count. Then the prison officials kept it quiet until they had time to search the farm thoroughly. So it was midafternoon before the warden let the information out and almost evening before Terry B. Blalock, the Baptist minister, showed up to make the obligatory pastoral call on Cecelia, bearing the news that his son had escaped from the prison farm.

Finney Blalock is one of those people who give Point

Blank a bad name. When he killed that woman down in Houston a few years ago, every paper in the state carried it in their headlines. Poor Terry B.— I don't know how many reporters asked him how it felt to be a Baptist preacher and the father of a cold-blooded murderer. Finney's mother Harva shut herself up in the parsonage until after the trial, but Terry B. had to go on performing his pastoral duties. And I have to hand it to the people of Point Blank. They rallied around Terry B. and Harva. Even those who weren't Baptist.

Still, everyone knew Finney for a rotten kid, and no one in Point Blank ever doubted his guilt. Not even his own people. He was a few years behind Lois and me in school—closer to Archie's age—but he was always in trouble. People in Point Blank called him a typical preacher's kid, but really it went beyond that. He broke into the Palmer's barn once, I remember, and took their best saddles and tack. What wasn't worth his while to steal he took his knife and slashed. The Palmers weren't Baptist, and Terry B. had a hard time smoothing that one over.

Finney dropped out of school during his senior year and headed for Houston where there was more interesting trouble for him to get into. After a while, the word came back that Finney was living off some woman down there. He was a handsome fellow if you didn't know too much about him. He had a way of looking at women— well, some women—like a hungry wolf. According to the rumors, he'd gotten at least one girl pregnant before he left Point Blank.

Nothing ever satisfied Finney for long, though, and soon he got to messing around with a young girl about half the age of the woman he was living with in Houston. The girl's parents found out and were going to prosecute him for corrupting a minor. So what did Finney do? Murders the girl, of course. That way she couldn't testify against him. That's the way his mind worked.

He might have gotten away with it, too, if he hadn't gone into a bar over at Cut-and-Shoot one night and started bragging about how he got the woman he was living with to help him get rid of the body.

That was the final insult for Point Blank. If he had just gone to Houston and dropped out of sight, it wouldn't have been so bad. But he made the other woman help him stuff the girl's body into a cedar chest—her hope chest I suppose—and bring it back to Point Blank where they made a half-hearted effort to bury it down along a little branch on the far side of Miss Mineola's ranch where renters from town often dump their trash. But Finney never was much for physical labor, and they didn't bury it deep enough. We had torrential rains that spring that washed the sandy soil away and exposed the chest. Loomis came across it on his way to work at Miss Mineola's one morning.

The Blalocks finally gave up on Finney then, I guess. Anyway, Terry B. didn't put up any money for a lawyer, and his son had to depend on a public defender appointed by the court. Of course, the Blalocks aren't wealthy people, and they'd already gone into debt making restitution for their son's theft and vandalism. Some people said that Terry B. went to see if Miss Mineola would help Finney out, but she turned him down. She wasn't one to back lost causes. So Terry B. just gave up. He probably figured by then that prison might be the best place for Finney after all.

Of course, Finney didn't see it that way. The Watson County sheriff said that when they told him down in Houston that he was being assigned a public defender, he just went crazy and tried to tear the place up. They had to put him in an isolation cell. At the trial, after sentencing, he stood up and yelled at his father that he'd get out one way or another and when he did, Terry B. had better be prepared to meet his Maker. Terry B. just sat there with his head down.

My neighbor who goes to that New Life Temple over in Pinehurst tried to convince everyone that Finney was possessed and that we ought to all fast and pray to get the demon to come out. But I'd known Finney too long to give credit for his meanness to anyone else but him.

The folks who sat around Miss Mineola's living room that afternoon drinking iced tea while the air conditioner rattled away in the window had no idea that they were in for another dose of Finney Blalock. Their minds were on a happier topic: who would be Miss Mineola's heir?

They all knew why Archie had changed his name from Sherpanine to Laudermilk and why he stayed in Watson County. But, realistically, what were his chances? There was still Miss Mineola's own grandson Maximillian to figure in—and her granddaughter for that matter, though no one expected much competition from her. To Miss Mineola, Muriel had been a mistake, adopted when Vivian thought she'd never have a child of her own.

After Vivian died, though, Max and Muriel's attention to their grandmother had slacked off considerably. They both lived in Houston, which might have been on another planet instead of just seventy-five miles away. If they came to see her more than once a year I'd be surprised.

Muriel had been married and divorced a couple of times and was working as a secretary somewhere in Houston. What Max did was always a little vague to us. All we knew was that he traveled a lot, and on those rare occasions when he did show up in Point Blank, he wore his shirt unbuttoned halfway down his chest and sported a lot of flashy jewelry.

Their grandmother didn't approve of what they probably called their "lifestyles." They didn't go to any church, Baptist or otherwise. Money ran through their fingers like water. Their family ties were loose at best. But worst of all, land meant nothing to either one of them. In fact, they only saw it as a nuisance. You had to pay taxes on it, whether you made anything from it or not. And it required a lot of work if it was to put anything in your bank account, work of a kind they weren't used to and had no intention of learning.

So you can see it wasn't necessarily simpleminded of Archie to hang on there in Point Blank. Miss Mineola was constantly changing her will, especially right after Christmas or her birthday, but she always kept secret just who was going to profit from her death. Even Cecelia didn't know what Miss Mineola intended to do with her fortune, though she's the one who had to drive the old lady to Bartholomew's office in Houston every time she changed her mind. So Archie probably figured he had as good a crack at Miss Mineola's estate as anybody, at least as long as he stayed in Watson County. Even if he didn't get all of it, he was betting that his Laudermilk name would bring him something substantial.

Then, of course, there was Cecelia. Everyone in Point Blank thought that if anybody got Miss Mineola's money, it ought to be her. She had waited on the old lady hand and foot for over five years, ever since her own mother died in the little house across the road. Actually, before that she had waited on them both, and it was always a toss-up which of the two was more demanding.

Cecelia's mother, Miss Flora, wasn't ordinarily high-handed like Miss Mineola, but there was a long history of hard feelings between the two, going back to when Miss Mineola had managed to gain control of her brother's portion of their parents' homestead. Miss Flora was one of the most Christian women who ever drew breath, but her religion was sorely tried when it came to her sister-in-law.

I don't mean that they were open enemies or that they shunned one another's company. Two old ladies living across the road from one another out in the country can't afford that kind of long-term ire. In the end, each of them was all the other had. No one else shared the same memories and understood the world the way they still did.

Miss Mineola would hobble across the road every day, leaning on her walking cane and calling fussily to Teensy, her graying poodle that Cecelia had to take in to the groomer's every month. She'd rap on the screen door of the kitchen with her cane and call "Flora? Flora?" in a quavery voice. She made a great display of never coming into the house until she'd been asked. While she was waiting for Miss Flora to come to the screen door, she'd turn around on the step and scold the little dog loudly.

"No, Teensy, no. You know Flora don't allow animals in her house. Now you just sit out here and wait for me." And the little dog would whine and cry piteously the whole time Miss Mineola sat drinking coffee there in the kitchen.

"Hush, Teensy, hush. You'll be all right," she'd call out from time to time.

And Miss Flora, who wore her white hair in a knot on top of her pink head, would steadfastly ignore the whole show, as though it were beneath her dignity to participate in such a ridiculous scene. Once, Lois told me, Miss Flora suggested to her sister-in-law that it would be kinder to the animal and certainly less distracting to them if she would simply leave Teensy at home when she came to visit.

Miss Mineola had thrown her hands up in the air in exaggerated horror. "Heavens, Flora. What can you be thinking? Teensy can't bear to be separated from me. You know that. At least she can still hear the sound of my voice. And that comforts her, poor little silly thing."

Miss Flora's face had turned a brighter pink beneath her white hair, but she never relented and let the dog come in her kitchen.

Her sister-in-law, on the other hand, liked to debate for the devilment of it. She would bait Miss Flora about first one thing and then another. Causes for the rising crime rate in the cities. Going to Mexico for cancer cures. Whether Jesus fed three thousand or five thousand with the loaves and the fishes.

Most of the time Miss Flora refused to be drawn in. She'd either agree Miss Mineola to death or she'd act bored and change the subject. She knew this was only a game to Miss Mineola, whereas when Miss Flora got into an argument, she meant business. She was a hot-blooded, passionate type, like all her family, the McHenrys. And she knew she might end up saying something she'd regret, while Miss Mineola, who was only amusing herself, would never regret anything.

The only time I ever saw Miss Flora get drawn in was once when I was out checking her water meter. She and Miss Mineola were sitting in the kitchen drinking coffee while Teensy whined and scratched at the back door.

"I've just about decided to start sending my tithe to Jimmy Swaggart, Flora," Miss Mineola said.

"You what?" Miss Flora set her cup down so sharply she sloshed the coffee over into the saucer.

"Jimmy Swaggart," Miss Mineola repeated, sticking her sharp chin out defiantly. "Don't you ever watch him, Flora? I mean to tell you, he preaches the Bible. And he don't mind calling a spade a spade either."

"Mineola Laudermilk," (Miss Flora always reverted to maiden names when she was riled), "how can you think of such a thing? You know how our little church here has to struggle to make ends meet."

"But just think, honey. When you send your money there, it goes out unto all the world. Just imagine—all-l-l the world," and she spread her arms out in a gesture meant to indicate the global scope of her money's audience.

Miss Flora, who hated to be honeyed by her sister-in-law in the middle of an argument, went over to the sink and snatched up a dishrag to wipe up the coffee she'd spilled. "I can't imagine you a-doing such a thing, Mineola. That's just—why are you doing it anyway?"

"I told you, Flora. Television is the way to reach the unsaved these days. When Jesus said, 'if I be lifted up, I'll draw all men to me,' it might just have been a prophecy."

"Of course it was a prophecy. About the cross. What in the world are you talking about anyhow?"

"Just listen to me now, honey, and don't get so worked up. It might have been a prophecy about TV antennas. You know how they stick up in the air. Well, maybe he was talking about being lifted up on TV aerials. Or even satellites. He could have even meant satellites."

"Mineola Laudermilk, you have absolutely lost your mind."

And Miss Flora picked up her cup and took it to the sink, where she nearly wore off the pink roses and the gold rim washing it.

In her heart of hearts she probably figured, as I did, that Miss Mineola, knowing that the Point Blank Baptist Church had depended on her contributions for years, thought they needed a reminder about which side their bread was buttered on. But angry as Miss Flora was, she didn't intend to trust her tongue just then. So she went on scrubbing the coffee cup, and when she finished that, she set to work on the pot itself. Meanwhile, Miss Mineola sat there smiling and humming "Blessed Assurance" to herself.

As for Cecelia, I don't really know how much expectation she had of her aunt. For one thing, Cecelia is one of those people who always seem too good to be true. Her husband had been in the Philippines during the Korean War and had picked up a rare tropical fungus that gradually ate away his legs till he had to have first one and then the other off. They lived in Houston then, and

Cecelia became their sole support while he looked after Lois at home. As she got older and he got sicker, though, it was Lois who looked after her father in his wheelchair. Cecelia would get up early in the morning and tend to him and then trudge off to work for the telephone company all day in downtown Houston.

Anyone else might have been bitter, but Cecelia remained cheerful and thankful for whatever relief she got from time to time. My mother used to fret about how Cecelia's life had been ruined by a bad marriage. Her set speeches on her friend's unhappiness had a way of making me uneasy. I felt like they were meant as subtle little sermons on the dangers of marriage in general—though she ought not to have worried on my account.

Cecelia didn't talk much about her husband after he died in the V.A. hospital in Houston and she moved back to Point Blank. She did tell my mother that he'd given his life to Jesus during that last year, after which they'd been very happy together. But I guess she knew most people in Point Blank would doubt that made up for the years of misery she'd already gone through. And then everyone knows that Cecelia tries to protect everyone. The orneriest so-and-so in the county would be safe if his fate were left in her hands.

All Cecelia had to live on was her pension from the telephone company and Social Security. I don't see how she could have helped but wonder from time to time about what Miss Mineola might leave her. A little extra money in the bank to fix the well when it went out or maybe even to travel some—she wouldn't have turned it down. Everyone knew, though, that Cecelia would have taken care of Miss Mineola those last years no matter if she'd been a pauper.

So you can see it was a toss-up as to who stood to gain the most from Mineola Magillberry's death. The deacons from the Point Blank Baptist Church were no doubt hoping she'd made a substantial bequest to the church. Indeed, all of Point Blank knew their lives would be affected by how she'd decided to parcel out her estate. If the land went to Muriel and Max, it would go on the market immediately. Several of the ranchers were probably already considering how they might get in ahead of development speculators. If the land went to either Archie or Cecelia, the ranchers might get themselves better lease terms than Miss Mineola had given. Given Cecelia's soft heart and Archie's soft head, either one could probably be talked around. Whichever way it went, there were sure to be some changes in Watson County.

All afternoon I could see the callers stop and gaze out across the fields as they made their way back to their cars and pickups, already adjusting to the idea of getting along without Miss Mineola.

I don't want you to think they were harsh or unfeeling. It's just that in Point Blank we accept the inevitable with more ease than city folks. Cities are supposed to be where people are most broadminded. But in a little community like ours, where everybody not only knows everybody else but is probably related to them some way or other, that's where you've really got to be broadminded. You've got to live with the idea of having a preacher whose son is a mad-dog killer or a community leader who buys herself a namesake. And no matter how many disappointments or jolts life brings, you've got to go on getting up every morning and making the best of things. Because that's how life seems to be, all marbled and streaked with the good and the bad.

Maybe that's why people in places like Point Blank read the Bible and still watch sex and violence on TV. All that's just normal everyday life to them, whether it's David lusting after Bathsheba or J.R. lying and cheating on "Dallas." They know people are capable of just about anything.

Of course when Finney killed that girl, the Houston

papers tried to make it sound like Watson County was full of backwoods perverts. But don't try to tell me things are different in Houston. Folks are just as odd there as they are here. I know. I read the papers.

CHAPTER • THREE

I'VE SINCE WONDERED IF I HAD LEFT Cecelia at that point whether things might have turned out differently. Finney Blalock might still be alive, for one thing. But who knows what would have become of Lois. And as for me, well, I would have just gone on keeping the books for the Water Board and sending in my column about Point Blank events to the *Somerville Courier* week after week. Nothing would have changed for me.

I certainly wasn't expecting my placid life in Point Blank to blow up in my face as I watched Terry B. climb out of his '78 Chrysler after all the other callers had left that evening. My mother used to say that Terry B. reminded her of an irresolute rabbit. As he made his way toward the house over the parched grass in jerky little steps, the comparison came back to me. Terry B. always wears a black wool suit, summer and winter, with dandruff on the shoulders. He has some kind of nerve disease that makes his hands tremble and his head move around on his neck like a chicken's. Cecelia stood holding the back screen door open for him, and as he came in he took out a big white handkerchief, wiped the sweat from his forehead and neck, then carefully folded it so that a fresh side was out before he put it back in his pocket.

"I'm so sorry to hear about Miss Mineola, Cecelia," he said, taking her plump, pink hand between his own white, trembling ones.

"That's real sweet of you, Brother Blalock," Cecelia said, patting him like a mother comforting a child. "But it wasn't a complete surprise. And she'd lived a long full life."

His eyes filled with tears, and he pulled out his handkerchief again and blew his nose. "I know. Oh, I know that, Cecelia. It's just that—" He seemed unable to go on.

Cecelia took his arm and steered him through the kitchen into the living room, and I trailed along behind them. But Terry B. didn't sit down. He stood there in the middle of the room, looking around, as if he couldn't remember why he'd come.

"Finney," he finally brought out. "It's Finney. They say he's escaped. Oh, my goodness, Cecelia. What are we going to do?"

"What?" Cecelia and I said together, and Lois, who was sitting at the desk in the corner, looked up and frowned.

"Finney, he's gone. They discovered him missing at the noon count. They only called me a little over an hour ago. I would have been here sooner, Cecelia, but for that. His mother, well, you know—I couldn't leave her alone."

"Poor Harva!" Cecelia said, pulling him down on the sofa beside her. "Lois," she said over the preacher's bent head, "would you mind getting Terry B. some iced tea?"

Lois got up and went out to the kitchen without a word.

"They don't really know when he got away," Terry B. went on. "All they know so far is that he was still there when they cleared the count at five this morning." He took out his handkerchief again and wiped his forehead and his neck. "It could have been any time after that, I guess, though it seems strange that he would try to escape in broad daylight. Of course, they searched the grounds first. He could have been hiding somewhere on the farm, and they didn't want to let it out to the general public till they were sure he was gone."

Lois came back from the kitchen with the iced tea and handed it to Terry B.

"I know this is just heartbreaking for you," Cecelia said.

He patted her on the knee with his palsied hand and said meekly, "Here you are with your Aunt Min passing away and you're comforting me. I don't know what we'd do without you, Miss Cecelia."

"Do they have any notion where he might have taken off for?" she asked.

"Not really. The other men in his cell claim they don't know anything about it. But of course that's what they would say. It's been so dry lately that they didn't find footprints. They've got the dogs out. They reckon he probably went toward the river. That's how they usually try to throw the dogs off." He didn't need to add that the river lay in the direction of Point Blank.

Everyone looked down at the floor. It was an awkward moment. Even Cecelia's spirits seemed dampened.

Finally Lois picked up a tablet from the desk and pulled her chair around to face the sofa. "Well, we've got funeral arrangements to make," she said. "Let's get on with it."

"There's not much to do," Cecelia said. "Aunt Min bought one of those Guardian Plans some time ago. Everything's probably decided already, except for the time." She took off her glasses and rubbed her forehead. She looked very tired.

"Today's Saturday," Terry B. said, pulling a pocket calendar out of his coat pocket. "And you don't want to do it on Sunday. They charge extra then. Do you want to wait till Monday?"

"I'd like to get it over with as soon as possible," Cecelia replied. "It's always a strain on everybody till it's over with." She paused and tapped her fingers on her plump knee, thinking, then shook her head. "But I guess you're right. Uncle Larry will have to come from San Antonio. And tomorrow might be too soon for him to get here. And then there's Aunt Min's grandchildren."

"I haven't been able to get either Max or Muriel," Lois told her. "I just left messages on their answering machines."

"You didn't tell them about Aunt Min!" Cecelia put her hand to her throat. "Oh, dear, that's no way for someone to find out—"

"No, Mother. Of course not. I just said to call back as soon as possible, that it was urgent. Not," she added, "that they'll be exactly devastated by the news. It's been almost a year since either of them has been out here. But we'll hear from them soon enough. This is what they've been waiting for."

"Now, Lois," Cecelia said.

"It's true, Mother. You know it's true. Everybody does. They can't wait to get their hands on Aunt Min's money."

"Maybe they have slighted their grandmother," Cecelia said in a conciliatory way, "but they haven't tried to worm their way into her good graces. No one can accuse them of that."

Lois shrugged. "As usual, you try to put the best face on it, Mother. As far as I'm concerned, they've neglected Aunt Min out of laziness, not lack of greed. But they're still counting on the status of grandchild outranking that of a niece. Or nephew."

Terry B.'s face had taken on the openly curious expression of a child during this interchange. "How much money did she have anyhow?" he asked.

Lois looked at him sharply, but Cecelia, not seeming to think the question out of line, answered thoughtfully. "I'm not really sure just how much she's got in different savings accounts or CD's, although I do keep her checkbook for her. I don't think there's all that much in actual cash money. Aunt Min put everything into land. You know how she was about owning property. She always said she was land-poor. In fact, that's what she and Max had that falling out about a couple of years ago."

"Really?" Terry B. obviously couldn't help himself.

"When she bought the Harrelson place over by the river. Of course, it was cheap, considering what the land market is around here right now. But Max told her it was going to get even cheaper. He said she was just throwing her money down a rathole."

"That's one time I had to agree with Max," Lois said reluctantly. "Not that Aunt Min asked for my opinion."

"She told him land was the only thing you could be sure there'd be the same amount of when you sold it as when you bought it," Cecelia said. "Of course she never considered selling any of it, once she got it. She did like leasing it though," she added.

"It was the closest she could get to slavery in this century," Lois put in. "She loved keeping that option to renew or not every year. It gave her a sense of power."

"Lois," Cecelia murmured.

"Remember when she almost refused to renew Bud's lease on the Hoffhine's land that time? I thought Evelyn would die."

Bud and Evelyn Wylie were Miss Mineola's best friends. Bud's in his eighties, and Evelyn, his wife, is always trying to protect him.

"Well, it worked out for the best in the end. Bud was a real gentleman about it. He understood Aunt Min better than anyone, I guess," Cecelia said. "He seemed to know she enjoyed a little tussle every now and then. It made her feel alive."

Terry B. nodded, as though recalling past tussles of his own with Miss Mineola.

"The extra charge wouldn't be any problem," Cecelia said, switching tracks so suddenly that we weren't sure what she was talking about for a moment. "But I know you have so many other duties on Sunday that it wouldn't be practical. And with this other problem that's come up …" She let the sentence trail off delicately. "So I guess we'll say Monday. It can't be helped. I'll check with the people at the funeral home to make sure that's okay with them."

She stood up, so Terry B. had to get up too, of course, and that meant he had to start making noises of condolence and leave-taking. I think he would have liked to sit there a while in Miss Mineola's big old house and gossip about her land and her family and her funeral arrangements instead of going home to face what was waiting for him.

Ordinarily, Cecelia would have sensed this too and would have kept on talking and serving iced tea so he could stay as long as possible. But she seemed to have something else on her mind tonight, something besides the funeral arrangements.

While Cecelia was seeing Terry B. to the kitchen door, Lois started pacing up and down in the living room. She's one of those people who want to do something in time of crisis. It's hard for her to sit still and let events take their course. When she gets edgy, she starts playing with her hair—it's dark and thick—sweeping it up in back off her neck and jabbing a haircomb into it. Lois doesn't wear much makeup—she doesn't need to since she has such dark, dramatic features—but her one small vanity is her haircombs. She likes ornately decorated ones with mother-of-pearl or turquoise inlays—that kind of thing. My mother always called them her "gypsy combs."

"Let's go into town and have a margarita, Beth Marie," she said suddenly. We could hear Cecelia out in the kitchen washing up the iced tea glasses from all the callers.

"And leave your mother here alone?"

"She'll be all right. Archie's out there in the trailer. I saw him come back a while ago."

"But, Lois, what about your Aunt Min?"

She looked at me, frowning, two little vertical puckers appearing between her dark eyebrows. "What about her, Beth Marie? She's dead. And you know as well as I do that Mother's not any more broken up about it than the rest of us."

"But still. I mean—"

"It's not the thing to do? Good God! Who cares? I've spent my whole life beating my head against that particular brick wall. Do you think it matters what people in Point Blank—" We heard Cecelia coming through the dining room, and Lois broke off her sentence, glaring at me like a guilty child.

"Sweetheart," Cecelia said, coming in drying her hands on a cup towel, "would you mind calling up Holcombe's to see if we can have the funeral on Monday? You're so good at dealing with people. And if they say Monday's all right, could you call Uncle Larry back and let them know? And then, honey, if you'd just look in that upstairs closet where Aunt Min stored her good clothes and see if you can find her something really nice for the funeral."

Without a word, Lois sat down at the desk and started dialing. I've seen her be downright charming with other people, but with her family, especially her mother, she's usually brittle and abrupt, as if she wants to let them know they don't have any claim on her. Now that she had something to do, however, I knew she'd be satisfied to stay.

"Would you mind giving me a hand in the kitchen, Beth Marie?" Cecelia asked.

I followed her back into the kitchen where a row of iced tea goblets were drying on a cup towel spread over the old linoleum-topped cabinet. Cecelia put her arm around me, hugging me close to her round, soft side, almost like I was a substitute for the daughter she couldn't hug. She only came up to my shoulder.

"What would we ever do without you, Beth Marie? You're such a blessing." She took both my hands in her warm, damp grasp.

We could hear Lois on the phone in the living room. Cecelia lowered her voice almost to a whisper. "There's something I need to talk to Archie about," she said, "something I need to ask him. Would you mind going out to the trailer and getting him? Tell him to meet me out in the barn. It's something I don't want to bother Lois about."

"Sure," I said. I felt sorry for Cecelia, having to walk on eggshells around her daughter. If Cecelia wanted to see Archie without Lois around, that could only mean it was about something Lois wouldn't like. Lois couldn't abide Archie and could never understand why her mother helped him out of one scrape after another. I suspected that Cecelia wanted to see him about that ledger entry Miss Mineola had written on her last day. "Talk to A. Call in note." No doubt she wanted to get things straight with him in case there were any questions about it.

The dusk had deepened enough for the security light to come on out at the barn as I made my way down the path to Archie's trailer. Even after the sun goes down, the August heat slackens only gradually here, and I lifted my dress by the shoulders and shook it slightly to pull it away from my damp skin. A breeze would have felt good, but not a breath of air stirred. The river is only about a mile from Point Blank as the crow flies, and the humidity begins to climb as the air cools off in the evening. I wondered about Finney and if he'd made it as far as the river. It made me a little uneasy, going by the empty barn, but as I rounded the corner I could already hear Archie's TV. He's one of those people who turn it on the minute they walk in the door.

Archie's old Ford pickup was parked right by the pre-formed concrete steps that led up to the door of his trailer. My mother had always been of the opinion that anyone who'd drive up in their own yard was no better than white trash. Not that the pasture around Archie's trailer was exactly a yard.

I stopped a minute on the top step to read the note he had taped to the front door. It was curling and dusty and had obviously been there a good while. With a black felt-tip marker he had written:

ROBBERS, WE KNOW WHO YOU ARE! WE HAVE A BAD DOG WHO DOES NOT BARK, BUT HE DOES BITE! WE HAVE A NEIGHBOR WHO KEEPS AN EYE ON US & HE IS A GOOD SHOT! SO COME ON IN IF YOU DARE!

I knew Archie wouldn't have heard me coming with the TV blaring and the air conditioner running, so I peeped in through the little window set in the upper part of the door to see if he was properly dressed. I didn't want him coming to the door in his underwear.

But what I saw shocked me worse than that. Archie stood on the other side of the little bar that separates the kitchen from the living room. He was pulling a drawer out, as if he were getting a spoon to eat the bowl of ice cream sitting on the counter. He paused, as though to gesture in the middle of a conversation. Whoever he was talking to was sitting on the sofa at the far end of the trailer, so I moved to the other side of the little window to see who it was.

Then I screamed. I couldn't help myself. It was Finney Blalock.

I don't know what came over me. Ordinarily I'm pretty calm in emergencies. Maybe it was all that had already happened that day. And then the shock of seeing them there together.

When I screamed, both men froze. Time itself

seemed to freeze for a moment. I had a hard time getting my breath again. Then just as Finney turned toward the door, Archie's hand came out of the drawer. It wasn't holding a spoon, but a pistol. And he shot Finney. Right through the head.

CHAPTER • FOUR

OF COURSE, BY THE TIME THE sheriff got there —they didn't send just a deputy this time—Cecelia had the situation in hand. Neither she nor Lois had heard the shot from the house, nor my screams, I guess. But Cecelia must have already started toward the barn to meet Archie because I ran full tilt into her as I was coming around the corner.

"What in the world's the matter?" she asked, grabbing my arm.

"He's shot," I cried. "Archie's shot him!"

"Shot who, Beth Marie? What are you talking about?"

"Finney. Finney was in the trailer with him. And Archie shot him."

"Lord have mercy," she whispered. Then in a steadier voice, "Beth Marie, get ahold of yourself. You hear me? Go on back to the house and call the sheriff. Call an ambulance. And hurry."

"But you can't...don't..."

But she was already making her way over the sandy path to the lighted trailer. "Go on! Hurry!" she called back over her shoulder.

I ran on toward the house. It was easier right then to

do what Cecelia said than to try to think. The screen banged behind me, and I called out to Lois as I came in through the kitchen. I could hear her upstairs rummaging around, so I called the sheriff's office myself. The dispatcher said they'd send an ambulance immediately and contact the prison officials too.

I didn't call up to Lois again just then. I wanted to sit there for a minute and pull myself together. Every time I closed my eyes, I saw the picture of Archie talking to Finney right before I screamed. And then the picture of Finney's head jerking sideways as the bullet tore into his brain. Whether my eyes were closed or open, I could still see it.

A few minutes later I heard a door close upstairs. I went to the bottom of the stairwell and looked up at Lois who had one of Miss Mineola's dark dresses over her arm.

"You're not going to believe this," I said shakily.

She held up the dress for me to see. "What?" she said offhandedly. "Is Archie suddenly prostrate with grief?"

"No. He's shot Finney."

I figured this news would shock even Lois who tries to be so blasé about everything, but I wasn't expecting her to take it so hard. She dropped the dress in a heap and swayed for a moment at the top of the stairs. I thought at first she might actually fall, but she only sat down suddenly on the top step.

"Say that again," she said hoarsely.

"Archie's shot Finney. Out in the trailer. Didn't you hear the shot up there? Or me screaming my head off?"

"No," she said woodenly. "The windows are closed and the air conditioner's too loud to hear anything outside." She still looked so unsteady that I took a step up toward her.

"No!" she almost shouted, and put up her hand. "No. I'll be all right. It's just so…I can't take all this in." She took a deep breath and stood up again. "Just a minute. I'll be right down."

I went back into the living room and waited for her. I wanted her to hurry. As long as I was talking, I couldn't see the picture of Archie and Finney.

After a few more minutes she joined me in the living room. "Now then." She sat down beside me on the couch and pushed her hair back from her face. She didn't try to pat me or anything the way Cecelia would have. She still sounded shaky, but astringent, the way you expected Lois to sound. "Tell me what happened out there."

"The TV was on real loud, so they must not have heard me coming. I happened to look through that little window in the door before I knocked, and I saw them. Or at least I saw Archie. And I would have gone ahead and knocked except that—" I stopped here. The implications of what I had seen were just beginning to dawn on me. Archie, obviously, had known that Finney was there. He had been talking to him as though they were just having an ordinary conversation, not frightened or surprised or anything. Which could only mean that he had been hiding Finney there in his trailer.

I looked at Lois. Then I looked back down at the floor, my eyes tracing the old-fashioned pattern of roses in Miss Mineola's carpet. I didn't want to think about this anymore right then, but Lois was watching me intently.

"Except for what?" she said, leaning toward me. And I suddenly felt like things were closing in on me, things I didn't understand. I wanted a little time to sort out what I'd seen and what it all meant before I went any further.

"Except that Archie shot him then," I said, and covered my face with my hands and shuddered. "It was awful."

Lois sat back and gripped her hands together in her lap. "Well. Finney was an escaped convict. Archie was just defending himself." She took a deep, shuddering breath. "Maybe Finney was even holding him hostage."

I took my hands away and looked at her. She wasn't paying any attention to me now. She was staring fixedly across the room and almost talking to herself, as though she were trying different possibilities out in her mind. She stood up and started to pace up and down the room.

"Of course," she said. "That must have been it. Finney was already in the trailer when Archie got back a little while ago. He was hiding in the bedroom or something. Then he surprised Archie. Not exactly hard to do. But he didn't know that Archie keeps his gun in that drawer in the kitchen. And when he got a chance, Archie shot him. That makes sense. Right?" She looked over at me quickly, as though remembering I was there. "Doesn't that sound like what happened to you, Beth Marie?"

Right then I saw the flashing lights of the sheriff's car coming along the road. "Look! They're here," I said.

"Good God. How did they get here so quick?" she said.

"They must have already been in this part of the county searching for Finney. The dispatcher probably radioed them."

"I've got to get out there with Mother," Lois said, heading toward the back door. "For heaven's sake, Beth Marie, keep calm. They're going to be questioning you, you know. But just tell it to them like you did to me." The kitchen door slammed behind her just as the sheriff's car pulled into Miss Mineola's long driveway.

I sat there on the couch alone, feeling more confused than ever. The scene she had reconstructed here in the living room, though it seemed the most reasonable explanation, wasn't exactly what I remembered happening. Maybe Finney had been in the trailer when Archie got back. Maybe he had surprised Archie there. That was certainly possible. But from what I had seen, Archie sure didn't look like any hostage, and if he had been taken unawares by Finney, the surprise had certainly worn off by then. When Archie reached in the drawer, I would never have guessed that it was to get a gun to shoot Finney.

All I could figure was that when I screamed, he must have panicked. But, of course, I hadn't screamed until I shifted positions and saw Finney sitting with his elbows propped on his knees on the sofa. I hadn't seen any weapon near him. Then he had jumped and turned toward the door at the racket I made. And then…but that's the part I didn't care to call up again.

Lois hadn't gotten it quite right. On the other hand, I could see how her description would fit what would be the most logical explanation. An escaped convict, a known killer. A prison guard who knew the danger he was in. What else would anyone expect?

Still, it hadn't happened that way. If I had to speculate, I'd say it looked like the two of them were just having a friendly chat when I first looked in, and that Archie had no intention of shooting Finney when he opened that drawer. He really was getting a spoon for that bowl of ice cream sitting on the counter. It was only my yelling suddenly like a fool that had startled him so that he grabbed the gun without thinking and shot. That's what I thought.

But I didn't know just what I was going to say to the sheriff. Lois had seemed so certain. Maybe she was right. Maybe it had actually happened the way she said after all and I had simply misinterpreted what I saw—or thought I saw.

Whatever her faults, Lois was my friend. Despite all her education and her life in the city, I was certain I knew her better than anyone else. Even better than her own mother, who made too many allowances for people. I've always had this feeling about Lois—that she was more fragile than people thought, and not just because she was so slight and small. People who have that brittle look about them usually break easily. The soft ones, though they may get deflated here and there, are the resilient ones. And Lois is definitely not soft. That's why I didn't want to tell the sheriff much until I knew what it was that she had on her mind.

Looking back, I can see that this probably wasn't the wisest choice, but nevertheless, if I had it to do over— knowing no more than I did then—I would do the same thing again.

I was soon startled out of these thoughts, however, by a knock at the back door. The sheriff had sent his deputy to fetch me out to Archie's trailer. This wasn't the same good-old-boy deputy who had been there before swapping stories with Archie when they took Miss Mineola's body away. This one was tall and slim with a little fawn-colored moustache and blond lashes.

"Miss Cartwright?" he said, and I knew right away he wasn't from Watson County, "would you mind stepping out to the trailer with me? I know you've had a terrible shock, but the sheriff has some questions he needs to ask you."

"Of course," I said and stood up a little unsteadily.

He took me by the elbow solicitously. "Have you been left here all by yourself then? After what you've just been through? Here. Let me get the door for you."

I smiled gratefully at him.

Out at the trailer, though, the sheriff wasn't being solicitous of anyone's feelings. Cecelia was behind the kitchen counter trying to comfort Archie, who of course was carrying on like some kind of soap opera star. Lois was standing by the refrigerator, with her arms crossed and her back to everyone. Finney's body still lay sprawled in front of the sofa where he'd been sitting right before I knocked. The ambulance attendants had arrived too and were standing by the front door.

"Can't you see we got enough folks in here already, Norton?" the sheriff said as we stepped through the door.

"This is the lady you wanted to see, sir. Miss Cartwright." The deputy didn't seem intimidated by the sheriff's sharp tone.

"All right. Take her on into the bedroom back there." He waved a meaty hand toward the other end of the trailer. "I'll be with you in a minute, ma'am."

The deputy and I went back to Archie's bedroom, which, as I would have expected, was a mess. Dirty clothes on the floor. Magazines and beer cans littering the nightstand and dresser. The bed, of course, wasn't made. The deputy looked around the small space, trying not to show his disgust, and then twitched the bedspread up across the mattress.

"I guess you'll have to sit here," he said. "I've got to help the sheriff, but it shouldn't take long."

"I'll be fine," I said. I was glad he hadn't called me "ma'am" like the sheriff. Was Norton his first or last name? I wondered.

I could hear them talking through the thin walls of the trailer. The sheriff was telling the ambulance attendants, somewhat testily, that they couldn't take the body before the coroner got there.

"And can you get him to shut up a minute, ma'am?" He must have been talking to Cecelia then. "I need to ask him some questions."

I heard Cecelia making indistinct noises, trying to get Archie to pull himself together, and then Lois's sharper voice came through clearly. "Come on, Archie. Stop being such a fool. Just tell the sheriff what happened so we can all get out of here. Finney, he must have surprised you. And you shot him to protect yourself. Right? Now stop your blubbering and tell the man."

"Ma'am, if it's all the same with you," this was the deputy's voice, "I think the sheriff would like for him to tell it in his own words." I noticed he called her "ma'am."

Cecelia murmured more urgently, and I heard the

sheriff swearing not quite under his breath. "That's all right, Norton," he said wearily, "if he doesn't want to tell us here, we can always take him down to the jail and hear it there."

Archie's sobs began to slow, for all the world like a child that's getting over a scolding.

"You do work for the prison, don't you, son?" the sheriff asked. "This kind of thing can't be all that much of a shock to you then, can it? Seems to me like your reaction is just a little bit excessive."

There was silence for a minute, and then I heard Archie say, his voice still shuddering, "It was just like she said. That's the way it happened."

"Fine. But why don't you tell us in your own words now?" Archie repeated almost exactly what Lois had said.

"That still leaves us with a few details to fill in though," the sheriff said. "When did you get back to the trailer here after going into town?"

"I don't know. I can't remember exactly."

"The television was going," I heard Deputy Norton say. "Can you remember what show was on?"

"No. No, I can't," Archie said quickly.

"A half hour," Lois broke in. "It couldn't have been more than a half hour before Beth Marie came out here. I'm sure of it. I was making telephone calls and saw his truck come up the driveway."

There was a long pause. Then the sheriff spoke again. "All right. So we'll say half an hour. So what happened when you first got back? Did you see Blalock right away? Was he hiding? What?"

Silence again. If Archie was making something up here, I knew it was putting an awful strain on him. Not that lying was anything new to him, but extemporaneous invention under pressure would certainly tax his capacities. I heard a crash, like something heavy falling to the floor, followed by a collective gasp.

"Oh, I'm sorry," I heard Lois say. "I didn't see that sitting there. Here. I'll clean it up." There was the rustling of what sounded like paper towels and water running.

"Yes," Archie said after a couple of minutes, a little less quavery now. "He was hiding. In the bedroom. I didn't know he was here at first. I came in and turned on the TV. I didn't hear anything else."

"I see. And then what?"

"Well. He came in and—"

"Where were you sitting?" the deputy asked.

There was a pause. Then, "In that chair there. That swivel rocker. I had my back to the doorway, see?"

"Go on."

"He came up behind me and stuck something in the back of my head—I thought it was a gun—and said not to move or yell or anything."

"And then?"

"Well, he just stood there for a while, and I didn't move or anything because I didn't know what he might do. I mean Finney has a reputation for being crazy—"

"You knew who it was then?" the sheriff asked.

"Well, I figured. I mean, he was the one that had escaped. And, yeah, I guess I recognized his voice."

"All right. Go on."

"I just sat there, and then I guess Finney got tired of standing so he went around and sat on the couch. He told me he wanted me to help him escape. He knew the dogs would track him here eventually. But after a while I began to suspect that maybe he didn't have a weapon after all, even though he kept his hand in his pocket like he was holding one. So I asked could I go to the kitchen. I hadn't eaten all day. I keep my gun in the drawer there, and I thought maybe I could get it out before he could notice. And about then there was this scream out on the front steps. It scared us both, I guess. That's when I grabbed the gun and shot him. I didn't know what he might have done and I wasn't taking any chances."

"Got all that, Norton?" the sheriff said.

"Yes, sir."

"All right. Well, ladies, you can take him on up to the house now if you want to and get him calmed down. We have some more work to do here right now. But we'll be wanting to talk to him again before we leave."

After they left, I heard the deputy talking to the sheriff in a low undertone. I couldn't make out what he was saying, but I heard the older man's reply. "Now listen here, son. Don't go making matters complicated. The prison people, they want their escaped convict back and we got him for 'em. That's all they're going to care about. And it's going to make us look good, finding him before they did. It don't matter to them that he's dead. This bozo here did the best day's work he'll ever do, getting rid of him. I can see he ain't too bright, and this Blalock character might've even talked him into helping him get away. I wouldn't be a-tall surprised. I don't know exactly how he come to kill him. Maybe they got in an argument or something. But I don't intend to inquire too closely into the matter neither. It's nice and neat like it is, and I for one would just as soon it stayed that way."

Deputy Norton said something else, but I couldn't hear what it was. The sheriff spoke again, sounding a little irritated now. "Well, look, why don't you go on in there and get that lady's statement. That'll give you something to do. I see the coroner coming now. We'll take care of things out here."

I only had time for a quick look in the mirror over the dresser before the deputy came in. Fortunately I'd put on a halfway decent dress before I came out that morning, but my makeup had faded a couple of hours ago.

He came through the doorway, filling up the entire frame for a moment, with the light behind him. I moved over—there was no place else to sit—and when I did, my hand slid over something scratchy under the rumpled bedspread.

"Sorry to keep you waiting so long," he said and sat down. The mattress sagged in his direction.

"That's all right." It came out sounding more breathless than I had intended, and I swallowed hard. I could hear the sheriff conferring with the coroner on the other side of the wall. The sheriff's voice was loud, but the other man only mumbled his replies.

"I know this can't be pleasant for you, so I'll try to make it brief." The deputy flipped open the pad in his hand.

"No, that's all right. Really."

"I guess we could use a little light in here," he said, and reached across me to turn on the lamp on the bed-side table.

When the light came on, I could see he had little freckles on the backs of his hands and the hair on his forearms was reddish gold. "Let's see now," he began gently, "do you have any idea what time it was when you got here to the trailer?"

"Well, not precisely. It was just getting dark though. Everything had been so confused up at the house, you know, with Miss Mineola dying. The people from the mortuary had come and gone. And Cecelia and Lois were trying to contact all the family members and make arrangements for the funeral. I stayed to help." My voice sounded better now.

"I see. So. What were you doing out here at the trailer?"

I felt the blood rising along my neck, and my hand closed over the prickly object under the bedspread.

"Mrs. Ramsey sent me," I said quickly, suddenly breathless again.

"For what?" He was writing something on his pad.

"I don't know. That is—" I stopped, trying to sort through my memory. This was getting complicated. "It was something to do with the funeral, I guess. She wanted to know if Monday would be all right with him."

He smiled encouragingly. "I see. Why didn't she just call down here? There's a phone, isn't there?"

I took a deep breath. My mind was racing. Why was I doing this? Why didn't I just tell the truth—that Cecelia had sent me to tell Archie to meet her in the barn? "The line was tied up. Lois was calling relatives."

Suddenly he laughed, and the lines at the corners of his eyes crinkled. "Relax, Miss Cartwright. You're not on trial. There's no need to be afraid. These are just routine kinds of questions."

I laughed weakly. "I'm sorry. It's just…like you say… all the excitement."

"Did you know the dead man?"

"Finney? Of course. All of us went to school together. And he's the Baptist preacher's son." I didn't add that I was actually a few years ahead of Finney in school.

"And the fellow that shot him?"

"Archie? Yes. He went to school here too. He was Mrs. Magillberry's nephew. Great-nephew, actually."

"So you were all friends?"

"Heavens, no!" I put my hands to my throat in a little gesture of consternation. "I never had a thing to do with Finney Blalock. He was dangerous even then. And Archie. Well, he was just Lois's cousin. But Lois and I, we've always been friends."

"I see," he said, writing on his pad again. Then he looked up, straight into my eyes, before I had a chance to lower them. "What's that you've got in your hand, Miss Cartwright? I believe you just pulled it out from under the bedspread?"

I looked down at my hand lying in my lap. It was holding one of Lois's fancy combs, the one with the cloisonné peacock eyes.

"Norton, come in here," the sheriff suddenly barked. "We've found something."

The deputy flipped his pad closed and turned to give me a narrow glance as he went through the door. I heard the men murmuring among themselves on the other side of the wall.

"Hell!" the sheriff said at last. "Well, bring her in here."

I was trembling when the deputy came to the door again. "Miss Cartwright?"

"Yes?"

"You want to come see if you could give us a little help here?" I wobbled a bit getting up, and he took my elbow to steady me. And before we left the littered bedroom he said in a voice too low for them to hear in the other room, "We'll talk about that comb later. Just the two of us."

I looked up at him and nodded meekly.

CHAPTER • FIVE

A SQUATTY LITTLE FELLOW IN A seersucker suit, who I took to be the coroner, was kneeling beside Finney's body. He had a case open beside him and a number of plastic bags filled with things I didn't want to think about. The ambulance attendants had gone outside to smoke while they waited. The sheriff was holding something in a handkerchief. He held it out; the deputy lifted his eyebrows. Then the sheriff held it so I could see.

"Do you know where these come from, ma'am?" It was Miss Mineola's watch, set with rubies, that she wore on Sundays or special occasions. Also several gold chains, some with those gold nuggets she particularly liked.

I felt like I was tiptoeing through a minefield. Miss Mineola's jewelry turning up on Finney could have all kinds of implications. For instance, that Finney must have been up at the house sometime after he had escaped. I decided it was time for me to get on the sidelines of this situation. I probably knew less about what was going on than anyone else, and here I was right in the middle of things.

"That looks like Miss Mineola's jewelry," I said. "At least, I've seen her wear the watch, and I know she had some of those chains and things. She liked to give them for gifts."

"I thought as much," the sheriff said. "Well, it looks like our escapee had been busier than anybody knew."

"Or cared to say," the deputy put in.

The sheriff frowned at him. "Don't go complicating matters now, Norton. This still doesn't change things. All it means is that Blalock broke into the old lady's house before he came down here. It makes perfect sense. He needed something he could sell. He had to have some money to make an escape with."

"It certainly looks like that might be the case, sir. But it does mean one more thing we've got to do." Deputy Norton spoke softly, but I felt like what he was going to say next would somehow complicate things a good bit.

"What's that?" The sheriff sounded as if he hated to hear the answer, too.

"We need to call the mortuary and tell them to hold up on processing Mrs. Magillberry's body. There'll have to be an autopsy now. If Blalock was there earlier today, in her bedroom, and if she was dead when her niece came home and found her, aren't folks going to wonder if maybe he didn't have something to do with her death? And to find out for sure, we'll have to have an autopsy."

The sheriff swore and turned his back for a minute. He even walked into the little kitchen, opened and shut the drawer that Archie had taken the pistol from, and then folded his arms across his chest. No one else said a word.

"That'll mean sending the body to Houston, you know," he said sulkily, as though this were some kind of defeat. "And that little justice of the peace over in Pinehurst—where is he anyway?—he'll have to order it. The family's not going to like it one little bit. And the funeral home people, they'll be madder'n hops."

The deputy didn't say anything to this, but only stood there looking at the sheriff stolidly.

"All right," the older man said finally. "I guess you're right. It might turn out to be even more complicated if we don't." He picked up his hat off the counter. "Call 'em up, Norton, right away before they get started on her. It may be too late already. I'm going back to town. Let 'em go ahead and get this body on out of here as soon as the j.p. gets here. But tell those yo-yos out there to make sure they bill this trip to the prison, not the county."

After the sheriff left, I didn't know exactly what to do. He had tipped his hat as he started out the door, but didn't say whether I should stay or not. I supposed that meant I was free to go. On the other hand, the deputy had said he wanted to talk to me about the comb I'd found. I wasn't sure I wanted to have that conversation yet. If I slipped away now, while the deputy was busy, I'd at least have some time to sort out this business about Lois's comb.

But just then the justice of the peace arrived, and the fellows from the ambulance followed him back inside. With so many people crowded into the living room of the trailer, I'd have to practically crawl over the body to get out. There was a back door, of course, but no steps there. If I took that way it might look like I was too eager to get away.

The deputy must have sensed my confusion. He looked up from where he'd been bent over Finney, conferring with the j.p., and said to me, "Miss Cartwright, if you'd just wait in the bedroom again, please. We're going to take him out of here now. There's no need for you to have to see any more of this tonight."

It would have been just as easy for him to say I could go on up to the house now. He obviously hadn't forgotten about the comb. But why hadn't he mentioned it to the sheriff?

I went back into the bedroom obediently, though I felt a little aggravated at being treated like a squeamish child. Not that I would have enjoyed watching them scrape up Finney's brains off the floor. I sat down on the rumpled bed again and fingered the comb in my pocket. It was Lois's all right. She was so proud of that hair, and the combs called attention to it. A number of people besides me would be able to identify it as hers, so there was no point in trying to cover that up. But what in the world was it doing here in Archie's bed? She had made a couple of trips to the trailer earlier in the afternoon to get ice. It must have fallen out then. But why had it turned up in the bed?

I listened to the sound of the gurney rattling through the front door, the deputy and the j.p. mumbling to one another, and finally the front door closing. The air conditioner was still rumbling away. Then the deputy stood in the doorway again. He hesitated before he came in, eying me closely.

"You don't have to worry," I said. "I haven't touched a thing."

"Good," he said. "I want to check for fingerprints in here. The trailer will be sealed off, of course. But I want to do this myself."

"What for?"

He sat down on the bed, not saying anything for a minute. "The sheriff, sometimes he . . ."

"You don't think he's thorough enough?"

"Well. He likes things to be simple."

"And you like them complicated?"

"Whether I like it one way or another doesn't make any difference. I just like finding out the way it really was, what really happened. If that's simple, that's fine with me. Most of the time it is. But I think this situation is different."

"Why don't you just tell him?"

He looked up at me, straight in the eyes, and then dropped his blond lashes. "That's not simple either. I've got a degree in criminology. And the sheriff—"

"He resents that?"

"Not exactly. He likes all the new equipment and hi-tech stuff. Nothing he likes better than running license plate checks through the state computer or getting a suspect's record faxed to us on the new machine we've got. It's just plain old deductive reasoning he doesn't like. If A happened, then B has to follow. That kind of thing." He smiled at me, crinkling the corners of his eyes, which I could see now were not exactly blue, but almost turquoise. Then the smile faded suddenly and he stood up.

"Like that comb, Miss Cartwright. I'm assuming you recognized it, or you wouldn't have been startled to find it. Nor put it in your pocket."

I drew out the comb. I knew I looked guilty as sin.

He looked at me sternly. "Is it yours, Miss Cartwright?"

"Mine?" I said, shocked. "Why in the world would you think it was mine?"

"Why else would you try to conceal it?"

"Do I have the kind of hairdo that would call for a comb like this?" I put my hand up to my short, straight, mouse-colored hair.

The stern look broke suddenly and he laughed. "I guess I don't know much about that kind of thing."

"Apparently not."

He sat down again and leaned forward over his knees as though he meant to speak confidentially. "Why don't you help me out here then? Maybe you've got some idea who it does belong to."

I suddenly felt like I'd been outmaneuvered. "I, uh, think it's Lois's comb. The girl—woman—that was just here." Lois would die if she knew I'd called her a girl. "Cecelia's daughter. Archie's cousin." I wanted to make it clear that Lois couldn't have been fooling around with Archie.

"They're cousins then?"

"Yes, well, second cousins anyway."

"Just second cousins?" The way he said it, I could tell he was discounting the implication I had tried to make. "He's a pretty good-looking fellow, wouldn't you say?"

"I guess so. Or at least I wouldn't be surprised if other people, people who didn't know him, thought so."

"But you don't?" He sounded skeptical.

"Archie?" I managed an incredulous laugh. "Archie, handsome as he may seem to outsiders, is practically the village idiot here in Point Blank."

"He didn't seem retarded to me."

"No. Not retarded. Just dumb. I don't know. Not real bright. He's always just feeling his way along. Trying to pick up on what's expected of him. Maybe he's just so lazy he doesn't want to go to the trouble of thinking for himself. It's hard to say. You have to know Archie to see what I mean."

"And you know Archie well?"

I looked at him sharply. "All of us were in school together. I told you that."

"All of us?" he repeated.

"All the kids here in Point Blank. Which included Lois and Archie."

"And this Finney Blalock character?"

"Yes." Again, I didn't add the part about Finney and Archie being a few years behind Lois and me. Nor did I say how many years ago that had been.

"I'm just trying to get it all straight," he said.

"Well, then, you can put the idea of any funny business going on between Archie and Lois out of your mind. She despises Archie. I think he's dumb. Cecelia thinks he's dumb. Everybody thinks he's dumb. But Lois despises him."

"That seems pretty extreme, don't you think?"

"You have to know Lois to understand that, deputy." We were really on shaky ground now.

He laughed shortly. "You seem to have an answer to everything. And my name is Norton. Now what about Lois? What would I have to know to understand why she despises her cousin Archie?"

I crossed my legs and stared at the toe of my shoe, frowning. "Lois is my friend, and I don't want to give you the wrong idea about her," I started, "but the truth is, Lois doesn't like many men. In fact, she probably doesn't like many people."

"Her mother?"

"Oh, her mother's just the opposite," I said. "Cecelia likes everybody."

"That's not what I meant," he broke in. "I meant does Lois like her mother?"

It struck me as a strange question. "Of course Lois likes her mother. She's her mother, isn't she? And everybody loves Cecelia."

"It's as simple as that, is it? Well. Tell me more about Lois and this phobia she has about men."

"I didn't say that!" I protested. "You make her sound like—" I didn't want to say what he made her sound like.

"Okay, then. This perfectly normal contempt she has for men."

I frowned at him and settled my skirt over my knees. "Lois has had a hard life. Her father was an invalid. Her mother had to support the family. Lois had to spend every summer up here with her grandparents away from home. It was a hard situation for a child to understand. I guess she blamed her father. She's always been a little down on men. Suspicious. She's never gotten over it. It's like she bears a grudge." I stopped and looked him straight in the eye. "You can understand that, can't you."

He shrugged. "Go on," he said.

"That's about it. Her father died. And he was sick a long time before that. After his death, Cecelia and Lois came up here to live. She was new in school, and of course all the other kids had grown up with one another. So she was the outsider. They didn't take to her much."

"Except for you. You made friends with her."

I shrugged.

"I think I understand that part. That's pretty simple."

I looked up at him sharply.

He smiled. "I just meant that you seem like a nice enough person, someone who might make friends with the underdog."

"I don't know that I've ever thought of Lois as an underdog. She frightens most people. She can cut you to ribbons with her tongue. She was the smartest person in school. And she didn't mind letting you know it either. That didn't help her make any friends."

"But her cousin Archie. Does she have more than her ordinary contempt for him? You said she despises him."

"She tolerates him, like everyone else around here does. To an extent. But she also enjoys showing him up whenever and however she can. For one thing, she always felt like Miss Mineola did too much for Archie and not enough for her and her mother when they really needed it."

"That's the old lady whose jewelry we found on Finney?"

"Yes."

"I see." He paused. "Did she dote on Archie? The old lady?"

"Oh, no. I wouldn't say that. If anything, she probably despised him almost as much as Lois did."

He frowned. "Maybe this seems simple to you, but I'm not following it. I thought you said that Lois resented Archie because the old lady did too much for him."

"That's right. Take the will, for instance."

"The will? You mean Miss Mineola—Mrs. Magillberry made Archie her heir?"

"No one knows for sure. But everyone expects Archie to get a pretty fair portion of everything. Archie certainly does anyway. Not everything, of course, though no one knows for certain, other than Bartholomew, her lawyer. If she'd let it out just how she intended to dispose of everything, then she wouldn't have had any more power over everyone, would she? So she kept it all pretty mysterious. But she had told Archie that he could expect to be taken care of the rest of his life."

"But why?" he said, showing his exasperation. "I don't understand. I thought you said she didn't much care for him."

"That part's simple. Because he changed his name to Laudermilk—Miss Mineola's family name. He'll be the only one who can keep it going."

"Of course," he said, slapping his knees in mock consternation. "That should have been perfectly obvious." He sat there for a minute, shaking his head. Then he nodded. "I can see why Lois might resent her cousin, but that still doesn't explain why her comb would be here in his bed. In fact, that complicates matters a good deal."

I couldn't disagree about that. I didn't know what to think about it myself.

"You don't have any alternative explanations to offer?" he asked.

"No," I said. "I wish I did. I just know it couldn't be what it looks like."

He sighed. "Miss Cartwright, I know you're a good friend of this person, but I think we need to find out the actual reason her comb came to be where it was. I'm being as honest with you as I know how. Would you help me try to find that out?"

"What do you have in mind?" I asked cautiously.

"You keep the comb for now," he said. "When you get the chance, sometime this evening if possible, ask her if she's lost one. Watch her reaction. Then show it to her. See how she responds. Don't tell her where you found it. If she just seems puzzled, then maybe it turned up here by some means she had nothing to do with. Maybe it dropped out and her cousin picked it up. Otherwise—well, we'll see."

Even though it was August and the air conditioner didn't cool the bedroom all that well, I felt myself suddenly go cold all over at the thought of what he was asking. Lois was my friend. I didn't want to be involved with trying to trick her. In fact, I wasn't sure I wanted to know how the comb came to be in Archie's bed.

"Miss Cartwright?" Norton said softly but insistently. I looked up at him and then away. "Don't you want to find out the truth here?"

I didn't say anything for a long moment. "I don't know," I finally replied. "It depends on what the truth is, I guess."

He slapped his thighs again and stood up suddenly. "Well, it's up to you. I could take the comb and ask her about it myself. But I wouldn't be as likely to find out as much as you would."

No, you wouldn't, I thought to myself. Under the best possible conditions Lois wouldn't be likely to take an immediate liking to a big, strawberry blond deputy who was as cool and self-collected as this one seemed to be. On the other hand, what if something unpleasant came out of all this probing? I couldn't, at present, imagine what that might be, but you never knew. Too many unexpected things had already happened today. To Deputy Norton it was just a matter of shining the cold, clear light of logic into all the dark corners and coming up with the truth. But he didn't know these people. He hadn't grown up with them.

Yet I found myself hating to disappoint him. It would be the pleasantest thing in the world to say yes and see him grin at me, the corners of those aqua eyes crinkling up again.

I took a deep breath and stood up too. "I'm sorry,

Deputy Norton. I just can't practice that kind of deception on my friend. You'll have to take care of this yourself." And I held out the comb to him in my slightly sweaty palm.

He didn't say anything, just took it from me with a curt nod. I couldn't make out whether he was disappointed, angry, or what. But I thought maybe, for just an instant before he shut down all the expression on his face, he looked surprised.

CHAPTER • SIX

THE NEXT MORNING I WOKE UP confused. I had been dreaming, and at first it seemed that the strange pictures still floating around in my head as I opened my eyes were only the dissolving shreds of dreams. Then it all began to come back to me—Miss Mineola dying, Finney escaping, Archie shooting him. Lois's comb and Deputy Norton. I groaned and rolled over, but I couldn't go back to sleep.

I turned on the radio while I ate breakfast and heard J. D. Fulp, the local announcer, reporting the details of what would probably be the lead story for days—Finney Blalock's escape and shooting.

J. D. has been doing the news on KSOM since before anybody can remember. His trademark is his absolute lack of expression and the way he reads in quotation marks around people's statements. He says he does it to avoid lawsuits.

"Sheriff Dooley reported that Blalock was quote dead at the scene unquote when he arrived. The deceased had been serving a life sentence at the Texas Department of Corrections for the quote murder of a young woman in Harris County in 1987 unquote. Prison officials have been quote unable to ascertain how the escape was effected unquote at this time. An investigation is quote ongoing. Unquote."

When J. D. began reading the obituaries, including, of course, Miss Mineola's, I turned the radio off and went upstairs to get dressed. It was Sunday morning, but I didn't feel like going in to Somerville to St. Barnabas. Everyone would be asking questions about the goings-on in Point Blank, and I felt like I'd already said too much the night before. Besides, I really ought to go out and see if there was anything I could do to help Lois and Cecelia.

I drove slowly on my way out to Miss Mineola's, letting my mind drift. August can be vicious in our part of the country, but we usually get some kind of break from the heat along about the middle of the month. Clouds were already building up from the Gulf at nine o'clock, high cumulus clouds with tops that might be fifty or sixty thousand feet up. Maybe we'd get a real gully-washer out of them.

The Packards were out cutting their second or third hay crop that summer. Used to be, people never worked on Sunday around here, but now it's like every place else. Sunday's just an extra day to catch up on chores. The hay smelled sweet, though, mixed with the sharper scent of the pines along the road. On the horizon I could see the fire lookout station sticking up above the treetops, abandoned now since they watch for forest fires from planes, or even satellites for all I know. When I was little, I used to think that being a lookout in that tower would be the ideal life, sitting up above the treetops looking down on all the world, like God. People think I'm crazy, I know, but I still like to climb up the old fire tower every chance I get. Up there you can hear the wind blowing through the pines and stretch out in the sun to read and be all alone with no one to bother you.

Maybe that's why I'm still here in Point Blank—the whole world grew away from me before I was old enough or smart enough to realize it. Lois feels sorry for me, living in this backwater little community. I try to take it in the spirit it's intended, but sometimes her pity galls me. She's tried everything to break me loose from here, including shaming me for "wasting my talents." That's a good one, Lois appealing to a biblical parable like that. Her idea of wasted talent is not getting paid as much as you think you ought to.

I often wonder what will become of Cecelia when she gets a little older, when she's in the shape Miss Mineola is—or was. Lois would never come back to Point Blank to take care of her. As for Cecelia, I'm sure she intends to leave it in the Lord's hands. With her, everything eventually converges on the Lord.

It occurred to me now that I never had found out why Cecelia wanted to see Archie in the barn the night before. And what did she have to confess to Bartholomew?

Suddenly the sweet smell of the hay and the comforting presence of the lookout tower looming above the trees were blotted out by the memory of yesterday's events. It wasn't only Miss Mineola's death. An old lady dying at ninety-four is as natural as cutting the hay when it's ready. But there was Finney. And the fact I'd been trying to forget—that the shooting hadn't happened the way Archie said it had. Or at least the way Lois had prompted him to say it had. And Lois's comb. Something was going on there that made me feel extremely uneasy. And the deputy. What did he think of me now after I'd refused to help him? And why did I care?

As I rounded the last curve and headed up the hill to Miss Mineola's big white house, I felt those questions, like the high-piled clouds, weighing ominously on the horizon.

I thought I'd be the first one at the house this morning, but already other cars were parked both at Cecelia's little house and over at Miss Mineola's across the red clay road. Nothing draws neighbors like death, my mother always said. A sleek little red sports car, obviously new, was parked beside a big white Lincoln, several years old. Those would belong to Maximillian and Muriel. I was surprised they had gotten here so early all the way from Houston. Bud Wylie's pickup was drawn up under the shade of one of Miss Mineola's prize pecan trees.

Bud and Evelyn Wylie had been Miss Mineola's best friends. Bud had been one of her pupils, in fact, way back when she taught school in Point Blank. Evelyn's his second wife, and though she's no spring chicken, she's a good bit younger than he is and fusses over him a lot—so he'll last longer, I suppose.

Inside, several neighbors, under Evelyn Wylie's supervision, were in the kitchen putting food away that members of Cecelia's church had brought. I spoke to the ladies, then went on through to the living room where Bud and the Lovingoods, an old couple who have a ranch down the road, were sitting on the couch making low conversation with Archie, dressed for the occasion in his best suit.

Cecelia was in Miss Mineola's bedroom with Maximillian and Muriel. I murmured my greetings to each of the neighbors, making sure I ended up close enough to the bedroom door to catch the conversation between Cecelia and Miss Mineola's grandchildren.

Through the open door I could see that Max, far from being dressed in his Sunday best, looked like he'd just come off the golf course. One of those gold chains his grandmother handed out for generic gifts hung around his neck, with a little gold squiggly thing on it, almost like a snake. A pair of large sunglasses was pushed up on top of his head, probably to cover his thinning hair.

Muriel, on the other hand, was dressed to the teeth in a black linen dress with a big white collar and a pair of black patent sandals with clear, lucite wedge heels three inches high. Inside the heels were little red artificial flowers that bounced around whenever she took a step. Neither Max nor Muriel could ever adapt to Point Blank.

Muriel was smoking, walking back and forth between the front bay window full of African violets and the bed where Cecelia was sitting in her best pink polyester dress that had Sunday written all over it. Muriel would never have smoked in the house while her grandmother was alive. However unconventional Miss Mineola might have been in her own youth, she never did take too well to other people's vices. And, of course, after she developed emphysema, no one, not even her good friend Bud, was allowed to smoke in her presence.

"Leave it alone, Max," Muriel was saying to her brother. "What's done is done. There's no use making a fuss about it."

"Hey. This is my grandmother we're talking about. Just about the only close relative I had left on the face of this earth. I think I have a right to be upset." He had his arms crossed over his chest and was working one heel up and down, obviously angry.

"Give me a break." Muriel turned and looked at him, her hands on her hips. "Just who do you think you're kidding anyway? As far as I can see, the only interest you ever take in relatives is when they die."

"Just what do you mean by that?" He took a step toward her. Everyone in the living room had gotten very quiet. All of us could hear Cecelia say, "Now, now. I know you all are both upset about your grandmother. I understand that. But we need to work this out as best we can for everyone."

"Everyone?" Max turned on her now. "What do you mean, everyone? We're her grandchildren, aren't we? Her closest kin? Shouldn't we be the ones to be consulted here?"

"Max, honey, I would have been glad to consult you. But I couldn't get you last night. And really there's not

· 70 ·

that much to consult about. She left explicit instructions with Bartholomew as to just what she wants—where to bury her, the funeral service, everything," Cecelia said.

"Just like her," Muriel observed, looking out the window.

"About this autopsy business," Max went on, "I'm sure that wasn't a part of her instructions. I don't see the point of that at all."

"Yes," Muriel said, turning back from the window and for once agreeing with her brother. "Why do they want to do that, Cecelia? That's gruesome. And we haven't even got to see Granny yet."

"I don't know why either. I was a little surprised myself. All I know is that the sheriff called this morning and said they'd have to do one and that means we'll have to set the funeral back. They won't get it done till tomorrow."

"Why not?" Muriel asked.

"Why, it's Sunday, sweetheart," Cecelia said.

Max laughed harshly and threw his hands up. "Right. I forgot we're in God's country."

Cecelia didn't say anything, only looked down at her plump hands in her lap.

"Well, I want an explanation anyway," Max said. "They can't perform an autopsy without the family's consent. Not without a good reason."

"So I guess they have one," Muriel said, stubbing out her cigarette in one of the saucers under an African violet. "Why get so worked up about it, little brother? Why so eager to get Granny in the ground anyway? Can't wait for the will to be read?"

The remark evidently hit home. Max swung the sunglasses off the top of his head. "I guess you wouldn't understand about this kind of thing, Muriel," he said coldly. "After all, blood is thicker than water."

Muriel stood there silent a moment, her face growing rigid. All of us in the living room held our breath. Finally she spoke, her voice trembling, "I think I'll go on back then, Cecelia, if you don't mind. I don't think I need to listen to this. You can give me a call and let me know when the service is going to be, can't you?"

Cecelia, who had been looking from one to the other in flustered anguish, her little round mouth puckered into an oh, blinked and said, "Sure, honey. You go on home. I'll let you know as soon as it's settled."

"Well, I don't know about you, but I'm going to get to the bottom of this autopsy business," Max said. "You all may not care what they do to Grandma, but I'm going to give that two-bit sheriff a piece of my mind."

I heard the screen door on the east porch slam behind him and then Muriel murmuring her good-byes to Cecelia and taking the same route out—to avoid having to speak to the rest of us, no doubt.

Cecelia came to the bedroom door and exhaled a deep breath. "I'm going to church now," she announced. "Brother Blalock'll be starting the service in another fifteen minutes and I ought to be there. Poor man. He needs all the support he can get this morning."

The Lovingoods, sitting there on the couch, raised their eyebrows and nodded. Then, realizing the best part was probably over, they struggled to their feet and told Archie that they'd best be getting to church themselves. They didn't seem in any hurry, though, and kept making small talk with Bud until they saw Max's little sports car pull away in a cloud of red dust, followed more slowly by Muriel's Lincoln.

Cecelia kissed me as she left for church, one of her soft little domestic kisses she's used to planting on whoever's handy when she's going out the door. My mother used to do the same thing. I guess it goes with their generation. Lois hates it. "It's so automatic," she says, "like some kind of Pavlovian response." I told Cecelia I'd go across to her house and see if Lois needed me for anything.

"Oh, sugar, would you mind?" she said as she started down the back steps. "I sure would appreciate it. She's been so upset. I think she was up crying half the night. I had no idea this was going to affect her so." And off she went with her Bible in one hand and her purse in the other, easing herself down one step at a time off the kitchen porch before she turned to smile back gratefully at me.

I hung around the kitchen for a while longer, helping Evelyn rearrange things in the refrigerator to accommodate the food the neighbors had brought in.

"Have they decided to have the dinner after the funeral over here?" I asked, trying to make conversation. Evelyn Wylie's not a person I know real well, and working with her in the kitchen like that seemed a little awkward to me. In fact, I was a bit surprised to see her helping out there. I always thought of her as more or less ornamental, even though I know she supported herself for all those years before she married Bud. And wherever Bud goes, she's right there beside him in his pickup. She goes with him everywhere.

Bud's so old now, of course, that he has hired hands to do the kind of work he had to do himself when he was young. Still, every now and then he goes out and helps with the feeding or the culling, just to keep his hand in. That's the one time Evelyn never goes with him.

"I suppose so," Evelyn said. "Cecelia said to keep as much of the food as possible over here. Hand me that macaroni and cheese, would you? It'll have to go in here too."

"I suppose I could take some of this over and put it in Cecelia's refrigerator, though," I said. "It looks like this one's about full."

"We may have to do that. Of course, we'll just have to cart it back over here tomorrow." She balanced a Jell-O salad on top of a bowl of potato salad.

"I'm not so sure about that," I told her. "It looks like

there's going to be an autopsy now. That'll probably delay the funeral."

"What?" She straightened up and turned to look at me with a face blank with consternation. The Jell-O trembled precariously in her hands.

"Cecelia told Max and Muriel just now. The sheriff has ordered one."

"Whatever for?"

"She didn't say. But Max was real upset about it. He said he was going to talk to the sheriff about it."

Evelyn closed the refrigerator door and came and sat down at the kitchen table, evidently giving up on fitting anything more into it. "Poor Minnie," she sighed. "Why can't they leave the poor woman alone?" She pushed a strand of gray hair back into the sculptured wave it had separated from. Evelyn's always done up so well it was almost startling to see even a stray hair loose. She wears polyester pastels, like Cecelia, but hers always come in color-coordinated combinations. Cruise clothes, Lois calls them behind her back.

She began to drum her nails on the table. "I wonder what's going on," she said. "No one said anything about an autopsy last night."

I shrugged. After last night, I was determined to keep my own counsel. "I'll take this platter of ham and that Jell-O salad over to Cecelia's, if you think that's all right," I said.

"What? Oh. Sure, honey. Go right ahead," she said. She stood up, smoothing her flowered overblouse across her trim little tummy. "Bud and I are going to gather up all that oxygen equipment and take it back into the medical supply place in town. We figured that would save Cecelia one bothersome job anyway."

"I'm sure she'd appreciate that," I said, balancing the platter of sliced ham on top of the bowl.

"Bud's already got it loaded in the back of the truck," she said, "so I guess we'll be going now. Go on now, honey, before that Jell-O melts and gets all over you." And she disappeared into the living room to collect Bud.

On my way down the driveway, I glanced in the bed of Bud's pickup. The long green oxygen cylinder was lying on its side. Bud had even wrapped the gauges in an old towel to protect them.

Cecelia's little house is a buff brick square, built on five acres of the old homestead. Her father's original portion had been a good deal more than that, but over the years his sister had whittled away at it till all that was left was a scrap of pasture. Cecelia's parents had planted fruit trees there that had developed into a pleasant small orchard, one that Miss Mineola had openly envied. Miss Flora had even accused her sister-in-law once of sending Loomis over to prune the peach trees with the intention of cutting them back so severely they'd never get any more fruit from them during her lifetime.

I knew from firsthand experience that Miss Mineola never forgot to bring up the fact that Cecelia's house was brick while hers was only wood. She never mentioned that the little brick bungalow could easily have fit inside her own house with plenty of room to spare. Every time she came over, making her way laboriously across the red dirt road, she'd always pause at the cement sidewalk leading up to the front door and lean with both hands on her walnut cane, shaking her head in wonderment. "My, my, my," she'd say. "Isn't that a fine house though. I sure do envy you this fine brick house to live in, Cecelia. Not like that old rundown frame house of mine." Then she'd sigh and start up the walk, saying mournfully, "Well, never mind. Maybe it'll last as long as I do anyhow. And won't nobody else want it after I'm gone."

I knocked on the door and then let myself in, not waiting for Lois to come. The Jell-O was melting, and I was so much at home here that I often didn't bother to wait for someone to open the door.

Inside, all the blinds were drawn. Maybe Lois was

still sleeping. I didn't know how I was going to ask her about the comb I'd found in Archie's bed, but I felt I should warn her that the deputy knew about it.

I took the food into the kitchen and put it in the refrigerator. I tried to be quiet, but she must have heard me.

"Who's there?" she called out. She sounded edgy.

"It's just me. Beth Marie." I closed the refrigerator door and looked up to see Lois standing in her bedroom doorway. She was in her underwear with a towel wrapped around her wet hair, and she looked awful.

"You just get up?" I asked, trying to sound cheerful.

"Beth Marie," she said, ignoring my question, "I need some money."

"What?"

"I need some money. Enough for a plane ticket to… well, to someplace."

"What are you talking about?" I said. Then I looked beyond her through the bedroom door. There was a suit-case, half packed, open on the unmade bed.

CHAPTER SEVEN

N EVER IN A THOUSAND YEARS would I have imagined the story that Lois told me as she finished packing her suitcase that morning. Even after all that's happened since, I still find it the biggest mystery of all, one that I haven't yet found an answer to. Probably because you don't solve people.

"I won't ask you to swear not to tell anyone, Beth Marie," she said, turning her sallow face toward me from the closet where she was pulling out clothes, hardly looking to see what she was holding. "There wouldn't be any point in it anyway. Somehow or other it will come out. I don't know exactly how. I can't think straight enough to figure it all out right now. Maybe it wouldn't have to. Maybe if I were calmer I could devise some way to cover it all up. I'm not good at scheming. I thought I was. I thought I could do this. And if he hadn't died, maybe—"

Here she stopped her breathless rattling, and her face froze. It hurt me to look at her. I felt cold all over as I sank down on the bed beside her suitcase.

"Lois," I said, trying to steady my own voice, "what are you talking about? I can't follow you. You're going to have to calm down, girl, and start at the beginning."

She laughed, sticking her hands into her dark hair

and shaking her head back and forth. "Yes," she said finally, and dropped down on the other side of the bed. "I don't have much time anyway. Mother will be back from church soon, and no telling who may come knocking at the door any minute. I've got to get away from here before noon. I can't see Mother again."

"Not see—? Lois, just tell me what's going on here." I tried to sound firm.

She took a deep breath and looked up at me. "I helped Finney escape, Beth Marie. He was going to Mexico. He had connections to get him to someplace in the interior where they'd never find him. I used the money I had for the fall semester in school to help him. I was going to follow him there later."

I stared across the bed at her. No words would form in my mind, much less in my mouth. This wasn't just unbelievable; it was nonsense, gibberish, as though she'd suddenly broken into another language. Finally I brought out lamely, "I don't understand. What are you talking about?"

She got up and began to dress. She moved wearily, as though she had worked hard all day and barely had strength to lift the dress over her head and button it up.

"Just what I said." Her voice was flat. "I don't expect you to understand. I don't have time to try to explain. These are just facts I'm telling you. You've simply got to accept them that way, like two and two make four. For God's sake, don't ask me why."

I made some kind of mental jerking motion, trying to push a reset button somewhere so my mind would start functioning again. "Lois," I said, "why don't we just get everything out in the open? Whatever you've done, tell the sheriff, tell your mother. Surely that's best in the long run."

She turned on me fiercely. "No!" she hissed. "Don't even think about it, Beth Marie. I'm leaving, and that's final. I don't know where I'll go or what I'll do, but

Mother...Point Blank...it's impossible. I can't stay here. It's like my life is over. Everything. Don't you understand?" She was practically screaming now.

"All right, all right," I said, trying to calm her. "But why, Lois? I don't understand. You've got to explain, give me some kind of reason. It's like...I can't fathom why you'd do such a thing. This is beyond me." I thought I had known this person, had her all figured out.

"You don't want to know, Beth Marie. Don't ask me why."

I sat there silently, staring at her. I knew if I kept quiet she was more likely to tell me than if I kept pressing her. She went to the bedroom window and stared out at the August fields turning yellow in the heat. She kept her back to me, so that I had to strain to hear what she was saying.

"I began writing to Finney over a year ago," she said. "I had this bright idea of using him as a case study for one of my seminar papers. I thought it would be a real coup. I mean, who in the academic world has personal access to that kind of subject for investigation? Here was a boy I'd gone to school with, a convicted murderer. You know his family, what the Blalocks are like. I thought it would make an intriguing study." Her voice began to catch at this point, and she stopped for a moment.

I kept quiet. I felt if I so much as breathed audibly I might upset the delicate balance that allowed her to tell me this.

"I only let Finney know in the most general way what I was doing. First, because I didn't think he'd be able to understand or even care about it. But also because I suppose I had some embarrassment about using him this way, displaying him as some kind of insect to be dissected and analyzed." She made a noise that almost sounded like laughing.

"Well, I was wrong. He was able to understand. In

fact, I guess it was what he expected from the beginning—that he was being taken advantage of. And in a way, he was right. But I didn't think of it that way. Not then." Her voice faltered again and she paused to take a deep breath. "But nevertheless he played along with it," she said, steadier.

She turned and looked at me suddenly. "You'll think it was for his own purposes, that he was trying to use me, too. That's what everyone's going to say, but it's not true. That's not the way it was at all, Beth Marie. I've got all his letters. I can prove it wasn't."

I shook my head almost imperceptibly to indicate I had no intention of disagreeing with her.

She turned back to the window. "I never did write that paper. Over a period of months, we wrote…I don't know…dozens of letters to one another. I had to go through all the rigmarole of getting on his official correspondence list with the prison officials, of course, and since they thought I was just using him as some kind of subject for a study, no one objected. But gradually I got to feel like I knew Finney in a way we had never known him in school here. We only saw the bad kid, the stupid kid. But he's not stupid, Beth Marie. He wasn't. He was…different. Fierce and majestic and daring."

I caught my tongue between my teeth to keep from speaking. The Finney I remembered was different all right, but "majestic" wasn't one of the ways I remembered him, though fierce or even daring might be true enough.

"He wrote me poems, Beth Marie. Most of them so sad they broke my heart. About lost children. He really opened up to me. I could see how he'd been afraid all his life. Afraid of nobody loving him. Afraid to love others. After a while, I could see I would never be able to use him for my seminar paper. Our relationship became much too precious for that kind of exposure. I couldn't betray him in that way."

I closed my eyes. I could already see it coming.

"Then after a couple more months his letters began to take on a different tone," she went on. "It seemed as if for the first time in his life he was feeling comfortable talking to another human being. They weren't so despairing and cynical any more. Once in a while he even made a joke—one that wasn't bitter. He began to notice things around him he hadn't mentioned before. What crops were growing out on the prison farm, the birds singing, that kind of thing. It was as though he were opening up to the world in a new way. His poems became, well, love poems. Addressed to me. They were as beautiful as the others had been sad. And now," her voice broke, "they're all I've got left."

"So you fell in love with him," I said as softly and noncommittally as I could.

"Yes," she said, lifting her head sharply, "and no one will ever believe me or understand. I'm sure you don't even believe me."

"How can I not believe you, Lois? Why else would you have helped him escape?"

She turned and looked at me narrowly now, obviously not trusting my response. "But you think I'm crazy."

I shook my head. "You know I haven't had much experience along that line, Lois."

"Everyone will think I'm crazy," she went on as though I hadn't said anything. "Even Mother." Then she laughed shortly. "One of life's little ironies," she said bitterly. "The phrase Mother's always using on everyone else to excuse their misdeeds—brain-damaged—she'll be saying that about me now."

"But how did you arrange it, Lois?" I asked. "How did you plan it?"

She started to say something, and then shook her head. "No," she said. "I'm not going to say any more about it. You know enough. You can see the predicament I'm in, why I've got to get away. That's all you need to know. The rest of it doesn't matter. None of it matters now."

"Lois," I said carefully, "did you lose a comb yesterday? One of those fancy combs with the mother-of-pearl inlay?"

She put her hand to her hair as though expecting to find it there. "I don't know. Why?"

"I've got to tell you this, Lois. It was found. That comb. Under the sheets in Archie's bed last night."

I watched her face closely. At first she only looked puzzled, as though she were thinking back, trying to remember. Then she flinched as if a sudden pain had shot through her. "Last night," she whispered. "Finney." And she dropped to the bed again, sobbing now.

I tried to comfort her as best I could, but my little pats looked pitiful, even petty, up against her grief. Her thin shoulders shook under my hand. I had never seen anyone weep so extravagantly and inconsolably before. After a while her breath began to come more regularly and the shaking stilled. She lay there for a moment more, and then her thin hands clenched into fists. She sat up and threw her hair back from her swollen face.

"I've got to finish packing," she said flatly.

She continued to cry quietly as she went on packing the suitcase, methodically picking up shoes, makeup, nightgown, and stuffing them into the bag any which way. She wept wearily and as though she herself weren't even noticing the tears. It was the saddest thing I had ever seen. I think perhaps she even had forgotten I was there.

I sat there silent for several minutes, trying to put aside all the questions ricocheting around in my brain so that I could deal with the situation at hand—what to do with her. I wasn't at all sure she was in her right mind. But I also knew she was fiercely determined about her course of action. Even rational, Lois was always stubborn once she made up her mind. It seemed to me that all I could do at present was to go along with her, maybe take her someplace out of the way long enough for her to at least get a grip on herself. And maybe give me time to figure out what in the world was going on. I wasn't sure just what she had or hadn't done. But I did know that what we both needed right now was time.

She clicked the suitcase closed and looked over at me. "Well," she said, her voice flat again, "are you going to help me or not?"

I stood up too. "Come on," I said. "Let's go to my house. We'll have to figure out just what we're going to do. This is Sunday, you know. Nothing's open. I mean not the bank or anything."

She looked at me doubtfully. I don't think she really trusted me, but she was in a tight spot and had no one else to turn to. And on top of everything else, she looked so tired, so bone weary, like she didn't really have enough energy to do anything but follow the only path that presented itself to her.

She picked up her purse—I carried the suitcase—and followed me out of the house, staying behind me all the way. I think she was suspicious that I might betray her somehow, by leaving a note for her mother or something. She needn't have worried. I had no idea what to tell Cecelia.

We drove to my house in Point Blank in silence. She was either too exhausted to speak or whatever attention she had was focused someplace far away. My own mind had begun to function a little better once it had gotten over the initial shock.

When I thought back over all that had happened yesterday, it was incredible to me that she been able to keep such tight control of herself. Only because I knew the force of Lois's willpower and the ability she had to seal off her emotions from her actions could I believe it even now.

On the other hand, the thought of Lois aiding and abetting a criminal, a prisoner, an escapee, was beyond my comprehension. She was such a stickler about rules and regulations. She prided herself on never having gotten so much as a parking ticket. There was something about clear-cut rules that appealed to her. She liked things well-defined. Lois helping a murderer escape from prison—well, it was unthinkable.

But there it was. And the only explanation was equally unthinkable: that Lois, so proud of her objective, analytical mind, had been taken in by the instinctive cunning of a criminal like Finney Blalock. Wild as it was, I had to believe her story about getting involved with Finney. She would never have helped him escape otherwise.

I don't have the sort of education Lois does, the kind that supposedly explains why people act the way they do. I only had two years at the state college in Somerville before Mother got sick and I had to move back home and take care of her. I did have one psychology course, but it didn't tell me nearly as much about how strange people can be as my English classes did. Dostoyevsky and Ezra Pound and Emily Dickinson—now *they* were strange.

Actually, for years after I came home, I tried to imagine myself as Emily Dickinson, stuck away in her little hometown there in New England. I even tried writing poetry for a while. But the illusion didn't hold up too well to my reality. Mother took up most of my time, and then they gave me the job of bookkeeping for the Water Board, which made it difficult to be a recluse. I guess I turned out more like Vinnie, Emily's sister, the one who had to take care of the household chores and wasn't as bright or creative.

I hadn't thought about Emily in a long time, but this morning, driving back home with Lois, she came floating into my mind in her long, white, diaphanous dress, like a large, languorous moth. That last year at college I had written my term paper on Emily. She fell in love with a preacher who moved off to California with his family and left her pining away with only her poetry for comfort. I had read every one of her poems—almost two thousand—even memorizing some. I hadn't thought about them in years, but this morning one came floating, along with the moth-like Emily, into my mind.

> *The soul has Bandaged moments—*
> *When too appalled to stir—*
> *She feels some ghastly Fright come up*
> *And stop to look at her*

That's just the first stanza, all I could remember word for word. But there was something about the story Lois had told me that reminded me of that poem. There's something else in the poem about a goblin-lover coming to smooth her "freezing hair" and sip from her lips. That's what I pictured when I tried to think about Lois and Finney; I saw her mesmerized, too appalled to stir. And there was no doubt in my mind that Finney was the goblin.

I could just recall a few more lines, now that I thought about it.

> *The soul has moments of Escape—*
> *When bursting all the doors—*
> *She dances like a Bomb . . .*

That was all though. I couldn't finish the line. I looked over at Lois. She certainly looked like a bomb right now, set to go off any minute.

In fact, I felt like the top of my own head was coming off from the effort to make any sense out of all these improbable events. The place for mesmerized moths and goblin-lovers was in books. They didn't fit in real life. They tore it open, dislodged all the pieces so that it looked as if it could never be put back together again. A bomb had gone off here in Point Blank, and no one except me even realized it yet. And I hadn't the least notion what to do. All I knew was that Cecelia needed to be protected from this. How that was going to happen, I had no idea. All I could do was try to delay the repercussion as long as possible, in the hope that some miracle might happen.

As I rounded the bend where the Packards were still out in their field haying, it struck me how different the world had looked earlier this morning. The tranquility had drained from the land. In fact, if I noticed anything about the scenery at all now, it was only that the clouds had continued to build from the south, looking both ominous and oppressive.

I turned off the main road that runs into Point Blank and took a narrow back road winding around one of the fields so that I could approach my house from the rear. The main road goes right by the Baptist Church, and I didn't want to chance someone seeing Lois in the car with me. I didn't even bother to explain this to my passenger who sat stonily beside me. She seemed to be in another world anyway.

"Go on in," I said, when I had pulled into the back driveway. We don't lock our doors in Point Blank unless we're going to be gone overnight. "I'll bring the suitcase."

She got out slowly, almost as though she were sleepwalking. She certainly looked like a soul caught in a bandaged moment right then. I watched her go up the back steps before I turned to pull the suitcase out of the back seat.

"You've got company?"

I hadn't even heard him come up behind me. He must have come around from the front of the house, staying off the gravel walk to avoid making any noise.

I jerked upright, hitting my head on the car door. "Oh!" I put my hand to my temple and swayed against the side of the car, more from shock than the blow. "What are you doing here?"

He caught me by the elbow and steadied me. "I'm sorry. I didn't mean to startle you."

"Then why did you slip up behind me like that?"

Even as I tried to sound angry, I heard my voice shake. Had he seen Lois?

The deputy ignored the question and stared at the suitcase. The sun was glinting off the chrome on the fender; the light stabbed into my head like an ice pick. Suddenly I knew I couldn't do this. I couldn't keep it all juggled in my head any more. However hard I tried, I couldn't protect everyone who needed protecting. Not Lois, not Cecelia, not anyone.

"Come on in out of the sun," I said wearily. Whether he had seen her or not, it didn't matter. I couldn't think fast enough to figure it all out. I couldn't put him off any longer. Whatever had happened would just have to come out.

He followed me inside, and I left the two of them in the kitchen, Lois's wild eyes following me up the stairs as if I had betrayed her. Maybe she even believed I had planned it this way.

I sat on my bed for a while, just holding my hands in my lap, feeling like a miserable failure. I could hear their voices faintly below, but I couldn't make out what they were saying. Any other time I would have tried to listen, but I felt like…I don't know, like I'd lost the right to.

After a while I went over to my bookshelf by the window and took out my copy of Dickinson's poems. I looked in the index and then turned to the page it listed, my eyes going to the last stanza as though I were searching for an oracle, a prophecy.

> *The Soul's retaken moments—*
> *When, Felon led along,*
> *With shackles on the plumed feet,*
> *And staples, in the Song,*
> *The Horror welcomes her, again,*
> *These, are not brayed of Tongue—*

It didn't make me feel any better.

CHAPTER • EIGHT

LATER, WHILE I WAS MAKING sandwiches for us in the kitchen, I was able to ask Norton why he had showed up on my doorstep. By that time Lois had gone upstairs to lie down in my room. She looked gaunt and exhausted. I doubt that she had slept all night.

The deputy sat at the table while I worked at the counter by the sink. I couldn't remember the last time a man sat at that little drop-leaf table, and my hands were unsteady from the unaccustomed domestic intimacy.

I noticed he had on a fresh shirt; I saw the precise laundry creases down the back when I went around behind him to open the refrigerator. He must live alone, I thought, if he sends his shirts out. Sunlight poured in through the casement windows and glinted off the short sandy hairs on the back of his neck just above the collar. He must have had a haircut recently.

I didn't know how much Lois had told him while I was upstairs. She had come up to my room after about thirty minutes, still looking haggard, but less wild. "I just want to sleep now," she said dully, and lay down on the bed and closed her eyes. I hadn't had the heart to ask any more questions or even try to explain that the deputy's sudden appearance was as much a surprise to me as it was to her.

I had come downstairs thinking he might have left, but he was still there, obviously waiting for me. I had had time to pull myself together, and I was wary now. There would be plenty of people intent on finding out who was to blame for Finney's escape, but hardly anyone would care about the hurts there aren't any laws to cover. I had decided that my part in this was to help Lois—and Cecelia—however I could. Norton was "the law," the term old-timers in Point Blank still used for a policeman of any jurisdiction. I knew it was better to have someone like him doing the job than some redneck good old boy. But I also knew I would have to be cautious around him if I was to protect my friends.

"She's resting," I said levelly. "I hope she can sleep."

"Yes," he answered. "She needs to."

I stood there at the bottom of the stairs, hesitant to say more.

"Can we talk?" he asked.

I could hear the cars starting up in the parking lot at the Baptist Church down the road. It must be noon and the service over. Everyone would see his car out in front. But they wouldn't know Lois was here.

"Are you hungry? I could fix some sandwiches."

"And coffee?" he added. "Coffee's what I need. I didn't sleep much myself." He followed me into the kitchen where it was brighter. I was surprised at how tired he looked.

"So," I said to him, getting the mayonnaise out of the refrigerator but keeping his face in view out of the corner of my eye, "what do you think?"

"About what?" he said, moving his shoulders wearily up and down.

I hesitated while I opened the jar. "About this whole situation." Both of us, I could see, were afraid of taking the first step that might reveal too much.

He laughed. "Well, if I knew what the whole situation was I might be able to tell you. That's the problem."

"I don't understand."

He hesitated now, obviously just as cautious about tipping his own hand.

"Look," I said suddenly, coming around the table and facing him squarely. It helped that he was sitting down. "I know that you want to find out the truth about all this. I don't blame you for that. I respect you for it, in fact. But you've got to understand my position, too. There are two women here—Lois and her mother—who stand to be damaged a great deal. I don't know all the facts myself. But I do know that I don't want their lives to be ruined—for nothing, for no good purpose. Just because—" I brought myself up short. I could feel my pulse pounding in my throat. I took a deep breath. "I don't want to play games with you. If I can help somehow without hurting them, then I will. But otherwise—" I turned back abruptly to cutting the sandwiches.

He sat there silently until I finished and put the food on the table. When the coffee was done, he got up and filled two mugs that he took out of the dish drainer by the sink. I sat down at the table across from him, determined not to say another word until he spoke.

"It's disastrous for a policeman to get personally involved in an investigation," he said finally. His voice sounded weary, but I was also gratified to catch the same note of uncertainty that I had heard in mine. "You can't expect that I could have the same concerns for your friends that you do. And if I did, that in itself would disqualify me from working on this case."

"I understand that," I said, but he held up his hand.

"Let me finish." He paused again while he looked at his cup. "Nevertheless, I respect your feelings about this. In fact, I've thought about that all night. What your friend Lois told me just now, about this Finney Blalock and how she was supposed to help him escape, I'm not too concerned about that. I suspect that he primarily needed her for ready cash when he got out. But she was only one part of the plan. As for the actual escape, she couldn't have helped with that. He needed help on the inside to actually get out. It's possible that help may have come from cousin Archie."

Here he stopped and raised his eyes suddenly, as though wanting to catch my reaction. What he saw must have reassured him, because he went on.

"But that's beside the point too. Blalock may have been shot because he wanted more from Archie. Archie may in fact have been surprised to find him there in his trailer. Maybe hiding him there wasn't part of the original deal. But Blalock could have threatened to expose Archie if he didn't give him more help—or money. I leave that to the TDC people to figure out. The county doesn't get messed up in the prison's problems if we can help it. But the crafty—and I think Blalock was probably very crafty—are frequently overcome by the stupid. By the simple reflex for survival." He didn't need to add that the stupid one he was referring to was Archie.

I began to feel hopeful, and picked up half a sandwich, pushing the plate over towards him. His theory about Archie helping set up Finney's escape would explain the scene I had witnessed last night, standing on the steps of the trailer. Finney might very well have made his way to Archie's and demanded more help—a hiding place, transportation to Houston, something Archie hadn't counted on. I didn't have any trouble believing that Archie, fearing discovery when I screamed, would take the easiest and quickest way out of the situation by simply shooting Finney.

"So," I said, "if that's the way it was—granted that Lois might have gotten money together to help him get wherever he wanted to go—then that's the end of it, isn't it?"

Norton smiled wryly and his fingers began to tap the table rhythmically. "You're awfully selective about who you want to protect here, aren't you?" he asked. "You want to save the ladies, but you don't seem to mind throwing old Archie to the wolves."

"Archie!" I exclaimed. "I wouldn't waste a lot of sentiment on Archie if I were you. There's not that much to choose between him and Finney when it comes right down to it. Except that Finney's clever and Archie's dumb. Well, maybe there's more than that, but, believe me, everyone in Point Blank thinks it's only a matter of time till Archie ends up inside the prison instead of guarding it. Especially now that Miss Mineola is gone. He only kept more or less inside the law because he didn't want to spoil his chances with her."

"Really?"

"Of course. Oh, he'll put on a big show of bereavement. He does have a theatrical streak. But you can bet he can't wait for the will to be read."

"I thought you said the will was a big mystery."

"It is. No one knows for sure what it says except Miss Mineola's lawyer. But still, this is Archie's one big chance. The only one he'll ever get. The rest who might stand to profit—her two grandchildren and Cecelia—they have other means of making it in the world. Archie doesn't."

"I understand Lois is writing her dissertation now?"

"Yes. Then she's supposed to do an internship in a psychiatric hospital next year. After that, she'll be able to set up her own practice."

"And rake in the big bucks?"

"Well. Make a respectable living. She's very sharp, you know."

He smiled a little crookedly at this. "I guess I haven't seen her at her best. Getting involved with this Blalock character is not my idea of sharp."

"No," I said staunchly. "You haven't seen her at her best, as a matter of fact. She is very bright."

"But not as bright as Blalock."

I guessed then that she must have told him everything. For some reason I felt embarrassed, not only for Lois, but for myself too. "I don't know about that."

He shook his head and drummed on the table again with his fingers. "I don't understand either," he said. "The whole phenomenon, I mean. Why do women—" He shrugged his shoulders in exasperation.

"You have to understand—"

"Yes?" he put in almost belligerently.

"She had a really miserable childhood."

"So? I thought she was supposed to be the brilliant psychologist here. Anybody ought to be able to see that some madman who's already killed one woman and threatened his own family is not exactly the safest person to go vacationing with in Mexico. My God!" he finally exploded. "She must be insane herself!"

I bit my lip. The truth of the matter was that only a couple of hours earlier I had been having much the same reaction. But I felt compelled to defend her now.

"It's like—" I paused again, looking out the window. The gold and red of the marigolds and geraniums I had planted along the border of the walk swam wantonly in my vision as I fought for words. "Like Archie, only in another way. Finney was her one chance."

"One chance?" he repeated. "I thought you just said she had a great career ahead of her."

I looked at him stonily. "You know what I mean. I'm not talking about careers."

"That's ridiculous," he said, waving my words away. "She's not bad looking. A little stringy maybe. But she must have plenty of opportunities."

"In case you weren't aware," I said acidly, "it's not always just a matter of looks. I'd say, as a matter of fact, that it's her intelligence that puts men off. They tend to feel threatened by her."

"Not just men. Judging from what I saw of her last night, she seems to feel pretty superior to the entire human race."

There was no point in my denying that. Most people felt that way about Lois. "Maybe," I finally said slowly, since it was just now occurring to me, "maybe Finney was the first one who wasn't put off. The one who felt equal to her. And maybe she liked that."

"You mean maybe she was just waiting for some man who could put her in her place?" His voice was harsh. "What is she—some kind of masochist?"

"I didn't say that," I protested. But his words had unnerved me. They sounded dangerously near a reasonable possibility, one I hadn't considered before.

"Women," he said. "They don't know what they want." And he drained his cup with a gesture that was somehow even more infuriating than his words.

I pushed my chair away from the table. "If that's all the light you've got to throw on the situation—" I began. But he held up both his hands in protest.

"No. I'm sorry. I didn't mean that. I'm just exasperated, that's all. Please. Sit down. I didn't mean to offend you."

"But it was offensive."

"Worse," he said. "It was stupid. I didn't mean to include you in that, of course."

I drew my chair back up to the table, but I made it clear I wasn't mollified. "Of course not. Some of your best friends are probably women."

"Look," he said and laid his palms carefully on either side of his empty cup, "I know I offended you. I'm sorry. I spoke before I thought. I apologize. I know that we probably have some differences of opinions about—any number of things. But I still could use your help on this."

"Am I supposed to be gratified by that request?" I could feel my heart thumping in my throat again.

His jaw tightened at that remark and he sat there a full thirty seconds before he replied. "What you feel about it is your business," he said finally. "I'm just stating a fact."

I allowed an equal amount of time to pass before I responded. Then I said, with what I hoped sounded like perfect self-possession, "But I thought you said the sheriff's department would leave this to the prison officials to deal with? I don't know what help of mine you need."

He turned his head and squinted out the window into the bright noonday sun. "It's not about Blalock," he said softly. "Not his escape or even his death. Although I still think there's something fishy about that."

"What then?" I was puzzled and even leaned forward a little to catch what he would say next.

He turned back from the window and looked me straight in the eye. "Mrs. Magillberry," he said. "I think she might have been helped out of this world a little too soon."

I sat back and stared at him. "But surely, if that's so, it would have been Finney. I thought you'd already decided that last night when you found the jewelry on him."

Before he answered, he got up and poured himself another cup of coffee. "This morning," he began, sitting down again, "that grandson of hers—what's his name?"

"Max? You mean Maximillian?"

"That's him. He comes storming into the office, demanding to see the sheriff. Well, of course, this being Sunday morning, the sheriff wasn't there. But Lurline, the dispatcher, didn't tell him that right off. She looked him up and down cool as a cucumber and told him we had a 'no shirt–no service' policy. He was furious, but he went back out to that little red Ferrari and rummaged around till he found a shirt. I was watching all this from the window in my office. When he came back in he was hopping mad. He wanted to know why the sheriff had ordered an autopsy on his grandmother."

I frowned, thinking back on the scene with Max and Muriel this morning. With all that had happened since then, it had nearly slipped my mind. "Oh, yes," I said. "I remember now. I was over at Miss Mineola's this morning. Both Max and his sister were there. I remember Cecelia telling them they'd have to put the funeral off till Tuesday because they couldn't do the autopsy till tomorrow. Muriel didn't seem too upset, but Max was furious. He wanted to know who had taken it upon themselves to order such a thing. He seemed to think it was some kind of, I don't know, either disrespect for his grandmother's remains or infringement on the family's authority. Probably the latter. He never showed Miss Mineola too much respect while she was alive. I don't know why he should start now."

"He didn't strike me as any prize family man."

"A spoiled rich kid," I said. "His parents left him plenty in a trust when they died."

"Does he work? Have a job?"

"Max? Oh, no. I think maybe he gambles. At least I've heard rumors to that effect. But mostly he amuses himself. The last I heard he'd taken up scuba diving. He goes to Mexico, the Caribbean, places like that, looking for new places to dive. A rough life."

"I see." He started drumming his fingers on the table again and stared out the window.

"So?" I said finally. "Cecelia told Max this morning she didn't know why the autopsy was ordered."

"No, she wouldn't," Norton said. "The sheriff hasn't told any of the family members the reason."

"Why? Surely they have a right to know. It was the jewelry wasn't it? Finding Miss Mineola's jewelry on Finney?"

"Did you say anything about that to your friend upstairs?" he asked, nodding in the direction of the stairwell.

"No. When I heard what she had to tell me this morning, it drove everything else right out of my head. It hadn't even occurred to me again till now."

"What about her mother? Or Archie? Anybody else?"

"No. I haven't told anyone."

"Good," he said. "It's important that it doesn't get out, not even to the family members. If no one lets that information out, it'll make our job a lot easier." He emphasized "no one."

"And please," he went on, "if you hear any mention of the missing jewelry, let me know. Or if anyone makes any inquiries about it. That can be important."

I nodded. Then I added, after thinking about it a moment, "But surely, if there was any—foul play—connected with Miss Mineola's death it would have been Finney that did it. I mean, you found the jewelry on him."

"Exactly."

"Isn't that what Sheriff Dooley thinks?"

"Of course." The deputy paused. "But if you could have seen that guy in the red sports car come storming in there this morning, you might not have been so sure. He was awfully determined there wasn't going to be an autopsy on his dearly departed grandmother—the one you've already told me he didn't actually care that much about."

I laughed suddenly. "The sheriff's right. You do like to complicate things. Max just likes to throw his weight around. But really. He wasn't even in the county yesterday afternoon."

"Maybe not. But a lot of other people were. I just don't think we ought to limit the options at this point."

I tried to think back to the previous afternoon, before I saw Archie shoot Finney. That scene had left such an imprint in my memory that it was hard now to recall the details of what had gone on before.

Cecelia had called me soon after she discovered Miss Mineola because she didn't know where Lois was. I had spent some time looking for her in Point Blank, but she was with her mother when I arrived. They'd already called the sheriff, and Archie was talking to the other deputy in the living room. The mortician had been impatient to get the body moved, I remembered. But the j.p., being new to the job, had insisted on going down his checklist methodically. He had wanted to see Miss Mineola's oxygen tank, and Cecelia had told him she'd moved it to the east porch. Lois was calling friends and relatives. Then later, after the hearse had left, there was something about a book. That ledger we found behind the bed. Lois had read the last day's entries, trying to make Archie angry. He'd tried to grab it away from her.

I checked through these jumbled scenes rapidly in my mind, editing them before deciding what to tell Norton. As far as I could tell, everything seemed fairly straightforward. But, of course, I hadn't known then just how Lois was mixed up in all this. Had she known that Finney had been in her grandmother's bedroom? Had she known about the jewelry? And how would that have affected her feelings?

I sighed, thinking of Lois asleep upstairs. Who would have guessed? Lois and Finney! How could you ever make any predictions about people?

"Yes?" Norton said, bringing me back to the present. "Do you remember anything else?"

I shrugged. "Nothing out of the ordinary. We found a ledger. I discovered it under the bed when we were cleaning up the bedroom. Miss Mineola kept it sort of like a diary, I guess. A business diary. There was something in it about Archie and a loan." I didn't say anything about Lois reading part of it out loud nor about Archie getting angry.

The deputy looked at me closely, obviously studying my face. "Okay," he said finally. "Maybe I'll look into that too." He scraped his chair back and stood up. "And if you think of anything else, you'll let me know, won't you?"

"Sure," I said, getting up and following him to the front door. I could see the clouds had dissipated. We wouldn't have any rain after all.

He turned before he stepped out onto the front porch and held out his hand. "Friends?" he said. And he held my hand a moment longer than necessary for just an ordinary handshake.

"Sure," I said again and smiled. I smiled because I felt suddenly guilty. I had just remembered one more thing. Cecelia's wanting to make a confession.

CHAPTER NINE

MY OWN FAMILY, BEING Episcopalian, would never think of having its funerals at Holcombe's, even though they might keep the body on display there for those who couldn't make it to the service at the church. But Miss Mineola, being Baptist, had been horrified at the thought of bringing a dead body—even her own—into a church, as though that defiled it somehow. My mother always pointed out to me that such an attitude was a theological inconsistency typical of Baptists.

"You'd think they were ashamed of dying!" she'd say. "I know it must be some kind of heresy. Something from the second or fourth century, I'm pretty sure." And she'd tell me to go look it up in the *Oxford Dictionary of the Christian Church*. But since she never could remember the name of the particular heresy or heretic, I never could find it for her. Besides which, I had noticed the Oxford Dictionary tended to give short shrift to Baptists.

Mother's idea of religious education for children was frequent consultation of this reference work, careful attention to the appropriate color for the liturgical seasons, and depositing me every Saturday afternoon for three months during my twelfth year at the St. Barnabas parish hall in Somerville for confirmation class. She read her parish newsletter and the diocesan monthly publication as soon as they came, clucking her tongue and muttering under her breath at various ecclesiastical decisions not to her liking. But I never knew what they were. Or when I did, I never could see what upset her.

We lived too far out for me to participate in any of the "youth activities" of St. Barnabas, except for confirmation classes, of course. So as compensation Mother let me go to all the Baptist picnics and "fellowships" in Point Blank, figuring I'd be safe enough there. But she drew the line at the Baptist summer camp. She was afraid I might be led to make some foolish emotional response if I were exposed to all that rhetorical intensity and rousing music for an extended period. She even had me read the article in the church dictionary on "Plainsong" after she heard me whistling "Do Lord" around the house.

As I went up the steps to Holcombe's Funeral Home that Sunday afternoon I wondered what Mother would think of Point Blank's current predicament. I still had a way of referring things to my mother in my head, whether I was buying a pair of shoes or voting for county commissioners.

There was no question in my mind, of course, about what she would have thought of Lois's involvement with Finney. But at the same time, her loyalty to her friends was unshakable. Would Mother have approved of my taking Lois home with me? That might have been going too far. And undoubtedly she would have wanted me to tell Cecelia the whole story as soon as possible. But then she was Cecelia's friend. If she had been in my position, with Lois as her friend, she might have acted the same way I had this morning. Except for the sandwiches. I wasn't at all sure she would have made sandwiches for the deputy.

I shook those worries out of my head as I opened the

big double door at the top of Holcombe's steps. I had to find out something from Cecelia now, before Norton talked to her again. But I had no intention of telling her about Lois and Finney. Maybe she could still be spared that.

I found her alone in the manager's office, sunk into a velour sofa. She was holding a long, legal-size document and frowning at it. When I tapped on the open door, she looked up, her frown turning instantly to a smile of relief.

"Thank heavens you're here, Beth Marie!" she exclaimed.

I kissed the cheek she turned up to me and sat down on the arm of the sofa.

"I'm so glad you're here," she said. "I guess Lois was too tired to come?"

I merely nodded.

"They gave me Aunt Min's Guardian Plan to look over here, but I'm not any good at this kind of thing. I thought she'd already made all the decisions, but I guess there's still some more." She held out several sheets covered with numbered paragraphs. "The manager's not in this afternoon since it's Sunday, but the girl in the office gave me this and said I should be looking it over and making some choices."

I took the pages reluctantly. "Like what? What kind of choices?"

"The coffin, for one thing."

"But I thought Miss Mineola already picked out a coffin."

"She had, bless her heart. That's why I feel so bad. But the secretary said they were out of that particular model right now. Well, honey, you know how Aunt Min felt about substitutes. I mean, whenever they ran out of coupon items at the grocery store, she never would let me take a substitute. If it was Mrs. Paul's Extra Crispy Fish Portions, then that's what she wanted. She wouldn't accept Gorton's or even fish sticks. So I wouldn't expect her to feel any different about her casket, would you? Not that she even liked fish. The only fish she'd ever even put in her mouth was in tuna salad."

I laid my hand on her shoulder to interrupt her rambling. "What kind of casket was it she wanted, Cecelia?"

She handed me yet another sheet, this one typed all in caps, obviously a product of the local establishment. "See here? This number seven?"

"PROTECTIVE, LINCOLN, COPPER, PAINTED, BLUE—$2999," I read from the list.

"The girl told me they've all gone up since Aunt Min took out this policy. It'd cost $606 more now," Cecelia said, "but she still gets it at the same price as it was when she bought the plan. That is, she would if they had it."

I scanned the list quickly. "Look at number eleven," I said, pointing to the item on the list. "PROTECTIVE, CHAPEL, STAINLESS STEEL, BLUE—$2799. That's practically the same thing."

"But it's stainless steel instead of copper, Beth Marie. And two hundred dollars less. I mean the more expensive one's already paid for, and I doubt that they'll give us a rebate. So Aunt Min might not think she was getting as much of a bargain as she'd hoped." She tilted her head to one side and looked at me with the bewilderment of a child who desperately wants to please but doesn't know how. I was glad Lois wasn't there.

I took a deep breath and let it out slowly. "Well, I think the protection and the color would probably be the most important features to Miss Mineola. And look at it this way. This one's probably gone up in price too. So she's still saving several hundred dollars."

She frowned as though weighing this.

"But if you're not satisfied," I added, "what you ought to do is wait and talk to the manager. That's probably best anyway."

Her round face brightened again. "All right then. I'll wait till tomorrow about that." She folded up the papers and stuck them inside her vast handbag, and I helped her up from the depths of the sofa.

"All I have to do now is pick out a viewing room," she said. "For when they bring Aunt Min back up here from Houston. Come on and help me, Beth Marie."

I followed her out into the main foyer where separate alcoves arranged on its periphery held caskets displaying the most recently departed citizens of Watson County. There were no doors on the alcoves, and the mourners from various families tended to get mixed together. In fact, the mood in the foyer was almost festive in a hushed sort of way. Relatives who hadn't met since the last funeral greeted one other with hugs and exclamations.

"Are you coming on out to the house afterwards?" a woman holding a baby asked another woman.

"We were just going to get a motel room here in town," she answered, squeezing the baby's plump knee.

"Heavens, no! We've got plenty of beds. And the neighbors are bringing in food."

"Well, if you're sure it won't be any trouble."

I followed Cecelia as unobtrusively as I could while she looked over the alcoves. The series of viewing rooms ended in a little formica and vinyl kitchenette with a coffee urn and a couple of tables. A place for the less mournful family members to retreat.

"Just what I need. Some coffee," Cecelia said. "Beth Marie, what about you?"

I poured both of us a styrofoam cup of what I hoped was fresh coffee and sat down across from her. No one else was in the room just then, and I hoped I could finally get down to what I had come here for. I waited for her to tear open the little pink packet of Sweet and Low and stir it into her coffee.

"I think maybe we ought to take the one nearest to

the entrance. What do you think?" she asked. "I know Aunt Min doesn't have much family left, but she knew lots of people in the county and they'll all probably be coming by, don't you think? It'd make a terrible traffic jam if they had to push past all those other folks. What do you think, Beth Marie? I sure wish I didn't have to make all these decisions. I don't know why she didn't leave all this to Max or Muriel." She shook her head and sighed.

"You know why, Cecelia," I said, and was suddenly struck by how much I sounded like my mother. "She knew those two would stick her in the ground any old way. They'd only be interested in getting it over with. You're the only person in the world she could trust to do things the way she wanted them done—even if it is a bother."

"How I wish it were all over with," she said with a groan. "After the funeral there'll be the will, and that's going to be even worse."

"Why? What do you mean?"

She looked up at me as though surprised I would ask such a question. "It won't matter who gets what. You know that. However Aunt Min divided things up, there'll still be a big wrangle over it. I just hope she left the same amount to both Max and Muriel, though they'll each think they deserve a bigger share. And if she left much to Archie or me, then they won't like that either. But if Archie doesn't get anything, then what's he going to do with himself?"

"Everyone knows, Cecelia, that if it were handled fairly, it would be you that got the lion's share. How many years have you taken care of her now?" I knew what her answer would be—I had heard this same conversation between her and my mother many times before—but it was like a litany from which none of the parts could be omitted or it wouldn't work.

"I would have taken care of her if she hadn't had a

penny," she said, laying her plastic spoon down. "In fact, it would have probably made it easier if she hadn't," she added unexpectedly.

"What do you mean?"

She shrugged her shoulders and looked, for the first time, so thoroughly disheartened that I almost faltered in my resolve. "I don't know," she said. "At least I wouldn't have had so many people looking over my shoulder all the time, trying to tell me what I ought to have done after I'd already done it." She sighed again and looked into her half-empty cup.

I could hardly bring myself to ask her my question now, but I knew I had to. Better me than someone else—someone who didn't understand her as well as I did.

"Cecelia," I began slowly. She looked up. "Remember last night, right after they took Miss Mineola away and the justice of the peace had left?"

"Yes?"

"You told me you had a confession to make, remember?" I could feel my heart beginning to beat in my throat again. I sat there silent for a moment, hoping she would respond without my having to say anymore. But she only puckered her forehead as though trying to recall where she'd misplaced something.

"You told me to get Bartholomew's number for you, remember? You needed to call him. You said you wanted to get something off your chest."

"I never got to," she said. "Terry B. showed up just about then. I guess it slipped my mind after that."

I sat there, looking over my styrofoam cup at her, waiting for her to go on. She shifted around uneasily in her chair and toyed with another packet of Sweet and Low. I didn't know whether I should mention how Max had raised a ruckus at the sheriff's office or about the jewelry they had found on Finney. It was getting sticky, trying to remember what not to say to whom.

"Well," she said finally, "I guess I better tell you. I

got my courage all worked up to tell Bartholomew yesterday afternoon, but then, after everything else that happened, Finney getting shot and all, it just didn't seem so important anymore."

"You can tell me, Cecelia," I said gently, and reached over to squeeze her hand encouragingly. How was I supposed to protect her if I didn't know what this confession was about?

Suddenly she laughed, and I drew back my hand, startled. I had been expecting her to cry maybe, but not laugh. She reached over and patted my hand now. "Heavenly days," she said, "I don't know whether I'm more ashamed of myself or angry, Beth Marie."

I stared at her while she kept on chuckling to herself.

"It's such a small thing, such a petty thing," she finally said. "But then it's not either. At least it was important to me. And it didn't seem so terrible at the time. It only seemed fair."

"What in the world are you talking about, Cecelia?" But there was no use trying to force her directly to the point. She always manages to tell things in her own way.

"How Aunt Min ended up with it, I don't know," she began. "It belonged to my daddy. I was there when my grandmother gave it to him. She was real sick by then, and her fingers had shrunk down to no more than bones. She was afraid she'd lose it, though her knuckles were so swollen there wasn't much chance of it coming off. But still it worried her a lot."

"What worried her, Cecelia?" I asked, trying not to sound irritated.

"The ring," she said. "The ring she always wore. I don't know if it was her wedding ring or not, but it had a little tiny diamond in it and garnets. Garnets are old-fashioned now I guess, but in Granny's day they were quite stylish."

I nodded to keep her momentum going.

"She pulled it off and gave it to Daddy, right there in

that same room where Aunt Min died—was it just yesterday? It already seems like a week ago." She sighed heavily.

"And?"

"That's all. She gave it to him. She said he was to have it. I believe my grandmother hadn't given it to him earlier because she didn't want my mother to have it. But by then Granny knew she was dying. She must have wanted it to come to me through my daddy."

"And?"

She looked at me puzzled, as though by now everything should be perfectly clear. "Well. He took it. He didn't give it to me then because I was still just a girl, and besides, if anybody was going to wear it, it should have been my mother. Still, he knew it would have caused a ruckus in the family if my mother had appeared with it on her finger. His sisters—Aunt Min and Aunt Hattie—would have had a conniption. So I guess he just put it away somewhere. I always meant to ask him what he did with it, but it was one of those things I never got around to before he died." She sighed again.

"But your mother must have come across it after he died."

"No. She looked for it. I remember she particularly wanted to find it for me. It was really the only thing I got—or would have gotten—from my grandmother. I mean something personal, you know. A keepsake. That's all it really amounted to."

"And your mother didn't find it?"

"No. She turned everything inside out looking for it, but she couldn't find it anywhere. Mother always suspected Aunt Min had managed to get hold of it somehow, but she was too proud to mention it to her." Here she stopped again and her eyes roamed the little coffee room distractedly.

"Go on," I said firmly, once again hearing the echo of my mother in my voice.

"Well. About a month ago it struck Aunt Min that the one thing she hadn't settled in her will to her satisfaction was the jewelry. Originally she had told Bartholomew to divide it up with everything else. But then she got to fretting over it. She wanted to make an exact inventory of it all. Not that there was anything especially valuable, except for all that gold stuff she buys that looks so gaudy. I never did see what she thought was so grand about all those chains and big old shapeless nuggets."

I nodded. "But you did want your grandmother's ring."

"I didn't even know for sure that Aunt Min had it. But if she did, I figured it belonged to me."

Cecelia took a deep breath. I could see this still rankled with her. "I guess I should have outright asked her about it. That would have been the thing to do. But I was angry!" She gave the table a restrained little thump with her pink fist. "It was so unfair. Why did she want it anyway? She'd never once worn it all these years since Daddy died. I guess she knew Mother would be all over her if she went that far. And, of course, we didn't know for sure she had it. It could have just gotten lost. But I figured that was why she didn't ask me to help her with the inventory the way she usually did. And if that ring got mentioned in the will, then there'd be no way I'd ever get it back." She shook her head and looked more distressed than she had all afternoon. "Isn't that awful?" she said, "to get that worked up about a silly old ring?"

I nodded to keep her from getting off the track.

"Anyway, last week I was putting Aunt Min's groceries away for her and accidentally overturned an old sugar bowl she keeps up on one of the top shelves of the cupboard over the sink. Something fell out of it and hit the floor, but I didn't pay it any mind until I got everything put away. I expected it to be an old button or something like that. But lo and behold, it was the garnet ring. I didn't know if she'd put it there and forgot about it sometime back or what. Anyway, I put it in my pocket and didn't say anything about it."

I sat back in my chair. "And that's what you were going to confess to Bartholomew?"

"Yes," she said. "I guess I should have confronted her with it outright. But she was getting so feeble, and a scene like that might have given her a heart attack or something. Besides, who knows how long it had been up there? It could have been years. She might not even remember putting it there. Anyway, I couldn't bring myself to mention it to her. It just seemed simpler to go ahead and take it. If she said anything about it, then I'd tell her I had it and that I felt like it was mine. I didn't even think about that inventory she sent Bartholomew. I don't know if that ring is on it or not. But yesterday afternoon it started weighing on me, so I figured I better let him know about it. I didn't think I'd be able to sleep with that on my conscience."

"And that's all?"

She had been rummaging through her black patent handbag for a handkerchief and looked up at me puzzled. "All of what?"

"All the confession?"

"Well, yes, it's all. What do you mean?" She almost sounded cross.

"I mean it's...such a small thing." Just the kind of thing Cecelia would torture herself with, I thought.

She clicked her purse shut and blew her nose. "It may sound like a small thing to you, Beth Marie, but let me tell you. The devil will use whatever device he can to get a toehold in your heart. It wasn't the ring itself that was the problem, you understand. It was what the ring represented—all those years of my daddy slaving away on this land and Aunt Min gradually eating it up all around him, till there was just this tiny little island that was left for him to stand on. That ring was like the little lamb that Nathan accused King David of stealing from the poor man, remember?"

I frowned, not being able to follow her leaps in logic. "A lamb?"

"You know," she said, waving away the question like an irritating fly. "Bathsheba and all that. Uriah. Daddy was like Uriah and Aunt Min was like King David. Look it up, honey. Second Samuel." And she started her preparations for getting up, one hand on the table and the other on the back of the chair for leverage.

"Cecelia," I said, when she was on her feet again.

"Yes, sweetheart?"

"Remember when you sent me out to find Archie and tell him to meet you down in the barn?"

She steadied herself by holding onto the counter behind her and took a moment to answer, as though she were searching her memory. "Oh, yes," she finally said. "Yes. I remember."

"What was that about, Cecelia? Why did you have to meet him in the barn?" I hated pushing her like that, but I figured I better get all the information I could out of her at one time.

"Oh, that," she said, propelling herself forward from the counter and starting back out toward the viewing rooms. "I'm afraid I can't tell you that, honey. That involves somebody else. I really can't tell you about that. It wouldn't be right."

CHAPTER • TEN

AS I DROVE BACK TO POINT BLANK, I told myself I didn't have any right to feel put out with Cecelia just because she wouldn't tell me why she'd wanted to talk to Archie. After all, I was concealing her own daughter's terrible secret from her. On the other hand, I was beginning to understand how exasperated my mother must have often felt with this friend of hers.

That stopped me cold. What I was doing? Turning into a replica of my mother? At times now I could almost hear her voice echoing in mine. The thought gave me cold chills. Not that I didn't love and respect my mother, you understand. I've always stood up for her when people make remarks about how she thought she was too good for a place like Point Blank. Still, I didn't intend to step into her shoes. I wanted...I didn't know what exactly, but something. Something my mother hadn't wanted. At least not that I ever knew about.

But I had to admit that Mother knew how to handle Cecelia. She used to say that her friend had "no sense of proportion," and that that deficiency accounted for her gullibility. Cecelia sometimes accepted the most implausible explanations at face value. For instance, when I called her up that evening and told her Lois had decided to spend the night with me, Cecelia acted as though it were the most natural thing in the world that two women in their thirties would be having a slumber party in the middle of funeral preparations. Actually, Lois had taken a double dose of some old Valium tablets of my mother's left in the medicine cabinet and I didn't want to rouse her.

I left her sleeping in my bed and moved into Mother's room, which, of course, only made me more aware of her influence. I took my copy of Emily Dickinson with me to browse through till I got sleepy. The book was a sort of talisman, I suppose. Mother never did like Dickinson. She liked Browning.

Reading Emily is like fishing. You can dip into her poems anywhere and come out with some little silvery sliver, something you never expected. Unfortunately, the first one I read that night made me think of Mother again. It began

I tend my flowers for thee—
Bright Absentee

Which reminded me of looking at the geraniums and marigolds that morning while I was talking to Norton in the kitchen. Their vivid colors had seemed to match my feelings at the time. But even the flowers weren't mine; they were Mother's. She was the one who had dug up the flower beds every February and gotten them ready for spring. She spent hours, days, trimming and mulching and fertilizing. Her greatest concern during her last long illness was that the flowers would be neglected and the weeds take over the beds she had worked so hard to keep up. So of course I promised her that I'd look after them. I sat by her bed while she dictated planting schedules and gave instructions about fighting thrips and spider mites.

I never minded tending to the flowers after she was gone. I had even learned a few things myself in the past few years and made some changes, digging out all that awful old monkey grass, for instance, and putting in vinca instead. But as soon as I read those lines addressed to the "Bright Absentee," I began to wonder if, once again, I was following in her footsteps, almost becoming her reincarnation. I drifted through the rest of the poem, all the lines about fuchsias and geraniums and hyacinths and roses. Then, ready to put the book away, I glanced at the last verse.

> *Thy flower—be gay—*
> *Her Lord—away!*
> *It ill becometh me—*
> *I'll dwell in Calyx—Gray—*
> *How modestly—alway—*
> *Thy Daisy—*
> *Draped for thee!*

Her *Lord* away? The bright absentee was obviously not a mother.

I laughed at myself and stretched, studying my bare foot. I'd see him tomorrow again for sure. Maybe they'd get the results of the autopsy and he'd come out and tell me about it.

If I closed the Water Board office at noon tomorrow, I could run in to Somerville and maybe find something more interesting than the Sunday dresses I'd worn the last two days. They were too—calyx gray. Somehow I didn't feel like being any modestly draped daisy. After all, it was summer. Why not something tropical looking? Something hibiscus-like.

I went to sleep that night thinking not about my friend Lois lying drugged in the next room, trying to escape her damaged life, but about floral prints.

The next morning, though, while I was still in my jeans and T-shirt, just finishing my second cup of coffee and feeling relieved to hear Lois running the shower upstairs, people started knocking on the front screen. Customers who hadn't paid their bill in two months showed up, checkbook in hand, wanting to know what had happened out at the old Laudermilk place on Saturday.

Maynard Wilkie, who used to run the feedstore before it closed up, had me go over the meter readings for the past six months while he quizzed me about Finney.

"You know me, Beth Marie. I don't claim to be a churchgoer. Never have been. And I don't aim to start being no hypocrite about it now. I've always felt closest to God out by myself on the lake. When it's quiet and peaceful, you know. But I have to say I went to services yesterday with Ruthie and the kids. I figured that if anybody ever needed the support of the whole community, it was Brother Blalock. I don't see how that man could get up there and preach like he did when his son had just escaped from prison and had his head blowed off. But he did it. He sure did it."

"Looks to me like these figures all match up, Maynard," I said, turning from the file drawer.

"Of course his voice sort of got quavery and broke sometimes, but you can't blame a man for that. Not one that's been through what he has. I mean if my Heywood ever went bad like Finney did, there's no telling how I might take on either." He opened his checkbook reluctantly and leaned his thick forearm across it while he wrote out the date slowly. "How much did you say that was now?"

I knew he wanted me to give him an eyewitness account of Finney's shooting, but I kept my remarks confined strictly to how many gallons of water he owed for.

As soon as he left, the Gorlack sisters came in together in their matching dresses. They have a way of talking exclusively to one another while referring to anyone else present in the third person.

"You did bring the bill with you, didn't you, Bess? Don't tell me you forgot it. We don't want to have to put Beth Marie to the trouble of looking it up."

"It's no trouble at all, Miss Luellen," I said, watching Bess rifle her dusty black patent handbag. "I don't mind looking it up for you." A little shower of old gum wrappers, hairpins, ballpoint pen lids, and grocery store coupons accumulated on the dining table as Bess rummaged for the bill.

"It was here when we left home, Luellen, I just know it was," Bess said hopelessly. "Do you think she'd be too angry if we asked her to look it up for us in her records? You know she keeps such good records."

I turned to my filing cabinet and heard Bess's purse shut with a click.

"And writes so well too," Luellen said, dabbing at her neck with a handkerchief that had fallen out of the handbag. "I guess she's going to have plenty to write about in her column for *The Courier* this week."

I silently copied out the numbers from their account and slid the paper across the table, smiling.

Luellen, the bolder of the two, actually made eye contact at that point, darting a glance at me before turning her attention back to her sister. "I don't know when we've had so much excitement in Point Blank," she said.

I handed her a pen as she reluctantly drew out their mutual checkbook. Luellen always carried the checkbook.

"Thank you, ladies," I said, taking the check and filing it in my cash box. They were just turning away, visibly disappointed in their mission, when I saw another car pull up outside. It had a star on the side.

I got up so quickly I almost upset the open cash box. The Gorlack sisters turned and stared at me. Then they saw Norton coming up the walk. They nodded to him like two heavy-head dahlias as he held the door open for them; then they trotted past him and down the walk with little short, self-satisfied steps. I could tell they were headed toward the post office to make their report.

I hadn't expected the deputy to appear this early in

the morning. I barely looked presentable, even for an ordinary day in Point Blank. He took off his hat as he came through the door, but he seemed preoccupied. Beyond him, I could see Ila Wanamaker coming up the walk, two children trailing behind her and one on her hip.

"I need to talk to you," he said grimly.

Ila's four-year-old, Mischief, burst through the front screen at that moment. It banged shut behind him, and Norton looked around, startled.

"Mischief, if I've told you once, I've told you a thousand times: don't go banging Miss Beth Marie's screen door like that. Now get yourself over here and watch your little brother while I take care of my business." Ila had already deposited the baby on my mother's best needlepoint chair seat. Mischief, his thumb in his mouth, stood staring up at Norton.

Ila plopped her diaper bag onto the dining table, pretending not to notice Norton at first. "I guess I better get caught up with my bill, Miss Beth Marie," she said. She'd never put "Miss" in front of my name like that before. Then she turned and looked at Norton and fluttered her hand up over her mouth. "Oh, my goodness. The deputy!"

Norton stared at the floor.

She waggled her hand at him. "I'm just being silly. Don't mind me. I bet you're out here on important business, aren't you, sheriff?" She jerked Mischief's thumb out of his mouth. The middle child, a little girl with white hair and red-rimmed eyes, broke a leaf off an angel-wing begonia by the window.

"Don't do that, honey," I said to her. "It's poisonous."

"Just checking out a few details," Norton said.

"Ah," Ila exhaled knowingly. "I've known Finney Blalock since—well, forever, sheriff. My Aunt Beulah married a Blalock. Finney was ahead of me in school, of course," she glanced over at me, "but I remember every little detail about him."

At that moment the little girl pushed the baby out of the chair, and its shrieks diverted Ila's attention.

"Why don't you wait in the kitchen," I said to Norton in a low voice while Ila was picking up the baby and scolding her little girl. "There's still some coffee. I'll be with you in a minute, whenever it calms down out here."

He nodded and disappeared quickly into the back hall.

Ila looked at me suspiciously as soon as she'd picked up the baby and sent the little girl outside. "Who was that masked man anyway?" she asked with a sly smile.

I must have flushed.

"You keeping him hidden away, are you, Beth Marie? Well, I can't say that I blame you." She shifted the baby to her other hip. "He is awfully cute." She sighed. "Remember to tell him I'd be glad to help any way I can, okay? I mean seriously. Used to be, Point Blank was the nicest place in the world for raising up kids, but any-more—" She mopped at Mischief's hair with a half-hearted maternal gesture.

"Did you bring your bill with you, or do you need me to look it up, Ila?" I asked.

"I guess I must have left it at home. No, don't go to any trouble. I'll just go back and see if I can find it." And she herded Mischief out the front door before I could pull out the file drawer.

I went to the front window to see if anyone else was eager to pay their water bill that morning, but for the moment the traffic to my dining room seemed to have slacked off. So I stuck the "Be back soon" sign on the front door and closed it.

I could hear voices in the kitchen as I passed the darkened stairway. Lois must have come down to make herself some breakfast and found Norton there. Some thing made me stop a moment and listen.

"Yes," Lois was saying, "she is conscientious. A regular little worker bee."

Norton asked a question at that point. I couldn't make out the words, but I could tell it was a question because of the way the tone of his voice went up at the end.

"Personally, I don't see how she stands it out here," Lois replied. "It would drive me crazy. She left college after only two years and lived with her mother here till she died. Never went anywhere else. Never got a real job. It's sad, really. I hate to see her wasting herself like this. She's really quite intelligent, you know. But I guess she just lacks the confidence to try her luck in the outside world. Point Blank is all she knows and all she seems to care about. I'm afraid she'll just turn into an eccentric old lady like her mother eventually."

I didn't wait to hear the deputy's reply. I didn't want to hear any more at all. I knew Lois's feelings—she had expressed them often enough. But talking about me to a stranger like that—as if she, of all people, were an authority on how to live your life. I felt angry, ashamed, betrayed. And I didn't particularly want to talk to Norton now either. I took a deep breath, dreading what I had looked forward to earlier, and went on through to the kitchen.

They were both sitting at the table, just as he and I had the day before, but he was leaning forward on his elbows, looking at her intently. She was wearing a floweredy silk kimono of mine that I save for when I'm traveling or visiting someone. Her long, dark hair was twisted into a tousled spray on top of her head. She had her bare feet propped up on the counter and the kimono poked down between her legs. She was running one finger slowly around the lip of her coffee mug. I could have snatched her baldheaded.

"Did you get some breakfast, Lois?" I asked, barely keeping my voice from shaking.

She slid her feet to the floor instantly. "Just coffee," she said. "I wasn't hungry." I went over to the stove and poured myself a cup.

The deputy had leaned back in his chair. I could see out of the corner of my eye that he looked uneasy. I didn't sit down but stood at the counter with my back to them, staring out at the geraniums and marigolds. I could feel my back growing rigid and I didn't trust my voice. I knew it was going to sound stiff.

"So. What can I help you with?" I finally asked him. Then it occurred to me that whatever it was, he might not want to talk about it in front of Lois. I didn't intend to make it easy for him though.

Lois must have sensed his hesitation. She stood up, pulling the kimono around her primly. "I'd better go get dressed," she said. "I wasn't expecting company so early. It's a capital crime in Point Blank if you're not dressed by noon, you know."

I still didn't turn from the window. I felt stiff as a poker, but I couldn't help it. Why had she been telling Norton about me? Had he asked, or had Lois volunteered to analyze my character for him?

He didn't say anything till we heard her footsteps creaking overhead in the bedroom. "I didn't come to ask questions this time," he said, as though reading my mind. He kept his voice low enough for me to tell that he didn't want anyone overhearing us.

"Oh?"

"No. I've got some surprising information."

I raised my eyebrows. "Really?"

"This is serious," he said. "I don't want anyone else knowing about it right now."

I shrugged. "If you don't want to tell me—" I let the sentence trail off.

"What is this?" he said, his own voice growing stiffer. "I thought you wanted to find out the truth here too. I thought you were going to help."

"Why not tell Lois?" I said, turning to face him. "She probably knows a lot more than I do. I mean, after all, I have very limited experience of the world." I sounded like a petulant child, but I couldn't stop myself. "Or maybe that's the point. Maybe you figure I'm so gullible I'll fall for this business about helping the forces of truth and justice."

He looked at me narrowly, and I turned back to the window. "Fine," he said, standing up suddenly. "Fine. If that's what you think, then I'm sorry to have troubled you. But I've got to say, I didn't expect this. Not from you."

I bit my lip. I wasn't going to make matters worse by asking what he meant by that. I sounded like a silly schoolgirl, and I knew it. The best I could do now was keep my mouth shut. Anything I said at this point would just make me look even more foolish. I wanted to cry with frustration, but I blinked hard and stared out the kitchen window at the flowers. I didn't intend to humiliate myself by crying too.

He stood there behind me for a minute, but I couldn't trust myself to speak. Finally he picked up his hat and turned to go.

"Just in case you come to your senses," he said from the doorway, "and just to show you—something—my good intentions, I guess, what I came to tell you was that they got the fingerprints from that jewelry they found on Finney Blalock Saturday night."

I turned and looked at him.

"Turns out his prints weren't on the stuff at all."

I opened my mouth to ask whose, but he went on before I could speak.

"Archie's," he said. "On every piece."

I stared at him. His jaw was clenching and unclenching as he stared back. My mouth was open, but I couldn't speak. The next thing I knew, he was gone.

CHAPTER ELEVEN

I SAT DOWN. I STARED FOR A WHILE AT the two half-empty coffee cups on the table. I wanted to put my head down on my arms and cry, but I didn't. I could hear Lois upstairs going back and forth across the floor. It sounded like she was packing.

I was actually grateful when I heard someone knock hesitantly on the front door. I thought for a moment it might be Norton coming back. But it was only another suddenly dutiful Point Blank citizen come to pay his water bill and ferret out whatever information he could about Miss Mineola and Finney Blalock. I took his check, smiled mechanically, and made small talk. When he left I went to work organizing my files. I wanted to keep busy, keep my mind occupied.

There weren't any more interruptions for the next half hour or so, and I had gotten all the way to the L's when I heard Lois coming downstairs. I didn't look up from my file drawer, not even when I heard her come into the dining room.

"Beth Marie?" she said tentatively.

"Yes?" I pulled out a card and studied it.

"Beth Marie, look at me," she said impatiently.

I looked up with what I hoped was a cool and imperturbable expression. She was wearing a navy suit, of all things, and had on heels. I frowned. "What are you so dressed up for?"

"I thought I'd go in to the funeral home. I just called Mother, and she said they might have the body back in Somerville by this afternoon. Not everybody knows about the autopsy. Someone ought to be there to explain. Uncle Larry might come from San Antonio. And other people in Somerville will be showing up at Holcombe's. Someone from the family should be there."

My surprise must have been evident on my face. "And you're going? To the funeral home?"

She dropped her eyes. "I haven't been much help, I know. And you probably think I'm not grateful to you for helping me out." She looked up and swallowed before she went on. "But I am, Beth Marie. I promise. I know sometimes I say things—" She looked down again.

I dropped the card back in the file. "You've been under a lot of stress," I said, as evenly as I could.

She gave a sardonic little laugh. "Sure. Well, anyway." She walked over to the front window, looked out, and sighed. "I tried to find out from your friend the policeman just what I might expect at this point. He wasn't very forthcoming. Wouldn't want to commit himself and all that." She turned away from the window and put her hands to her temples.

"Look, Lois—"

"Everyone in Point Blank seems to feel it's time I pulled my weight in this particular little scenario. Did my part. Played the dutiful daughter. The bereaved niece. So I guess I'll go along. At least for right now."

"It'll give you something to do," I said lamely.

She laughed her mirthless little laugh again. "Sure, Beth Marie. Something to do. Who could ask for more?"

I bit my lip and didn't answer.

"Well," she said, taking a deep breath and picking up

the overnight bag she'd brought downstairs with her, "if I could borrow your car to drive in to Holcombe's. That way I won't have to face them at home again right now. There's no telling who'll be there at the house. It would help a lot. And I'm sure someone will be coming back this way this afternoon who could return it to you. I'm planning on staying for the duration. Let Mother rest and all that." She smiled at me grimly.

What could I say? My anger was getting diluted with pity. She'd been through a lot in the past few days, even if the trouble was of her own making. There was no point in my being petty, I decided. Besides, Cecelia could certainly stand the help. A gesture like this from Lois would mean a lot to her.

"Sure," I said, forcing a smile. "The keys are in my purse by the phone. Don't worry about it. I wasn't planning on going any place anyway." I'd already given up my shopping plans.

I closed the office at noon and walked down to the post office to pick up the mail. I went the back way again, by the Packards' field, so that I'd have time to think. I didn't want to run into anyone else until I had time to put together Norton's information about the fingerprints with what I already knew.

There must be some logical explanation, I thought. After all, Archie had been there in the trailer with Finney for who knew how long before I discovered them together. Maybe Finney had shown the jewelry to Archie. Maybe he had been bragging about what he'd done, or maybe he was using the jewelry as a bribe to get Archie to give him some further help with his escape. Archie could have taken the jewelry and looked it over and then returned it to Finney. That was the most obvious explanation. But in that case, why weren't Finney's fingerprints on it too? Norton had been very definite about Archie's prints being the only ones they found on the jewelry.

I squinted in the noon sun and watched the waves of

heat shimmer over the freshly cut hay stubble. It had smelled sweet yesterday, but today it had already dried and the only smell was the dust from the road.

The other alternative I was more hesitant to frame in words. I put it to myself in the form of a question just to try it out. Could Archie have stolen the jewelry from Miss Mineola's room himself and later put it in Finney's pocket after he'd shot him? He was capable of that. But if it had happened that way, Archie must have done it after I ran from the steps of the trailer and before Cecelia got there. There would have been plenty of time, even as slow as Archie's mind sometimes worked. But wouldn't he have thought about his fingerprints being on the jewelry? Maybe not. It was entirely possible that, like a little boy caught holding stolen cookies behind his back, Archie would have merely stashed them in the first place he thought of. It probably never occurred to him that the sheriff would check for fingerprints, much less do an autopsy on Miss Mineola.

And they wouldn't have, I remembered suddenly, if it hadn't been for Norton.

By the time I reached the post office, the dust raised by passing cars and trucks had settled into the creases of my clothes and stuck to my damp skin. I felt grungy outside and in. How had women ever survived in this heat wearing long dresses that covered them up from ankle to elbow? I pulled my clinging shirt away from my skin as I stepped inside the post office, letting the cooler air dry me off.

"It's the humidity," an overalled farmer leaning on the counter said, as though on cue. A chorus of three women chimed their agreement.

Out of the corner of my eye I could see all four of them look at me furtively as I bent to look into the little window of my mailbox, yet none of them said a word to me. After twenty-five years I was still an outsider here, the daughter of that uppity Episcopalian woman who had always thought she was too good for Point Blank. And I had proved my isolation by refusing to tell anybody anything about the shooting out at Miss Mineola's. I never would fit in here.

While I turned the little brass dial on my box, they went on talking. I might as well have been invisible.

"I wish I knew when to plan for it," one of the women said plaintively. "I was going to make a lemon meringue pie, but I ain't a-going to make it and have it set around for two or three days till they decide to have the funeral. It'll go to weeping, sure as the world, in this weather. And then be as flat as a flitter by the time it gets put out for anybody to see."

"Why don't you just make up a casserole and put it in the freezer," another one said. "It'd have plenty of time to defrost before they're ready to eat. If the funeral's at ten, they won't get back to the house before noon. Surely they'll let us know by this evening. They can't just keep everyone hanging on like this."

"I heard the Baptist church was going to fix a whole ham and some brisket though. I thought that was real nice, them going in on the meat like that. That's the biggest expense."

"As much as Mineola Magillberry's done for that church, it's the least they could do for her. And after all, it's most likely going to be just one big Baptist potluck anyway. You know the whole congregation's going to turn out for something like this. There's not much family of hers left. Just Cecelia and her daughter and Archie and them two grandchildren from Houston. How much can they eat anyways?"

I pulled my mail out of the box and took it over to the table to sort through it.

"I heard her brother Larry might come too."

"I don't know as that wife of his'll let him come or not," the farmer put in. "He ain't been in too good a health, I hear."

"Well, if I was her, I'd sure look after him. Lord knows we got enough widows in this world now."

"Ain't that the truth? I was down to the Grandper-sons Center in Somerville last week for the forty-two game and, I swear, it seemed like to me they was a dozen women for ever man."

The farmer chuckled at this and gathered up his mail. "I gotta get home with the mail before the wife goes a-hunting for me."

The women watched him go with a look of open longing. Two of them were widows, and the other one was divorced. Through the post office window I could see him climb stiffly into his pickup and then spit casually out the window as he pulled away. The shortest woman let out a slow sigh like a long-pent secret. "Ruby Hopkins ought to go down on her knees every night and thank the good Lord she's still got her husband."

"Lord, Lord, ain't that the truth. So many times I think if I could just have Delmer back—"

"Don't none of them know what they got till it's gone. It gets so lonely."

They started drifting toward the door. Just as they opened it, Bud Wylie's pickup pulled up outside.

"They's some that gets a second chance though," the short one said, looking at her companions meaningfully.

"Evelyn?" the divorcee said. "It was her first chance, don't forget."

"I reckon he was worth waiting for. She's sure lived the high life ever since she married Bud."

"And didn't even have to raise his kids. I call that too much sugar for a dime."

"Well, she's made him a good wife. I swear, that woman'd do anything for him. It's might near idolatrous the way she takes on over him."

"I hear he's been pretty broke up over Miss Mineola's passing. You'd think—but she must've been ten years older than him."

"That's been the only fly in Evelyn's ointment, having to play second fiddle to Miss Mineola so long."

"Well, Evelyn stuck it out, and now she's got Bud all to herself."

"Like I say, she ought to thank the good Lord every night."

Bud touched the brim of his hat as he passed them coming up the steps but didn't stop to talk. He looked grim.

"Hello, Bud," I said when he came in.

He looked startled. "Beth Marie," he said, "I didn't expect to see you here. I thought you'd be out at the house with Cecelia."

"Oh?"

"You heard, didn't you?"

"Heard what?"

"About them coming and getting Archie. That new deputy. They took him in to Somerville. For questioning, he said." Bud paused and frowned. "I'd a thought you knew that already."

"No. No, I didn't," I said. The word must have gotten out that Norton had been by my house earlier.

I watched as Bud retrieved the mail from his box. "The deputy didn't say why they wanted to question Archie?" I asked.

"I reckon not. Evelyn's been out there with Cecelia this morning. She called and told me about it."

"Are you going out there now?"

"I hadn't planned on it. Evelyn's got her own car. I figure I'd just be in the way. 'Course, if there was anything Cecelia needed me to do, I'd be only too happy to oblige." His forehead puckered as though he was uncertain as to whether he might have missed some social signal, and it occurred to me how much husbands and wives in Point Blank depended on one another. That's why you got married. You depended on the other person to supply your deficiencies, and vice versa. And that's why they were so alone, so amputated, when they lost their mates. Mate was a good word for that kind of marriage. Like socks or gloves, what good was one without its mate?

"No, I'm sure Cecelia wouldn't hesitate to say if she needed you, Bud," I reassured him. "But would you mind taking me out there? I might be of some use to Cecelia myself, and Lois borrowed my car to go in to the funeral home."

The pucker faded from his forehead, and he looked relieved to be given a task he could do. "Sure, Beth Marie. No problem. I'd be glad to run you out there. I'm pretty much at loose ends right now anyway. I've already taken the oxygen tank and all that other paraphernalia back to the medical supply place." He seemed eager to show that he'd been helpful.

I followed him out to the truck, and he opened the door on the passenger's side for me. The hot vinyl seats still smelled new, I noticed, even though Bud had bought the truck about six months ago. I was used to crawling over all kinds of tools or greasy farm machinery parts when I rode in local pickups, but there wasn't even a good coating of dust on Bud's dashboard. Another sign of Evelyn's part in this marriage. She obviously kept the interior clean for him. He, of course, was responsible for washing the outside. A tacit but clear division between men and women in Point Blank.

Bud eased gingerly into the driver's seat, hauling himself up by holding onto the steering wheel as though it were a saddle horn. "Guess I got throwed one too many times," he said. "Used to, the rheumatism didn't bother me excepting in the wintertime. Now, seems like it's just as bad in the summer."

His face sank back into its grim mold as we bumped along the road out to Miss Mineola's. He was obviously taking her death hard. I tried to think of something distracting to say.

"Did the Packards get a good cutting off their hay this time?" I asked as we passed the field of drying stubble.

He rubbed his chin reflectively. "Packard does okay, I guess. But not as good as I expect to," he said. Then he smiled. "Many a time I've tried to talk her into selling me that place, but she always put me off. I just about had her talked into turning a-loose of it Saturday night a week ago. We was playing dominoes at her house, just like we always did." He chuckled to himself. "When I took the last game with a deuce-trey, that made her mad. Swore she'd never sell me a square inch if I was the last man on earth. Even threatened to call up some development company the next day. That's how peeved she was. It upset Evelyn right smart. She don't understand Minnie the way I do."

I only nodded and said nothing. I seriously doubted that any development company would be interested in property out here in the nether reaches of Watson County. Not when River Oaks mansions in Houston were being auctioned off for a song. However, I've lived in Point Blank long enough to know the passionate devotion some people here have to land, especially older people like Bud and Miss Mineola. Refusing to turn loose of it would be about the worst threat she could make. For Bud Wylie and Mineola Magillberry other forms of wealth existed only to be turned into land holdings. This was the passion they shared. Land was solid, substantial, real in a way that stocks and bonds and even cash weren't. Land was territory, autonomy, power. It was a kingdom.

"What do you think will happen to it now?" I asked. "Who'll inherit it?"

"Them no-good grandkids of hers, most likely. Maximillian, for sure."

"Not Cecelia or Archie?" I asked.

"Oh, they'll probably get something. But not the land. Min would want that to go to her own blood."

"You think so? I thought she was upset with Max. Maybe even had written him out of her will altogether. There was a note about changing her will in that ledger of hers we found behind the bed."

"No," he said, shaking his head. "She was always threatening, sure. But nobody knew Min like me. She never woulda done nothing like that. Not with her land. I'd bet my life on it. My life savings anyway." And he gave one last, appraising look at Packard's pasture in his rearview mirror and chuckled.

I had to wonder how much he told Evelyn about his business deals. Would that be another of those divisions of responsibilities that Point Blank marriages were built on? Evelyn, a northern city girl, had none of that land-lust bred into her. Land deals probably weren't included in her side of the partnership.

About halfway out to Miss Mineola's we came up behind Terry B. inching along the road in his Chrysler. The shocks are just about shot on it, so he drives as slow as possible through the labyrinth of chuckholed county roads his parishioners live on. When he saw us, he pulled over and waved us down.

Bud edged the pickup alongside the Chrysler.

"Say, would you folks mind doing me a favor?" Terry B. was already climbing out of his car. "I was supposed to deliver this here electric roaster out to your wife, Bud. Then, come to find out, she was out at Cecelia's. She volunteered to cook the briskets for the funeral if we could get it to her from the church. But the wife and me, we've got to go into Somerville to sign some papers about—about our son."

"Sure," I put in quickly. "Whatever we can do. You just let us know." Poor Terry B. Everyone was paying attention to Mineola Laudermilk and her funeral while the Blalocks were being left to cope as best they could with their own son's death. Bud must have felt bad too because he had already climbed down from the truck and come around to hoist the large electric roaster out of Terry B's trunk and load it in the back of the pickup.

"Thanks so much, folks," Terry B. said, slamming the trunk shut so that the whole automobile rocked. "I sure appreciate it."

"Don't mention it," Bud said, pulling on the front of his hat brim.

While he was climbing back in the truck I asked Terry B. when Finney's funeral would be. "I'd like to come. If you don't mind."

Terry B. stared down at the ground. "We'd be real pleased if you could do that, Beth Marie. I would, I know. And I think it'd mean a right smart to his mother. I'm not for sure yet just when it'll be. We've got to get some things straight with the prison officials. But I'll sure let you know when I find out."

"Good. I'll be there," I said.

"God bless you," Terry B. called as we pulled away.

Bud said nothing. He wasn't a churchgoer and had little use for a Baptist or any other brand of preacher. That had been his first wife's area of expertise and would have been Evelyn's too, except that she wasn't religious herself. I had heard her tell Cecelia as much, as though religion were some minor proficiency you inherited, like perfect pitch or being double-jointed. In any case, Bud probably thought Finney should have been disposed of long ago in the same way mad dogs are done away with.

Several cars were parked in Miss Mineola's drive, including Evelyn's big white Lincoln. Bud looked uneasy, and I knew he didn't want to go in and face all those people. I wasn't surprised when he said he thought he'd go back in to Somerville.

"Somebody needs to check up on Archie," he said. "I don't know who'll look after that boy now that Min's gone. I'll go ahead and put this here roaster in Evelyn's trunk though. No telling when I'll get home, and she might want to get those briskets to cooking this afternoon."

He pulled his truck up behind her car. "Here," he said, pulling an extra set of keys out of his pocket, "would you mind unlocking the trunk for me?"

I took the keys and climbed down out of the truck. He left the motor running while he went around to let the tailgate down. The lid to the Lincoln's trunk popped up smoothly. As I had expected, Evelyn kept her own trunk as clean and neat as she kept the cab of Bud's pickup. The only thing in it was a plastic container of windshield washer fluid and something bundled up in a clean towel. I started to move both of these aside to make room for the roaster.

"Watch out! Here I come," called Bud, sliding the roaster off the tailgate.

I made a grab for the plastic jug with one hand and the towel with the other. I only got a corner of the towel though, and as I hurriedly jerked it out of his way, the bundle came unrolled. Inside was a plastic tube connected to a kind of clear green masklike thing.

"I'm sorry," I said, rolling the bundle back up.

Bud set the roaster down with a grunt and turned to look. "What's that?" he asked.

"I don't know. Looks like some attachment that might go with the oxygen tank."

"My gosh. I thought I'd got all that stuff," he said, taking it from me and flipping back the towel to look. "Guess this must be something they overlooked. Anyway, you won't mind letting Evelyn know I've put the roaster in her car, will you, Beth Marie?" he said as he closed the trunk.

"I'll tell her," I said. "And thanks for the ride, Bud." I could see he was anxious to get away before someone came out that he might have to talk to.

It was a little ironic, I thought as I went up the back steps to Miss Mineola's kitchen, that the old house was such a hub of activity now that she was dead. No telling how long it had been since there were this many cars in her driveway at one time. I supposed it was easier for Cecelia to be receiving the callers over here at Miss Mineola's. She couldn't have fitted more than a few people into her little living room across the road.

I halfway expected to see Muriel back at her grandmother's house today, establishing her own territorial expectations, but there was no sign of her amongst the half-dozen people scattered around the living room. The Gorlack sisters were there, however, and cast a triumphant, forgiving look my way when I came in. They'd found out about Archie being hauled off to the sheriff's office before I had.

Cecelia's face lit up when she saw me. "I'm so glad you're here, Beth Marie," she said. "I was hoping you could help me decide what dishes we should use tomorrow."

Evelyn, who had just come from Miss Mineola's bedroom with a dust rag in her hand, looked surprised to see me there.

"Hello, Beth Marie," she said. "I thought you'd have the Water Board open today." That's the kind of pointed remark that shows you Evelyn isn't from around here.

"I had such a land-office business this morning that I figured I could afford to close this afternoon and come help Cecelia out," I said.

Evelyn turned to Cecelia. "Why didn't you say something to me about the dishes, honey? I would have been happy to help."

"But you've done so much already, Evelyn. You haven't stopped a minute since you got here this morning," Cecelia said. "I don't know what I would have done without you."

"Well," Evelyn said, "let me know when you need me. I'm almost through in the bedroom."

It had been easy enough for me to pick up on the fact that Cecelia wanted to speak to me in private; that was the real reason for her bringing up the dishes. In the kitchen, she leaned against the drainboard, looking stricken. "Beth Marie, do you know why they've taken Archie off to jail? This is terrible!"

"They haven't taken him to jail exactly, Cecelia. At least not the way I understand it. Bud said they just wanted to ask him some questions down at the sheriff's office. That's all I know about it."

"Are you sure about that, Beth Marie?" She sounded uncharacteristically stern.

"Yes, ma'am."

"And you don't have any idea why they want to question him?"

She had me there, of course. As kind as she is, she was still a mother and had the maternal instinct for sniffing out evasion.

"I'm not sure that I'm supposed to say anything about this."

"About what?" Her eyes were searching my face intently. When I didn't answer right away, she added, "You know as well as I do that boy doesn't have good sense, Beth Marie. And Aunt Min is going to hold me responsible if anything happens to him."

"Cecelia," I said, "Miss Mineola is dead."

She brushed my comment aside with her plump hand. "Honey, you know good and well that doesn't make one bit of difference. It's not like she doesn't know. And one of these days I'm still going to have to answer."

"But not to her, for heaven sakes."

That brought her up short. "Well," she said slowly, "I can't help it. I still feel responsible. I need to know what kind of trouble Archie might be in."

Just then there was a terrific rattling at the back door. "How the hell do you get this door open," a thin, angry voice demanded.

"If you'll wait just a minute, I'll get it," another voice, stronger but equally irritated, said.

"Get that damn dog out of my way," the first voice said. "I swear to goodness, why don't they have that miserable excuse for an animal put out of its misery." There was a whomp and then the sound of Teensy's yelps receding toward the barn.

Cecelia started for the back door in a jerking hobble. "Uncle Larry!"

CHAPTER • TWELVE

CECELIA'S UNCLE LARRY WAS ONLY four years younger than his sister, Miss Mineola, and dry and bent as a dead limb about to blow off a tree in the next high wind. His antique clothes hung on him as though there were nothing more than a wooden scarecrow frame inside them. His yellowed, collarless shirt was open at the neck and his unpressed black wool pants were held up with old-fashioned galluses. His wife, Beulah, a younger woman of only eighty, plucked the black wool hat from his head as he came through the door. He snatched it from her hand.

"Get that chair out of my way, woman," he cried in a high-pitched, reedy sound that would have been a bellow in his younger days. She was maneuvering a chair behind his frail legs for him to drop into. "Good God! What you trying to do, kill me?" And he lurched for a bench along the wall, collapsing onto it sideways.

Beulah, who would have made two of him, hovered about him, trying to anticipate his every wish. As if to spite her, Uncle Larry often changed his request in mid-sentence. She never seemed to notice his outbursts, except occasionally when her lips contracted a fraction of an inch. She kept up a constant tuneless humming noise, almost under her breath but not quite, just enough to give herself, if not others, the idea she was paying no attention whatever to his tirades. She accepted Cecelia's greeting kiss as though it were an interruption to her concentration and kept her eyes trained on her husband.

"Heavenly days," Cecelia was saying, "I didn't know—I'm so glad you all could come."

"I got the old woman up at four o'clock this morning and told her we was coming to Minnie's funeral," Uncle Larry said, perching his hat on his thin knees.

"Four-thirty," Beulah said, momentarily interrupting her humming. She said it low enough that he couldn't catch it.

"What'd she say?" he asked, directing his question to Cecelia. "Is she disputing my word?" He turned an angry glare on his wife who was folding her sweater neatly on the back of her chair.

"I'm just so glad you're here, Uncle Larry," Cecelia interjected quickly. "It must have been quite a drive for you though."

"Same distance for me as for anybody else," he said sourly. "Now what I want to know is, where's the body?" The way he said it, you figured what he wanted was to assure himself that a hoax hadn't been played on him and that his sister was actually and irrevocably dead. "I always knew I'd outlive her," he went on, "that is if I stayed far enough away from her. Outlived 'em all, that's what I've gone and done." He slapped his bony knee in satisfaction.

"She's up at the funeral home in Somerville, Uncle Larry. Remember? Where we had Aunt Hattie when she died." Cecelia stopped, and I could see her wavering as to whether or not to tell him about the autopsy. "They don't have her quite ready yet," she said finally.

"Funeral home," he repeated with querulous disapproval in his voice. "I don't see what we need with no funeral home. Mama and Daddy was laid out right in there in the front room."

"Well," Cecelia said weakly, "I guess they just do things different now, Uncle Larry. There's all these laws, you know."

"Laws, my hind ear," he fumed. "The law won't pay no attention, long as you bury 'em deep enough. And quick enough if the weather's hot." At that point he began to look a little befuddled. "This is August, ain't it? How long ago'd you say she died, girl?"

"Saturday, Uncle Larry. She died on Saturday."

"And what day is this?" he said, frowning up at her. It was obvious this was a genuine question.

"This is Monday."

"Monday? Why, it's time we was getting her in the ground then. This is the third day. You can't keep a body around that long in this heat."

"He don't even know where he is sometime," Beulah announced with sudden triumph. "Wakes up in a different world everyday. I have to tell him what day it is ever morning, and before dinnertime he don't remember."

Cecelia looked at me beseechingly.

"I'll go call the funeral home," I said. "Maybe I can find out when they'll be ready."

I had to go back into the living room to call. I asked to speak to Lois. There was a lengthy wait as the woman went to look for her. "I'm sorry," she said when she came back, "there's no one here by that name."

"Really?" I felt my throat begin to tighten.

"And I've been here ever since we opened this morning."

"If she comes in, could you tell her to call home right away?" It was only after I'd put down the receiver that I realized I'd forgotten to ask if they'd received the body back from Houston.

Evelyn, who was serving as hostess to the callers in the living room, looked at me quizzically. I nodded toward Miss Mineola's bedroom and she followed me in there.

"Is something wrong?" she asked.

"I don't know," I said carefully. "I thought Lois was at the funeral home. She borrowed my car to go up there this morning. But they say they haven't seen her. I just hope nothing's happened. And Uncle Larry's just arrived. He and his wife are in the kitchen with Cecelia—wanting to know where the body is. They're giving her fits. Could you go tell her—I don't know—tell her the funeral home is hoping to get the body back by this afternoon. That's certainly no lie."

"What should I say about Lois?" Evelyn had worked hard all morning, and she looked as concerned now as if this were her own family's problem. The room was cleaned and polished to a fare-thee-well and the curtains drawn back to let in the light. She'd even put a little vase of pink rosebuds on the nightstand beside Miss Mineola's bed.

"I don't think we ought to bother Cecelia with anything else right now. It looks to me like she's going to have her hands full with those two in there. If you can stay here and sort of run interference for her, take care of the visitors and the phone calls anyway, I'll run up to town and see if I can find Lois and also check on when the body will be back from Houston. I'll call and let you know. Uncle Larry's going to be raising Cain till he sees the body."

"And Archie," she said. "What about him? Why did they take him in to town to question him?"

"Oh, no. I'd completely forgotten about him. Well, Bud said he was going to the sheriff's office," I said, evading her second question. "Maybe he'll know something. I'll go by there too if I don't run into him at the funeral home."

"I can't believe all this is happening," she said. "I don't know why we couldn't have a nice quiet dignified funeral for Min and get it over with. This is so hard on Bud, you know."

"I guess I'll need to borrow somebody's car if I'm going into town," I said, ignoring her comments. "I could drive Lois's if only she'd left me her keys."

She took the hint immediately. "Here, take mine," she said. "Bud knows where to find me if he needs me. And why don't you just slip out the east porch here, Beth Marie. If you go out through the kitchen you'll just get Larry all stirred up again. Be sure that porch screen catches though. It's loose in this dry weather. Make sure it's closed good. Otherwise the wind will catch it and start it banging back and forth."

I had never driven a Lincoln Continental before. I felt like a little girl sneaking off on some forbidden adventure as I slid into the white leather seat. If Evelyn kept Bud's truck tidy, she kept her own car immaculate. The radio was turned to one of those elevator music stations from Houston, but I didn't dare change it. A pair of pink-tinted sunglasses lay in the front seat and a box of pink tissues was in a holder under the dash. Did Bud really like all this Mary Kay femininity?

But I knew that wasn't quite fair to Evelyn. After all, she was also an EMT on Point Blank's volunteer ambulance crew. She'd been a nurse before she married Bud, and there had been some accidents where her efficiency and skill had saved the day.

I wasn't the only one impressed by Evelyn's Lincoln. As I pulled into the parking lot at the funeral home, an attendant emerged from the side door and hurried across the blazing asphalt to open the door for me. I didn't see my own little six-year-old Toyota anywhere.

The attendant herded me through the side door and directly to the director's office. "No one's here at all from the family," he said, sounding vaguely reproachful. "Though we have had some calls from someone called—Maximillian?"

"Her grandson."

He raised his eyebrows carefully. "He sounded… impatient."

"Yes, well. He's not in charge of the arrangements."

"I didn't think so. He sounded quite concerned

about the delay, however." He hesitated a moment as though, given enough time, I might divulge some interesting bit of information. "He assured me that he would be back up here by noon. Of course, the body's not back yet from the forensic lab in Houston. But we expect it this afternoon. Although, they always build up a backlog over the weekend, so we can't promise anything."

I guess he thought since he wasn't dealing with a member of the family he could afford to be a little less delicate.

"In which case," he went on, "we could schedule the funeral for tomorrow morning. That is, if it's all right with the family."

"Oh, I'm sure it would be," I said, thinking of Uncle Larry out at Point Blank. "And when would the body be ready for, uh, viewing."

He frowned and consulted a chart on his desk. "Of course, it depends on how early we get it back. Say if it got here by two or three this afternoon, we could be ready to go by, oh, seven this evening. But I can't promise anything, you understand. Everything hinges on the folks down in Houston." He looked at me keenly. "If it were to be a case of poisoning or anything like that."

"Heavens, no!" I exclaimed. "I mean, I certainly don't expect that."

"Of course not. But then that's what autopsies are for."

"I'll let her niece know then," I said and picked up my purse to leave. "And if Lois Ramsey, her great-niece that is, should come by, would you tell her to call home right away?"

"Certainly, certainly," he said, slipping back into his comforting mode. "Anything we can do to help, you just let us know."

It wasn't until I was safely back inside the fortress of Evelyn's car and felt the icy air blowing over me that I allowed myself to think about Lois. I had no idea where she could be. Or rather, I had two ideas, and I didn't like either one of them. She had either taken my car and run away or she had plans to disappear in some other way I didn't like to think about. And what was I to do? Keep quiet? Wait? It wouldn't be much longer now till other people began wondering where she was.

I pulled into a 7-Eleven that had a pay phone outside and tried to call her apartment in Houston. She would have had plenty of time to get there by now. I stood in the blazing sun, staring at the cloudy streaks on the glass of the telephone enclosure and listening to the phone ring in Lois's apartment. I counted twenty rings.

There was only one thing to do, I decided, sliding back inside the consolation of Evelyn's Continental. Only one other person knew why Lois might be likely to disappear. And much as I hated showing up on his doorstep, he was also the one who could do something effective about searching for her.

Still, I sat in the parking lot of the sheriff's office over behind the First Methodist Church for a good ten minutes before I could get up my nerve to go in. All right, I finally said to myself, what have you got to lose at this point? You already made about as big a fool of yourself this morning as you're likely to make. He's seen the worst. So why worry about it?

Because Lois has got your car, dummy. He's going to think it's very strange if you say nothing about it. It'll look like you were in collusion with her. Aiding and abetting, or whatever they call it.

So just go in and file a missing car complaint with whoever's on duty. There's no need to talk to *him*.

I was still struggling with what to do when a shadow fell across the white leather upholstery and a knuckle tapped at the window. I fumbled for the button to lower the window, then realized I had turned the ignition off. Before I could collect myself, he opened the door himself.

"Aren't you getting hot sitting out here in the sun?" he said, grinning at me.

I slid out without saying anything. Then I reached back inside and collected my purse before I closed the door. "Are you always sneaking up behind people?" I said testily.

"We have special training in it," he answered. "Come on in and cool off."

I followed him into the building and down the hall to his office, watching his back for any sign of a swagger. He stepped aside to hold the door to the little cubicle open, and I hazarded a glance at his face. He was staring at a poster on the opposite wall announcing a training program in computer searches for criminals.

As soon as the door was closed we both spoke, simultaneously.

"I need your help," I said.

"I've got news for you," he said.

We looked at one another in the moment it took us to sort out what the other had said.

"Okay, you go first," he said.

"Why does that make me suspicious?" I smiled lamely.

He shrugged. "Damned if I know," he said. "You've got to be one of the most suspicious women I've ever met."

"When you hear what I've got to tell you, you may think I'm not suspicious enough."

He cocked an eyebrow. "Really? Let's hear it then."

"Lois is gone." I waited a moment for his response, but all I saw was his lips tighten ever so slightly. "She borrowed my car about mid-morning, saying she was coming into town to the funeral home. She thought it was time she did her familial duty. But according to the people at Holcombe's, she never showed up there at all."

"Maybe she went back to Houston. Maybe she suddenly felt like she needed to get away by herself. And took your car simply because she felt her need was greater than yours. That wouldn't be out of character for her, would it?"

"I already called her apartment. No one was there."

"Or at least no one answered."

I shrugged now, a little impatient at his pointing that out, though I had to admit it was possible.

"On the other hand," he went on, "it's just as likely she's run off somewhere. She doesn't strike me as someone who's likely to stay around and face the music. Maybe she decided to take off for Mexico on her own. Either way, we better put out an alert for her. We'll check the airports first. That's the easiest place to begin."

"Oh," I said, except it came out like a squeak.

"Yes?"

"It's just that, well, that sounds so criminal-like. So serious. I didn't intend to get her in any trouble. I just wanted to find her."

"Look," he said, taking me by the shoulders with both hands and giving me a gentle shake, "you've got to get it into your head that it's not you that's making it serious. She's made her own bed. I mean, look—she's taken off with your car. Don't you think you have a right to feel angry about that? All you're doing is what any ordinary citizen would do."

"But we're not ordinary citizens. We're friends."

He sighed and let go of my shoulders. "You drive me crazy," he said, turning his back and going around behind his desk. "First you feel one way and then it's another. First you want one thing and then you want something else. Sit down. I've got more to tell you. And when you hear it, you may see that I don't have any choice at this point. I've got to find her."

I lowered myself slowly into the chair across from his desk and stared at him. "What? What is it? What have you got to tell me?"

"Archie," he said. "Remember cousin Archie? No one seems especially concerned that the sheriff hauled him down here this morning to ask about those fingerprints of his on the jewelry we found on Blalock. I guess everyone feels generally relieved to have poor old Arch conveniently out of the way."

"And what did he say about the fingerprints?" I asked as levelly as I could.

"He lied of course. You're right about one thing. Old Arch is as dumb as the day is long. We had to get blowups of the prints from the jewelry and have him compare them with the ones the prison had on file for him, pointing out the precise duplication, before he finally gave in and admitted that he was the one who had taken the jewelry out of the old lady's room."

"And then he put the jewelry in Finney's pocket after he'd shot him?"

"Yes. That too. The reason for that was not immediately clear, however."

"I would suppose it was so that Finney, who wouldn't be able to defend himself, would be blamed when the jewelry was discovered missing. Even Archie could come up with a simple plan like that."

"But there was no reason for Archie to get rid of the jewelry if that was all there was to it. Even after it was discovered missing, Finney would have been blamed. Even if it was never found, folks would simply think that he'd stashed it someplace. Archie could have kept the jewelry just as well as planting it on Blalock."

"All right. Maybe. So?"

"The reason Archie says he wanted to get rid of the jewelry was that he didn't want to be connected with an even bigger crime. A much bigger one."

I said nothing, waiting for him to go on.

"Archie says that he'd gone up to the house to talk to his aunt. She had called him as soon as she saw him come in from work that morning and said she wanted to see him. He told her he'd be there after while, that he needed to get some sleep first. He wasn't in any hurry to have this conversation, I take it, since he expected it to be about some money he owed her. Anyway, his story is he woke up hours later. Took a shower. Took his time. Finally, he ambled up to the house. She didn't answer when he called out, so he went on into the bedroom. He said she was already dead."

I sat there a moment, letting all this sift into my mind. "Dead?" I repeated.

"Curled up in a ball like your friend Mrs. Ramsey said."

"And he didn't tell anybody, raise a cry or anything?"

"No. He said he figured his cousin would take care of everything herself when she got home."

"But he went ahead and took the jewelry anyway."

"Yes. Said he hadn't intended to beforehand, but there it was." He paused and looked at me closely. "He said something else too. He said he heard a noise in the house. Upstairs. Hardly anyone ever goes up there, he said. He took off with all that gold jewelry still in his pockets, afraid he'd be caught with the body. He went into town but couldn't make up his mind what to do with it. Later, after he'd shot Blalock, he decided that Mrs. Magillberry's jewelry being found on an escaped convict would be pretty good insurance in case there were any questions about him having been there in his aunt's bedroom."

"But no one else was in the house. Or if they were, they haven't mentioned it—or Archie's being there either."

"No, they haven't, have they?" he said, leaning back in his chair. "I find that very interesting in itself."

"The night Miss Mineola died. Lois went upstairs—" I didn't finish the thought aloud. But I could still see her standing at the top of the stairs, holding up her hand to stop me. It had been several minutes before she came down. Why hadn't she wanted me up there?

CHAPTER • THIRTEEN

BABBITT'S CAFE IS JUST AROUND the corner from the sheriff's office in Somerville. I was a little nervous about going there with Norton. But anyone from Point Blank who saw us together would have been more likely to make something of it if we'd gone to the Holiday Inn or even the Mexican restaurant over by the college.

That late in the afternoon all the people who work around the courthouse square had already come and gone on their coffee breaks and the dinner trade hadn't started yet. A couple of lawyers, already finished for the day, sat at an oil-cloth covered table discussing county politics, and Levi, a town fixture with a waist-long grey beard who lives at the Good Samaritan Mission and collects aluminum cans, was drawing out his cup of coffee as long as possible at the counter. Other than that we were alone.

Norton was a regular there, of course, and the waitress smiled on him proprietorially as she shuffled toward us, plastic-covered menus in hand.

"What's the special today?" he asked. He'd taken off his wide-brimmed hat as we came in and I could see where it had made a damp dent circling his hair.

"Chicken-fried steak, same as it always is on Monday. Mashed potatoes and gravy. Choice of vegetables. English peas, corn, or snap beans." She was already writing on her order pad.

"Beans," Norton said, handing back the menu. "What'll you have, Beth Marie?"

I suddenly realized I hadn't had anything to eat since that morning, which accounted for the dull headache I'd developed. Still, I didn't think I could face a slab of fried beef with white flour gravy on the side.

"Do you have salads?" I asked.

"Combination. Comes with the meal," the waitress said, reaching up to smooth the hairnet over her new perm. "Thousand Island, Eyetalian, or Ranch."

"A sandwich," I said, flustered. "I'll have a sandwich. A club sandwich. And a glass of milk."

"I'll see if we've got that," she said as she took my menu.

"If not, then just a hamburger," I called after her. She gave no sign she'd heard.

"You ever been in here before?" Norton asked.

"Sure. My father used to bring me in here when I was a little girl. It was a special treat to come with him. We'd sit at the counter and I got to twirl around on the stool."

"Maybe you've changed and she doesn't remember you," he laughed.

"A lot's changed since then," I said, more seriously than I had intended.

"Yeah. Well."

There was a long silence during which I watched Levi at the counter pour his coffee into his saucer and then part his long moustaches with two fingers of one hand and insert the saucer between his whiskers with the other hand. I was thinking about the call Norton had made to the Houston airport from the sheriff's office. He'd asked them to check their records for a flight booked by a Lois Ramsey that day. He wasn't really surprised, he said, when they'd given him a negative answer. It wasn't likely she would have bought a ticket in her own name if she were running away.

"I have the airport police searching the parking lots for your car," he said. "But we'll need you to sign a stolen car report if we're going to make a wider search than that."

"Oh. Well—I don't think I'd want to do that just yet," I said, fiddling with my knife. "I mean she might—"

The waitress came shuffling back to the table and carefully put a thick white platter down in front of Norton. "Watch it now. That's hot." She smiled at him. "I'll get your coffee right away, hon."

"Thank you, ma'am," he said and winked at her.

She put a red plastic basket down on my side of the table without any comment. It had a hamburger and fries in it. He started to call her back, but I shook my head. "Don't bother," I said. "It doesn't matter. This is fine."

Nevertheless he got up and went to the counter. When he came back he had the glass of milk I'd ordered. "Good for your nerves," he said. "You didn't want the club sandwich anyhow. They think it's a Yankee invention here. What've you got against chicken-fried steak anyway?" he asked, as though trying to cheer me up.

"We never had it at home," I said. "My mother thought it was barbaric." I laughed in spite of myself. "That's why Daddy came in here."

We both ate silently for a few minutes. He seemed to be as hungry as I was.

"At what point did Archie say he heard the noise upstairs?" I asked once my headache began to abate.

"He says it wasn't until he'd already stuffed his pockets with all those chains and things. He'd gone back to look at the body again, to reassure himself she was really gone, I suppose. Also, he gave me a bunch of bull about making a little farewell speech to her—how much he appreciated all she'd done for him. That's when he heard the noise upstairs, like someone moving around. He knew hardly anyone ever went up there, he said. The old lady was too infirm, and Mrs. Ramsey wasn't able to get up and down the stairs very well either. Anyway, he was scared of being caught with the body, so he slipped out through the kitchen and took off for town. He must have debated about putting the jewelry back, though he didn't say that. He probably went into town to try to get rid of it as quick as he could, then figured maybe that wasn't a good idea either, at least not right away."

"You sound like you believe him."

He shrugged and waited till he had swallowed before he spoke again. Then he wiped his mouth with a paper napkin and said slowly, "It's hard to say. All that about finding her dead when he came in might be a lie. It's just as reasonable to think she was asleep and woke up to find him rifling her jewelry box. Which would have pretty much sealed his fate with her. And there's that note in the ledger book you mentioned, the one about calling in the loan. That's no doubt what she wanted to see him about and why he took his time getting there. In either case, he would have been glad to see her dead."

"But why would he have volunteered to tell you that story then? No one's come forward yet to say they saw Archie there."

He tipped his chair back and folded his arms across his chest. "As you say, old Arch isn't too bright. People like him panic easy. When he heard they'd taken her body in for an autopsy, he figured he better make a clean breast of it. Whoever was upstairs might have seen him there, and if they discover she didn't just die in her sleep, then he could be in a lot more trouble."

"I see."

He leaned forward in his chair again. "Of course, if she woke up and he hit her over the head or smothered her with a pillow or something, you'd think there'd be some sign of a struggle or some bruising. And there was nothing on the j.p.'s report about that."

"Well, Cecelia had sort of straightened her out and fixed her up a bit before he got there."

"In that case, she couldn't have been dead long."

"I suppose not."

He stared out the front window at the afternoon glare. "Of course, there's always the chance that the old lady simply died a natural death at the same time an escaped convict was wandering around the premises and a relative was stealing her jewelry. But I personally don't think we ought to go on that assumption. That'd call for some mighty big coincidences. Especially since it appears that your friend has now taken off for parts unknown. And I believe you were going to mention something about her having gone upstairs that night?"

I picked at my french fries. "It was just—well, she'd gone upstairs to find a dress for Miss Mineola to be buried in. All her best clothes were stored away up there. She hadn't been anywhere to wear them in years." I paused, trying to remember clearly. "Lois was coming down the stairs when I told her about Finney being shot. It must have been a terrible shock to her. I didn't realize how terrible then, of course. But I did notice she was so shaky that she sat down on the top step. I started to go up to her, but she almost shouted at me to stop. I went back in the living room and she came down in a few minutes."

"Do you think there might be another reason she went upstairs?"

I folded my napkin. "Finney," I said. "It could have been Finney that Archie heard up there earlier."

"And," he pressed gently on, "your friend Lois might have had to get rid of any signs of his presence."

I sat there in silence, running my fingernail along the napkin crease.

"In fact, she might have been up there with him

when Archie came. Didn't you say her mother called you when she couldn't find her?"

"But you don't think Lois—"

He held up his hands as though to ward off my question. "I'm not speculating about anything right now. I want to wait until the Department of Corrections people get through questioning Archie about Finney's escape. They're with him now. I figured as long as he was in a confessional mood, we might as well get as much out of him as possible."

"Did you say anything to them about—"

"Lois being involved in the escape? No. That's their territory, and they don't like the county edging over into it. Besides, I figured I might as well leave that to Archie. That is, if he knew anything about Finney and Lois. He didn't mention her in our little discussion. And Archie strikes me as the kind of guy who wouldn't miss a chance to implicate someone else if he thought that would take the heat off him."

He wadded his own napkin into a tight little ball and chunked it onto his empty plate before going on. I held my breath, afraid of what was coming next. I could tell he was trying to find a merciful way to put it.

"I think we've got to consider some other possibilities here," he finally said. "If he is telling the truth about the old lady being dead when he got there, and if it was Blalock and your friend upstairs, well, I can't help looking into the implications of that situation." He paused and then went on. "And I've got to say, it doesn't look good, her taking off like this." He looked at me closely and then lowered his eyes. "I'm afraid there's not going to be much use in trying to protect her any more, Beth Marie."

The gentleness with which he said all this and hearing him say my name like that took me by surprise. Before I knew what was happening, tears were stinging my eyes. I blinked them back rapidly.

"You can see that, can't you?" he added. I nodded my head quickly, but I couldn't speak just yet. I felt like I was deceiving him. He was probably thinking I was upset about my friend, when in reality it was his own kindness that had taken me off guard.

"Well," I finally said, making a surreptitious dab at my eyes with my napkin, "what I've got to do first is get Evelyn's car back to her. She probably thinks I've taken off for parts unknown myself." I tried to make it sound like a joke, but he didn't smile. I concentrated on the golden fringe of his lashes rather than looking him directly in the eyes, but I had to drop my own gaze again.

"I'll run you out there," he said as he came around the table to pull my chair out. "And I'll tell Mrs. Ramsey about her daughter if you want me to."

I must have visibly cringed at the mention of telling Cecelia because he took hold of my arm and didn't turn it loose till he had to get his wallet out at the cash register. The waitress eyed me sourly. I pretended to read the headlines of the newspaper lying on the counter.

"Ever thing all right?" she said, handing his change back. He either wasn't paying attention or intentionally ignored the question in his hurry to push the glass door open for me.

He almost pushed it into Max, who had just come around the corner from the sheriff's office. Miss Mineola's stocky little grandson looked, as always, like a banty rooster spoiling for a fight. I could feel Norton bristle beside me.

"They told me I might find you here," Max said. His eyes flicked to me briefly, but I wasn't sure he even recognized who I was.

"Something I can do for you?" Norton asked stiffly.

"I was in hopes you'd have this business about my grandmother cleared up by now." Max rocked from one foot to the other, his fists on his hips. "Come to find out, this stupid autopsy still isn't complete. Not only that, but now you've got my cousin locked up. I just want to know what the hell's going on."

Norton's jaw tightened, and I could almost physically sense him shift into his official-capacity mode. "We have no control over the coroner's office or the forensic laboratory in Houston, sir. Perhaps you'd like to check with them directly."

"Don't pull that bureaucratic bullshit on me. I know when I'm being given the runaround."

Norton's nostrils twitched. "I'm sorry about the delay with the autopsy, but there's nothing we can do about it."

"What about Archie?" Max demanded. "I understand you've been putting the screws to him down here. What's all that about?"

"The Texas Department of Corrections is in charge of his questioning—not the sheriff's department. I'm afraid I can't discuss that with you right now."

"What do you mean, not discuss it with me? I don't have any intention of 'discussing' it, and certainly not with some two-bit deputy like you. I want to talk to whoever's in charge."

"Max!—" I started to intervene, but at that moment a large hand was laid on his shoulder.

"Say. Calm down here, fellow. No need to get yourself so worked up." It was Bud Wylie. He'd stopped his pickup and hopped out when he spotted us, leaving the door open and the motor still running. "Beth Marie. Sheriff." He nodded twice in our direction but kept his gaze trained on Max. "Glad to see you could get back up here, son. Your Uncle Larry's out at the house. I know you'll be wanting to see him."

Max looked startled at first, then his face settled into its usual sullen expression. I let my breath out slowly.

"I've just been trying to find out what's going on," he said to the older man. "But I don't seem to be able to get any straight answers."

"You're just going to have to ease up on yourself

some now, son," Bud went on in a soothing tone. "You know your grandmother wouldn't want you making a scene about this."

I wasn't so sure of that myself. Miss Mineola had caused plenty herself as I recalled. But Bud seemed to be having an effect on Max.

"But what about Archie? How come they've got him down here?"

Bud cast a quizzical glance at Norton, who gave an almost imperceptible shake of his head while staring steadily at the sidewalk. Bud seemed to understand the small signal instantly, and it struck me that both he and Norton operated by that same masculine code of communication that didn't require words.

"I reckon we're just going to have to leave that up to the sheriff for right now, son," Bud said. "I've just been over there and seen Archie. He's doing okay. He'll probably be out of there later this evening."

"I'm sorry I haven't gotten Evelyn's car back to her yet, Bud," I put in quickly to help divert the conversation. "I was just headed back to Point Blank."

"Don't mention it," he said, though he looked at Norton and me closely. "I guess Lois still has your little Toyota, does she?"

"Well, actually she found out she had to go back to Houston quite suddenly. Something having to do with school. She took my car rather than going on back to Point Blank to get hers."

Norton, still staring stolidly at the sidewalk, said nothing.

"Oh? Well, I brought Evelyn back into town with me. She wanted to get her hair done before the funeral. She's at the beauty shop now. We thought maybe we'd go ahead and pick up the car since it has the roaster in it. We didn't realize Lois had taken off like that."

"Yes. Well." I cast about for a way to get off the subject of Lois. "That thing we found in the trunk this morning," I added quickly, "doesn't that need to be returned to the medical supply place? I think I can still make it over there before they close." I looked at my watch. "That is if Max doesn't mind taking me by there."

Bud rubbed his chin, already grown stubbly by late afternoon. "I reckon that'd be all right, Beth Marie," he said. "That would save me an extra errand."

I followed him to the Lincoln, Max and Norton trailing behind, unlocked the trunk, and took out the towel-wrapped bundle. Then I handed the keys to Bud. "Tell Evelyn I appreciate the loan of her car."

He nodded and went back to his pickup. Max and Norton were still standing there. I didn't know what to say.

"I'll call you this evening," Norton finally said, as though sensing my confusion. "We'll, uh, make plans." And he gave a little tug to the front of his hat brim and sauntered off toward the sheriff's office, leaving me alone with Max.

Max was tight-lipped as he opened the door to his little red car. He obviously hadn't relished backing down from his confrontation with the deputy, and he didn't know quite what to say to me now. I gave directions to the medical supply store in one of the more run-down strip malls in Somerville, and he followed them silently. He pulled up in front of the building, straddling the line of a parking spot, and got out of the car as if he intended to come in with me.

I felt uneasy. Max wouldn't hesitate to tell others how to take care of their business. Besides, anything to do with his grandmother he obviously considered his business, at least now that she was dead.

I could see a woman behind the counter inside the shop, but the door was locked, and when I knocked, she only pointed up at the clock on the wall and shook her head. Max stepped in front of me and rattled the door.

The woman frowned and mouthed the words, "We're closed." I might have gotten her to open the door if I'd been by myself, but when Max swore and hit the door with his open palm, she pursed her lips, raised her eyebrows, and snapped out the lights inside.

"Damn stupid cow," he said, turning away.

"That was smart. That was real smart, Max," I said. My headache was coming back. I wished now I hadn't been so eager to help. Then Norton could have taken me back out to Point Blank himself.

Max was already climbing back in the car, his face turning a dark red under his tan. "This town is the black hole of the universe when it comes to intelligence. It digests brain cells. You live here for very long, you end up with a vacuum between your ears."

Before I even had the passenger door closed, he threw the car into gear and was spinning out of the parking lot. He whipped in and out of the traffic in town, and after we were out on the highway he put his foot to the floor, passing everything in sight. He hung one elbow over the door and watched the road narrowly. I would have preferred having the air conditioner on instead of the top down, but I didn't dare speak up. He was angry enough as it was.

We'd just turned off on the county road when he said, still not looking at me, "You know anybody in real estate around here? Personally, I mean."

I thought a minute, trying to keep my eyes off the speedometer. "No. I know who some of them are, but I don't know any of them personally. Why?"

"Some secretary called my sister last week and left a message on her answering machine. Said she was calling for some development company."

I shrugged. I didn't know of any business in the area that called itself a development company.

"She said they'd made an offer on some of my grandmother's property out here. They wanted to check with us—why, I don't know. It got Muriel all upset. Both of us figure Granny's not—she wasn't—really competent to be making those kinds of decisions in her condition."

"Did Muriel call them back?" I asked.

"No. The stupid fool erased the message by mistake. She resets the machine every morning as she's going out the door to work. She says she was in a hurry and didn't remember about the message till it was too late. Didn't even get the name. At least that's what she says."

"You don't believe her?"

"That she's capable of doing something so stupid? Sure. But also, she might just be doing it for some other reason. Trying to get me upset, maybe. Or maybe she did call this place back and found out something she doesn't want me to know about."

"Why would she have said anything at all to you about it then?" I asked.

He glanced over at me and shook his head. "You don't know Muriel, do you? I doubt if she could keep from letting her little brother know she was in on something he wasn't."

I felt his narrowed eyes rake my face as I stared straight ahead. "I just thought I'd check with you," he said. "You seem to know pretty much of everything that's going on out here. In fact, you strike me as having a lot more on the ball than the rest of these yokels. I thought you might be able to help me." And he reached over and patted my knee clumsily.

I jumped as though I'd been touched by a snake. "No," I said. "I can't."

He put both hands back on the steering wheel and laughed. "Nervous?" he said. "Don't worry. No need to be."

I was thoroughly rattled by the time we pulled up in Miss Mineola's drive. He swung the car onto the lawn in a way his grandmother would never have allowed. I scrambled out muttering a brief, "Thanks." I just wanted to get away from him as quickly as I could. Then I remembered the towel-wrapped bundle I'd put on the floor by my feet. I opened the door again, and we both reached for it at the same time.

"I can take that back," he said, almost like a command.

"I will," I said, and tucked it under my arm. "I told Bud I would."

He opened his mouth to protest, but then shut it suddenly. "All right," he said with a smirk. "Have it your way, little lady."

CHAPTER • FOURTEEN

CECELIA WAS SITTING IN THE DINing room alone, looking through a stack of sympathy cards that had already arrived. Larry and Beulah were napping, she said. Max had followed me in, and, with scarcely a nod in her direction, walked through to the living room and switched on the television set as though he lived there.

Poor Cecelia looked as if she was on her last leg. Her hair hung in damp tendrils around her round face and her brow was puckered in deep furrows.

"Aunt Min's still not back from Houston," she said anxiously, as though Miss Mineola were only late getting home from a shopping trip. "People have been calling all day wanting to know when the funeral's going to be. I told the ones that called this morning that it would probably be tomorrow. Then when they didn't get through with Aunt Min down in Houston, I had to call them all back and tell them it would be Wednesday at the earliest."

"I'm sorry I wasn't here to help," I said.

"Oh, sugar, you've already been so much help. I don't know what I'd do without you." She pushed one of the damp strands of hair back behind her ear. She didn't mention Lois's name, but I could tell she was feeling tired and deserted, whether she would admit it or not.

I sat down with her at Miss Mineola's big walnut dining table and started idly sifting through the stack of condolence cards. I didn't know how to begin what I had to say.

"I guess Lois must have had to go back to Houston," she said tentatively.

I took a deep breath. "Probably," I said.

She looked at me closely, waiting for me to go on. She could tell there was more.

"Honestly, Cecelia," I finally said, looking up. "I'm not sure where she is."

"But she's still got your car?"

"I guess so. They're trying to find it now." I couldn't bring myself to say "the sheriff's department."

"Maybe she went back to her apartment. But why would she do such a thing without telling you?"

I shrugged. "I called her apartment. No one answered. I think Lois was...very upset, Cecelia."

"Upset?" she repeated. "Not about Aunt Min?"

I knew this would be the hard part. Did I tell Cecelia that her daughter had made some kind of romantic hero out of Finney in her imagination, that she'd even tried to help him escape? That she'd fallen for his line about their running away to Mexico together? Would Cecelia even believe me if I told her?

I couldn't tell her that Lois and Finney had been, well, together down in Archie's trailer right while Miss Mineola lay dead—or murdered—up in the big house. And I certainly couldn't tell her that they might have even been upstairs in Miss Mineola's own house when Archie found her. Norton wouldn't want me saying anything about that.

Cecelia looked at me steadily for a long time. I listened to the whir of the ceiling fan turning slowly above the table.

"Does this have anything to do with Finney Blalock?" she finally asked.

"I think it might."

"I was afraid of that."

I must have looked startled.

"Oh, sugar," she said, smiling at me but looking sadder than if she'd been crying, "I know everybody thinks I'm just a gullible fool, and maybe they're right. But even if she's not too bright, a mother can always tell how her child is feeling. I've known for a long time that Lois was unhappy."

I murmured something about Cecelia being a fine mother, but she ignored me.

"One of her letters to Finney Blalock came back a month or so ago," she went on. "She mailed it from Houston, but she'd put one of my address stickers on it, so they returned it here to my post office box. If she'd written out the return address, I'm sure she would have put her own in Houston. But she uses those little stickers of mine on her bills a lot of the time. I guess she just slipped up and stuck one on that letter too. Anyway, as luck would have it, that one came back. I don't know why. If I'd known it was hers, I never would have opened it. It had things in it I'd just as soon not have read."

I kept still, hoping she would finish the story without any more prompting from me, but it was a long time before she said anything else.

"I'm afraid she's done something very foolish," she finally added, so low I almost couldn't hear her.

"I didn't know anything about this, Cecelia," I said. "Believe me. She only told me yesterday." I felt like I owed her as much of the truth as I was sure of. "Lois was beside herself about Finney. I took her home with me, hoping she could pull herself together. She spent the night at my house last night, just like I said. And this morning she'd calmed down. She seemed more reasonable. She got dressed and asked if she could borrow my car to go in to the funeral home."

"Did she help Finney Blalock escape?"

"She wasn't very specific about that." Which was the truth.

Cecelia put her elbows on the table and leaned her forehead in her hands. "Lois needed a mother like yours," she said. "Someone who could have understood her better than I can. I don't even know what she's talking about half the time. I try to ask her questions about her work at school and all, but most of the time she doesn't even bother to answer me. So I've just given up asking. I know it must be frustrating for her, trying to explain things. Your mother—now she was smart. She could have understood."

"Cecelia, please. None of this is your fault. Don't try to take responsibility for it."

"Oh, I'm not, honey. But I can't help but think, maybe, if so many things had been different. A long time ago."

"We could all say that, couldn't we?" I felt the firmness creeping back into my own voice, and again I wondered if it were a borrowed firmness, learned from my mother, or if it were truly my own. "Lois has hurt you, I know. She's hurt me too. But most of all she's hurt herself. Give her a chance to lick her wounds. Then we'll see. Don't worry. She's all right. It's not as though she's disappeared forever." I was speaking more hopefully than I felt.

Cecelia looked up and smiled at me like a reassured child. "You're right, Beth Marie. I'll just have to trust the Lord to take care of her right now."

"That's right," I said encouragingly, all the while wondering what kind of plans the Lord might have in store for somebody as hardheaded and willful as Lois. I got up and went over to put my arms around Cecelia. "Right now you've got all you can handle right here in this house. Would you like me to stay out here with you tonight?"

"Heavens, no, honey. I'll be just fine. I've got Uncle Larry and Beulah and Max here with me. And Muriel called to say she'd be here in the morning."

"Great," I said, pulling away. "Just what you need."

"And I'm sure Evelyn will be here bright and early. She's been a big help."

"Okay, then," I said reluctantly. "If you promise you'll go to bed early. And in your own house where you'll rest better. Let Max take care of his aunt and uncle over here. He's certainly made himself at home."

She only smiled at this, and I could tell it was meant to reassure me without her having to tell an out-and-out lie. She'd probably put the old couple in the extra downstairs bedroom, send Max upstairs, and sleep on the sofa herself. Miss Mineola's room would be off-limits for guests until after the funeral.

After assuring her that I'd let her know the minute I heard any news about Lois, I left through the kitchen to pick up the towel-wrapped bundle I'd left there on the table. I slid it into a paper sack I found under the counter. I didn't want to bother Cecelia with another detail right now. I'd get it returned tomorrow somehow.

Slipping out the door, I cut around behind Miss Mineola's big white house and angled through what used to be the field where she had once kept her spring calves. Then I climbed through the barbed wire at the edge of the field, certain no one had spotted me from the house.

I hadn't wanted to ask poor Cecelia to run me home, and I sure didn't want to ask Max for another ride. It was only a little over a mile back to my house in Point Blank, and now that the sun was going down, the heat had slacked off some. Besides, walking always seems to help my thought processes, and there was plenty I needed to think about.

The dust puffed up in dry clouds around my sandals as I walked, and I watched purple martins sailing high overhead, searching the last slanting rays of light for mosquitoes. Late evening in summer had always been one of my favorite times as a child. You stole your last moments with playmates then, waiting to be called in for the night. The world was cooling off and it was the best time for games like Run, Sheep, Run. The lengthening shadows made it easier to hide, and dusk made the chase more dramatic. Nothing afterwards had ever exceeded the sheer physical thrill of those moments. Your heart started pounding, your breath came in quick gasps, your senses were heightened above their everyday slackness.

How different the child's game was from the real thing once you grew up. The thrill faded from life. Everything grew tamer and less dramatic. Or was it that way for everyone? Did life feel like that to Finney when he had committed his terrible crimes, when he tried his escapes from prison? Was that why he did those things, for the thrill of it? And was that emotional charge what had lured Lois into such a crazy alliance with him? Were they only playing out the games of childhood, but without the protection of a make-believe world, one that would dissolve when some voice called them in for the night, out of the darkness?

Remembering those summer evenings, I could catch a glimmer of what Finney and Lois might feel. They were both willful people. Their lives didn't follow the usual patterns. A deflection here, a decision there, hardly recognized at the time—a person's life was made up of such small increments, it seemed. And it could suddenly take a direction you hadn't anticipated.

I wasn't sure that's what accounted for Archie though. It was hard to think of anything very subtle connected with Archie. Possibilities seemed to dawn on him all of a sudden. At which times he would take major leaps. Leaving his family in Hawaii and starting a new life here. Changing his name. Shooting Finney. That's why it wasn't such a strain to imagine him rifling Miss Mineola's jewelry boxes when he found her asleep. Or doing away with her if she had waked up. Anyone else might have made up a plausible enough story to get out of such a sticky situation, but Archie wasn't good at thinking on his feet. He could only react. Suddenly and desperately, as he had when he shot Finney in the trailer. He never stopped to consider the consequences.

Which is why I still leaned toward thinking Miss Mineola had caught him stealing the gold chains and nuggets and that he had reacted, immediately and violently, maybe choking or smothering her. Supposedly there had been no sign of a struggle. Cecelia said she had found her aunt curled up in a ball, the kind of fetal position that old people draw up in when they're dying. But no one else had seen her that way. She was all straightened out by the time anyone else saw her. Maybe Cecelia had in fact found signs of a struggle and had covered them up, especially if she had any suspicion that Archie had been there. That would explain why Cecelia had wanted to talk to Archie alone in the barn that night. I could see her trying to protect him.

On the other hand, Cecelia wasn't the kind of person to break or even obstruct the law. What would she do if she had to make a choice between protecting Archie and breaking the law?

But she hadn't got to talk to Archie that night. Or since then either, as far as I knew. Had she been telling the truth about how she'd found Miss Mineola? I shook my head. What a question to be asking about Cecelia. Still, if anything could ever induce her to tell a lie, it would be the need to protect someone else. I had already seen her distraught today over the promise she'd made to Miss Mineola about looking out for Archie.

On the other hand, maybe Archie was telling the truth. Even Norton, who apparently liked to leave no stone unturned, no complication unconsidered, seemed inclined to believe him. At least he never lost an opportunity to point out my readiness to use Archie as a scapegoat. For the first time it occurred to me to consider that accusation seriously. Was I anxious to make Archie a scapegoat? After all, as Norton said, it made a certain amount of sense to believe Archie about what had happened in that downstairs bedroom. Maybe she was already dead when he came in. Maybe he did indeed just help himself to the contents of those jewelry boxes and then take off for town. Callous as it sounded, I could believe it of him. His comment about leaving Cecelia to take care of things had the ring of truth to it. It was the kind of remark only Archie could make.

That interpretation would take care of all the complications generated by my other speculations. The only question left unanswered then would be who Archie had heard upstairs. And the answer to that now seemed clear. It must have been either Lois or Finney or both.

If Miss Mineola had already been dead, what difference would their being upstairs make? Yet Norton said he found all those simultaneous events too coincidental to ignore. And Lois suddenly disappearing with my car certainly clouded the picture. Could she have had anything to do with Miss Mineola's death? That, of course, was impossible. Not Lois. Finney, maybe, but not Lois.

These thoughts had carried me clear to the pasture where the Packards had by now rolled the hay into huge round bales higher than my head. They must be wondering if they'd still be making hay in that field next year. Whether they could keep the lease would depend, I supposed, on who inherited Miss Mineola's land. If it were Max or Muriel, the Packards could forget it. If a development company was interested, either one of them would unload it as soon as possible. On the other hand, if Archie were to get it, he might be guided by someone like Bud. Bud might even be able to buy it from him. Of course, if Cecelia got the land, she'd just go on letting the Packards rent it forever, if that's what they wanted.

The only one who seemed concerned about the will was Max. I was sure that was the only reason he was impatient about the autopsy and the delay with the funeral. He was anxious to get to the important part—what he stood to gain from his grandmother's death. It must be weighing on everyone's mind, though, as often as Miss Mineola had changed her will. Cecelia seemed completely unconcerned, but then that's what you would expect from her. But Lois and Archie, what were they thinking? Or Muriel, for that matter?

It was just dusk as I unlocked my back door. The heat that had built up during the day rushed out at me, and somehow I hated to go in and face the big, empty rooms. I put the paper sack down on the kitchen table and went into the living room to switch on the air conditioner, wondering if Norton might have tried to call me with news of Lois. He hadn't liked being left on the sidewalk in front of Babbitt's when I got in the car with Max. He might even call to make sure I'd made it safely home. For the first time in my life I wished I had an answering machine.

I needed a shower badly after my hike home across the fields, but before I went upstairs to the bathroom I took the phone off the hook. That way, if he called while I was in the shower, at least he'd know I was home now and maybe call back.

I had just pulled off my dusty sandals and jeans when I thought I heard a car in the back driveway. It was getting dark now, and I didn't see any lights when I peeked out the bedroom window to the backyard. I was probably just imagining things. Anyway, Norton would probably call before he came all the way out to Point Blank. Still, as soon as I was out of the shower and had wrapped my wet hair in a towel, I ran downstairs again and put the phone on the hook. It was then I heard, softly but quite distinctly this time, the back screen door close.

For a moment I stood there frozen. I hadn't locked the back door after I came in. Someone had been in my house while I was upstairs. My first impulse was to run to the back door, but all I had on was the towel around my hair. I started for the stairs. Just then there was a knock on the front door. What was going on?

I raced up the stairs again, grabbed my old chenille bathrobe, and glanced out my bedroom window again. There was no one there now, at least not in a car. I went downstairs slowly, holding my robe together tightly at the neck, turned on the front porch light, and looked out through the little window in the front door. It was Norton.

"Thank God you're here," I cried with sudden relief, throwing the door open and pulling him in. "Or was it you? Did you come in the back door first? Without knocking?" I ended almost angrily.

He stared at me. "What in the world are you talking about? I just got here. Just now."

I stared at him for a long moment. "And you didn't see anyone else? Anyone leaving?" I felt suddenly weak.

"No. What's the matter? Here." He took me by the arm and moved me toward the sofa. "Now tell me what's going on."

"Someone was just here. I'm certain I heard the back door close as I came down the stairs. I was taking a shower," I finished lamely, resettling the towel that was coming unwrapped from around my wet hair.

"You left the back door unlocked?" His grip on my arm tightened.

"I forgot to lock it again when I came in." I tried to hold the damp towel in place with my free hand.

"And you were here by yourself!"

"You don't have to yell at me," I said hotly. The fear and relief were finally catching up with me and I was afraid I'd start to cry next.

"That's great. That's just great," he said, turning loose of my arm as I sank onto the sofa. "You're just the kind of woman law officers are supposed to protect, even though you act like there's not a thing in the world that will ever happen to you. Way out here in the boonies and you don't lock your doors, not even when you're taking a shower. I can't believe it. You probably don't even pull the shades when you get undressed."

"Now just a minute," I said, standing up again. "For your information, I do not undress in front of open windows. And people often leave their doors unlocked out here, at least until they go to bed. Men and women. You sound like you're trying to make me responsible for someone slipping into my house, like I was the guilty one!" I yanked the towel off my hair.

He didn't say anything else, but I heard him go into the kitchen and open and close the back door several times. When he came back, I had gotten hold of myself again and was sitting on the sofa. He sat down in a chair across from me and leaned forward, his hands on his knees. I ran my hands through my wet, tangled hair and crossed my legs carefully, tugging the edges of the bathrobe together.

"I didn't mean to get you upset," he said in a low, even voice. "You just caught me off guard."

"I'm all right."

"Now tell me again what you think you heard."

Even though I didn't like the fact that he said "think you heard," I started at the first, telling him how I'd walked home from Miss Mineola's, come in the back door, and gone upstairs to take a shower. I left out the part about the phone. "I thought I heard a car just as I was getting undressed, but since I didn't see any lights from the window, I figured I was mistaken. Then when—

I was coming downstairs, I heard the back door shut. I wasn't mistaken about that, I'm sure."

"I don't guess you've looked around yet to see if anything's missing?"

"No. You came right after that."

He looked around the room as though for some telling sign left by the intruder. "Why don't you go get dressed. Mind if I get some ice water?"

I shrugged. "Help yourself."

Upstairs, I stood surveying the possibilities of my closet in confusion. Originally I had intended to put on my nightgown and read a while in bed. I was still a little put out with the tone he'd taken with me. But it was pretty unnerving to think someone had sneaked into my house while I was upstairs. Norton had probably scared them off, driving up when he did. I ought to be grateful, I supposed. Still, he didn't have to talk to me as though I were a child.

I finally put on some shorts and a T-shirt, old ones I wore when I worked in the flowerbeds. Emily's gray calyx, I thought. I combed out my damp hair and went back downstairs where I found Norton in the kitchen, clinking ice cubes in his glass.

"Everything look all right in here?" he asked. "Anything missing?"

I looked around. "What would anyone take from a kitchen?" I asked. "I don't even have a microwave."

"Where's your purse?"

"There on the hutch," I said. "That's where I always put it when I come in." I went over and opened it. "Wallet, keys, everything's here."

"Must not have been a burglar then. Even if he were scared off, he would probably have grabbed your purse."

"Wait," I said, frowning, "there was something else."

He turned and looked at me, waiting for me to go on.

"There was a paper sack. Sitting there on the table."

"A paper sack?"

"Yes. It had that thing in it, some kind of mask, for Miss Mineola's oxygen. That's what's gone."

Neither of us said anything for a while. Then he went to the back door again, bent down to give it a closer look, and then stepped out onto the back steps. "Why don't we sit out here where it's cooler," he called to me.

I followed him out and we sat down on the top step together. It was completely dark now. The light from the kitchen made a yellow bar that fell across us and out onto the grass.

Norton was frowning. "I wonder," he said and then stopped.

"Wonder what?"

"Nothing. Just if I've made a mistake."

"Mistake?"

"Archie," he said. "We let Archie go. The TDC people were through with him for the time being. He's suspended from duty, but they agreed not to hold him or even charge him right now. I told them he might be more helpful to this investigation—useful's more the right word, I guess—if he were free to move around. If he thinks he's going to get off easy, he might make contact with someone else or do something that would give us more information about all this. He still has to check in with them every day, and they'll keep a watch on his trailer out there. Still—" He didn't finish the sentence but just shook his head and frowned.

"Still what?"

"Well," he rubbed his freckled hand across his face, and I noticed for the first time how tired he looked, "maybe we shouldn't have been so quick to release him."

"You think it might have been Archie who came in here tonight?"

He shrugged.

I leaned back on my elbows and studied that possibility for a moment. "But why? And why would he take that sack?"

He shrugged again. "All I know is he'd been released in plenty of time to get back out here. That's all I'm saying. Maybe we made a mistake. Maybe he was more involved in this than we thought."

"Well, what did he tell the TDC people about the escape? Did he say anything about Lois?"

Norton looked at me and then looked away again, shaking his head. "Is that all you're worried about?"

"Of course not. But it's one of the things. And it could have a bearing on...on the other thing too, don't you think? I mean, just conceivably?"

"I guess you're right. Anyway. They wouldn't like it if they knew I was letting this information out—and you must keep quiet about it—but Archie says he had Finney in the trunk of his car when he left the prison unit. They didn't tell me how he managed that. There's some things they absolutely don't want getting out. Anyway, he let Blalock out in the woods down on the far side of the cemetery. As far as Archie knew, that was the end of it for him."

"Why—"

"Money," Norton said before I could even frame my question. "Finney paid him. Half up front, half when they got to the cemetery. The money was in a coffee can hidden in one of those plastic flower dealy-bobs on one of the graves."

"So he hadn't expected Finney to show up again at his trailer."

"No. He says he thought Finney would be long gone by then. He expected that whoever left the money there in the cemetery had probably arranged to pick him up there too."

"Lois?"

"You have any better suggestions?"

I didn't respond to that, and after a moment he added, "Blalock was clever. He kept the two parts of the escape separate. Not trusting either Archie or Lois, he didn't let one know about the other's part in it. Probably figured it was safer that way. And that's why neither one of them was able to give the other away Saturday night."

"But Lois had been at the trailer earlier. Getting ice that afternoon."

"But remember that Archie took off for town right after he left with the jewelry, hoping to get rid of it as soon as possible."

"And you think it was then that Lois and Finney—"

"Yes. I think they were upstairs in the house when they saw Archie come up to see Miss Mineola and a little later leave and drive away. That's when they went to his trailer."

"But why? And did they know about Miss Mineola then, do you think? About her being dead, I mean?" I stopped.

He leaned his elbows on his knees. His face was in the shadows. "I think that's why Blalock took it into his head to go down to Archie's trailer. He must have figured he had something on Archie. Something he could use."

"So you think Archie really did—do away with Miss Mineola?"

"Not necessarily. Blalock could have killed her himself. Or maybe she saw him. Then again, maybe Blalock saw Archie take her jewelry. If so, he'd know he had the perfect setup to blame the old lady's death on Archie in case he got caught. Either way, whether it was Blalock or Archie who killed her, Blalock would know he could pin it on old Arch."

"That's too many choices," I said. "It's too confusing. It's like a maze." I leaned forward myself now so I could see his face in the bar of light from the kitchen. "And what about Lois?" I asked.

"I was wondering when you were going to ask about her," he said.

CHAPTER • FIFTEEN

IT WAS A LONG TIME BEFORE NORTON left that night, almost midnight, and he didn't want to go then. But I insisted.

"Whoever it was has already got what they wanted," I told him. "They won't be back."

"You don't know that," he argued. "You don't know that they even knew what was in the sack when they grabbed it."

"Don't be silly. Why would anyone take a brown paper sack unless they wanted what was in it?"

"People do all kinds of weird things," he said, scowling. He'd followed me into the kitchen while I made iced tea. Then we went back outside and sat on the steps again watching the lightning bugs. He wanted to know about my mother and father, if I had any brothers and sisters, what I wanted to do next.

I told him how we'd come to Point Blank after the doctors said my father needed peace and quiet for his damaged heart, which, even so, had failed him after a few years. But he had loved those years in the country, and had taught me to love it too. That's why I stayed.

"I never believed that explanation Lois was giving me this morning. You know that, don't you?"

I shrugged and made a face.

"But seriously. What's your idea of a really good time?"

I hugged my knees and stared at the pinpricks of light hovering just above the grass. "The fire lookout tower. There's one just on the other side of the cemetery. I don't know if you've noticed it. I like to climb up there and look around. Of course, you're not supposed to. It's been condemned. Kids go out there sometimes. And me. People in Point Blank think it's weird, I guess, or think I'm weird. They're always teasing me about climbing up in my tower. Bud Wylie told me he'd build me a tree house or a jungle gym if I really needed someplace to play. But I love it there. It's peaceful. A good place to think."

"Then you ought to go to the mountains sometime," he said. "You'd love it. I go every chance I get." And he described some of the backpacking he'd done. It was pleasant to talk about something besides death and autopsies for a change.

Norton had called out to Miss Mineola's while I made the tea. Uncle Larry had answered, and Norton had to shout the questions at the top of his voice several times before he could get any information. Max, it turned out, wasn't there. He'd left, saying he was going back into town. And Cecelia, he thought, had gone back to her own house to sleep. Uncle Larry said he hadn't seen her since he got up from his nap. What time was it anyway, he wanted to know. And who was going to fix his breakfast?

As soon as Norton had hung up the telephone, I could see he'd made up his mind that the person sneaking into my kitchen had been Max. But he didn't bring it up again till later when we were sitting on the back steps.

"It stands to reason," he said then. "He saw you leave, followed you home, and waited till he saw the light go on upstairs. Then he snuck in the open back door and took the sack."

"But why? That mask thing was in the car with us all

the way back to Point Blank. Why didn't he take it then if he wanted it? And why would he want it anyway? It doesn't make sense."

"I don't know why. If we knew that, maybe we'd know all we need to clear up these so-called coincidences. It only proves there's something fishy though. Maybe he didn't want anybody to know he wanted it."

"Why?"

"Don't you see? Somehow he doesn't want to be connected with that mask. Didn't you tell me this character does diving, snorkeling, something like that?"

"Yes. But this mask was just green, transparent plastic, real soft and flexible. It didn't look like you could use it for diving or anything like that."

"Of course not. But he knows about this kind of thing, you see, because of this hobby of his."

"What kind of thing?" I asked, frowning. "What are you talking about?"

"Pressurized gasses and breathing apparatus. That kind of thing." He stood up and ran one hand through his strawberry hair. The creases in his shirt had gone a little limp in the day's heat, and I knew he must be tired. Should I offer to let him sleep on my sofa? I tried to pull my mind back to Max and the mask.

"We don't know where Max was Saturday, do we?" he asked and then said, not waiting for an answer, "Supposing he came up here, waited for Mrs. Ramsey to leave, then went in and gassed the old lady."

"Why would he do such a thing?" I leaned back and crossed my arms, looking skeptical. Then I frowned as I remembered another detail. "He did ask me about a message someone had left on his sister's answering machine. Some development company interested in buying their grandmother's property. He says Muriel erased the message by mistake so they never got the name of the company. He wanted to know if I'd heard anything about it."

Norton rubbed his forehead. "Wasn't there something in that diary of Mrs. Magillberry's about changing her will too?"

"Yes. But who knows how? She changed it every few months, according to Cecelia. And she kept all the changes secret."

"Maybe there's some connection here that might give him a motive. Maybe he wanted to stop his grandmother from selling off his inheritance."

"I don't think so. She would have been doing both Max and Muriel a favor by selling it off. They much prefer money to land."

"Well," Norton said lamely, "that's what he told you."

"So why should he have told me anything at all?" It seemed to me Norton was grasping at any straw that would make Max look bad. Still, when I thought of how Max had put his hand on my knee in the car, as though to thrill me into some kind of confidence, I shuddered.

Norton looked at me. "Like I said, people do all kinds of weird things, and as far as I can see, he's our best bet for who took that mask this evening. I think I should stay here with you."

I laughed, and then said, as lightly as I could, "What would the neighbors think?"

"Don't be a fool, Beth Marie. This is potentially very serious. I'm just doing my job."

"I beg your pardon," I said, stung by his humorless tone. "A fool?"

"You're just like all women," he said and stood up. "You want to be protected, but as soon as the immediate threat has passed, you act like this is some kind of game."

I felt my face turning red in the dark.

"Like I say, I'm just doing my job. Lots of people don't like the job I do. Sometimes even the ones it's meant to help."

We were both standing by now.

"I'm sorry if you thought—" I began stiffly.

"Don't say any more." He held up a hand. "We're both tired." There was a long pause. Then he picked up his hat off the step. "I have some things I need to check on in town. But please," I could feel him staring at me though he'd stepped back out of the light, "be sure to lock your doors after I'm gone."

I stood there, waiting till I heard his car start out in front and drive away. Then I went inside, locked the back door, turned off the lights, and locked the front door. "Damn him," I whispered to myself all the way up the stairs. Several times I caught myself starting sentences out loud. "Why did I ever—" But as soon as I heard my own voice, I stopped. I am not going to think about it, I told myself silently. I am going to put the whole sorry business out of my mind.

I picked up the book of Dickinson's poems and began paging through, looking for something like "The Soul selects her own Society" or "How happy is the little Stone That rambles in the Road alone." But I couldn't find them. Instead, I came across another poem, one less familiar but even better. I read it over and over till I could say it to myself after I had turned out the light:

The Heart is the Capital of the Mind —
The Mind is a single State —
The Heart and the Mind together make —
A single Continent —
One is the Population —
Numerous enough —
This ecstatic Nation
Seek — it is Yourself.

Well. I wasn't necessarily ecstatic, but I was single and I was enough. Who needed him?

Still, I had troubled dreams all through the night and was waked early the next morning by a call from Harva

Blalock, telling me that Finney's funeral would be at ten o'clock that day. I promised her I'd be there. Then I went out to water the flowers that were drooping along the borders in the heat, determined to keep the deputy out of my thoughts.

I tried going over last evening's events systematically. Cecelia had gone home early last night. Was it possible she came over, found me in the shower, and took the oxygen mask to return herself when she found it on the kitchen table? In the sunny light of morning that seemed much more reasonable than any explanation either of us had thought of last night.

I finished spraying the marigolds, turned off the water, and went inside to call Cecelia and put my mind at rest about that particular point anyway. It was only eight, but Cecelia was an early riser. If Miss Mineola had still been alive, Cecelia would have already fixed her breakfast and had the dishes washed by now. I tried Cecelia's house first, and when I got no answer there, I called the big house across the road. I was surprised when Uncle Larry's wife answered.

"Cecelia?" Beulah shouted into the phone. "No, she's not here. Said she had to go up to the funeral home. They got the body back last night she said."

"Oh? You've seen her this morning then?"

"Of course I saw her. She slept right here last night."

"Really? Your husband said she'd gone home for the night."

"That old fool? You can't count on him to get any-thing straight. He doesn't hear too good, you know. No, Cecelia was already up and ginning around when I woke up this morning."

"Do you know if she went anywhere last night? In the car, I mean."

"Now that you mention it, I think maybe she did. When they called her from the funeral home to say they had the body back."

I thanked her and hung up. So, I thought, she'd gotten a call from Holcombe's, stopped by to see if I could go with her, found me in the shower, and decided not to bother me. Just like Cecelia. Then she'd noticed the paper sack on the table, saw the oxygen mask in it, and decided to take care of that errand herself. A simple explanation.

Norton and I had both been tired last night, overwrought, imagining things. I suddenly felt much lighter, relieved of the disturbing thought of some stranger sneaking in my house. Norton had been wrong.

That was no excuse for the high-handed way he'd talked, but that didn't matter anyway. Not to me—a single continent, an ecstatic nation. Who needed that kind of emotional turmoil? It was silly. Silly in small doses, disastrous in large ones. That's what had intoxicated and ruined Lois.

Poor Lois, I thought. Where was she today? And—it suddenly hit me—where was my car? Had they found it yet? Finney's funeral was scheduled for ten this morning. How was I going to get there without a car?

I sat beside the phone for a moment, debating with myself. Then I dialed the sheriff's office in Somerville. Lurline, the dispatcher, answered. Yes, she said, they had located my car. Come in at nine when the business office opened and pick it up. "Unless," she added, "you want—"

"That'll be fine," I broke in. "I'll pick it up at nine."

After I hung up, though, I realized I still had the problem of getting to Somerville. Cecelia was tied up at the funeral home, and I certainly didn't want to ask Max to take me in. While I dressed for Finney's funeral, I debated the options and finally decided to call the Wylies. Bud or Evelyn would probably be willing to give me a ride. They'd want to go to Holcombe's anyway as soon as the funeral home had Miss Mineola all fixed up for viewing. I still hadn't explained anything to them about Lois, but by now they must have begun to suspect something funny was going on.

Evelyn answered the phone. "You mean you're going to close the Water Board Office again?" she asked when I told her I was going to Finney's funeral.

I silently reminded myself that Evelyn was not from Point Blank. "The Blalocks are expecting me to be there," I said. "And there'll be few enough people at the funeral as it is."

"Yes, you're probably right. Well, of course, I'll be glad to take you in since I'll be going to Holcombe's myself. I'm almost ready now. I'll be over in half an hour."

We floated into town in her Lincoln, and I noticed the big car had the same effect on Evelyn that it did on me. She edged out smaller cars and went through two yellow lights. The only vehicle she deferred to was a logging truck. She didn't have on her Point Blank polyester pants this morning either, but a linen suit. And her gray curls had been freshly done up yesterday afternoon at the beauty parlor. I started to mention the problems with the oxygen mask, but, remembering her remark about my closing the Water Board, I decided not to. There was something about Evelyn that always made me feel incompetent.

"By the way," she said as she waited for a light to change, "Bud went in and got Archie last night when they were through questioning him. The boy had tried to call Cecelia, but she wasn't home. It's probably just as well, though. Archie needed a man to talk to, you know? He's lived around women too much, I think. I'm not sure it was the best thing for Minnie and Hattie to take him away from his family. It seems to have—I don't know—arrested his development or something."

"Maybe so," I said. Actually, I wasn't sure a developed Archie would have been an improvement.

"He has such a terrible temper," she went on, making a left turn from the right lane. "He throws tantrums like a small child if he doesn't get his way. I even feel a little uneasy having him in the house—"

"In the house?" I broke in.

"Yes. Bud brought him home after he picked him up in town. It was late and he hadn't eaten. You know how Bud is. He didn't have the heart to take him back out to that terrible trailer where—where it all happened. So Archie spent the night with us. I'm sure Bud felt like it was the one thing he could still do for Minnie. He feels a kind of obligation towards the boy now that she's gone."

I asked her to drop me off at the florist shop on the square so I could get something for Harva and Terry B. It was only a couple of blocks from the sheriff's department, but I didn't mention that fact.

"Are you sure you don't want me to wait?" Evelyn asked.

"Oh, no. Terry B.'s picking me up here," I lied.

"I'll go on then," she said. "Cecelia can use all the support she can get right now. I'm sure she'll be glad when all this is over. Maybe she can go on a long trip somewhere. Forget all about it for a while."

I didn't tell her that wasn't Cecelia's way.

Evelyn glanced at me through her pink-tinted glasses as I climbed out of the car. "I can't imagine why the sheriff wanted to question Archie anyway, can you, Beth Marie? Unless it had something to do with Finney escaping."

"Maybe that was it," I said, figuring that didn't really count as a lie.

"I thought you might know something more about it than the rest of us," she said, arching her eyebrows over the tops of her sunglasses. "You and that deputy seem to be seeing a lot of each other lately."

I stiffened. "Things aren't always what they seem," I said. I could feel a flush creeping up my neck. "We don't really have much in common. I don't imagine I'll be seeing any more of him."

She smiled in a kindly, sympathetic way. "Well, I hate to say it, but he's probably not what your mother would have wanted for you either. Not your type at all."

I shrugged. I really didn't want to stand there on the sidewalk discussing my love life—or lack of it—with Evelyn. She waggled her fingers at me as she drove away—as though we had some kind of secret together.

I went into the florist shop and ordered a potted plant sent out to the parsonage in Point Blank. Then I slipped out a side door and walked up the street to the sheriff's office.

Lurline, wearing a brown and yellow striped polo shirt and green eye shadow, was at the front desk eating a doughnut and drinking coffee. As I signed a paper for the release of the car, I could feel her watching me.

"You want to see Norton?" she asked offhandedly, taking my car keys off a pegboard behind her desk and handing them to me.

I looked as blank as I could. "No, I don't believe so. Do I need to?"

She shrugged and lifted her eyebrows. "Suit yourself. I don't know what's going on, but he sure has been a ring-tailed tooter ever since he come in this morning."

"I'll just take the car," I said stiffly. "I have a funeral to go to right now."

"Oh, yeah. That convict that got killed out y'all's way. He a personal friend of yours?"

"I went to school with him. And I know his family."

"Y'all sure got all kinds out there at Point Blank, don't you?" she said good-naturedly.

I've always admired people like Lurline. They say exactly what they think, and what they think never seems all that complicated.

"You want me to tell him you been here?" she called after me as I was leaving. I pretended I didn't hear. It wasn't until I was halfway to the cemetery that I realized I'd forgotten to ask Lurline where they'd found the car.

The Blalocks were only having a graveside service for Finney. I guess they figured there wouldn't be many people show up anyway and it would save on expenses, not having to use Holcombe's chapel. Finney was being buried in what's commonly known in Somerville as Peckerwood Hill, the burial ground for prison inmates. It sits up on a pine-covered rise on the east side of town close to the railroad tracks and across from a concrete plant that's been shut down ever since the end of the oil boom.

Several notable outlaws are buried there, I understand, but the prison officials don't like to have much publicity about the cemetery in case some of the town's college students should take it into their heads to steal the headstones as trophies. At the bottom of the hill are the older graves, marked only by nameless white concrete crosses. Higher up, the graves have markers with rounded tops like cartoon tombstones. These are concrete too, but they have names inscribed on them along with the date the inmate died. Only a few have birth dates.

Harva and Terry B. were already there, sitting in their old Chrysler with both doors open to let the air flow through. Beside it was a little Chevette that belonged to their daughter who teaches school in the next county. She hadn't brought her husband or children. On the other side of the Chevette was a pickup belonging to a younger brother who'd just gotten out of the Marines. I pulled up into a shady spot under a pine tree and got out. As though they had all been waiting for me to appear, the family members began emerging from their separate vehicles.

There was no canopy over the open grave like Holcombe's puts up to shelter the mourners from the sun or the rain, or maybe just to soften with a man-made structure the sense of elemental nature and all that implies at a time like this. The casket sat on two sawhorses beside the grave, a single spray of white carnations laid out on top. A backhoe was parked down at the bottom of the hill, ready to go to work again as soon as we were finished. Nearby was a white TDC van with a guard in grey and a trusty in white leaning against it. I supposed they were there to operate the backhoe.

Harva had been crying. She clutched a wad of Kleenex, glued into a tight ball by now, that she used to daub at her eyes and nose during the service. But there were no extravagant outbursts of emotion. The sister, in a heavy navy dress, possibly the only one she owned suitable for a funeral, had her lips pressed firmly together; and though she bunched them up from time to time, she never opened them except to say "Amen" at the end of the prayers. The brother kept his chin pulled in as close to his neck as he could get it, a habit learned in the military no doubt, and kept his eyes steadfastly on the ground except when he nodded to me as I joined them. It was as though they had already exhausted whatever feelings they had for Finney long ago and were now having to draw on an emotional account they'd just as soon spend some other way.

All except Terry B., who kept casting his gaze about in a bewildered way as if he were still unable to take in the fact of his son's death. But, then, he'd probably been bewildered about Finney ever since the boy got big enough to start getting into serious trouble.

"Dearly beloved," Terry B. began when the five of us had made a semicircle around the grave. Then he stopped and blinked at the middle distance as though his mind had suddenly gone blank. I felt sorry for him. Baptists don't even have a prayer book to go by at times like this. They just have to make it all up, which must be a terrible strain, even when it's not your own son you're burying. Neither of his children gave him the slightest sign of encouragement but only stared stolidly at the ground about to receive their brother's body. Harva put the Kleenex ball up to her nose.

Terry B. cleared his throat and opened his Bible to a place he had marked beforehand. "'The voice said, Cry. And he said, What shall I cry? All flesh is grass, and all the goodliness thereof is as the flowers of the field.... The grass withereth, the flower fadeth: but the word of our God shall stand for ever.'"

He paused a minute and looked around at us while we contemplated the grass withering under the Texas sun. There was an audible sob from Harva. He reached over and patted her awkwardly on the arm, looking at the rest of us apologetically.

A light breeze fluttered the thin pages of his Bible. He turned a page and held it down with his thick fingers while he read on. "'Who hath directed the Spirit of the Lord, or being his counsellor hath taught him? For I beheld, and there was no man; even among them, and there was no counsellor, that, when I asked of them, could answer a word.'"

The daughter cut her eyes over toward her father. This was a highly unusual scripture to read at a funeral service, even for Baptists. But then Finney was a highly unusual individual. My guess was that Terry B. had looked long and hard to find something that would come as close to the truth of the situation as possible. What he was trying to say to this pitiful little group gathered around his dead son's body was that he was as mystified as the rest of us. He'd done his best to raise his children right; was there any explaining why one should turn out a schoolteacher, another a Marine, and a third a murderer? I believe Terry B. would have been willing to accept the responsibility for the mystery of Finney if anyone could have pointed out to him just where precisely he'd gone wrong.

He closed his Bible now and bowed his head, a signal we were about to pray. The prayer had fading flowers and withering grass in it too, along with the valley of the shadow of death and the sun shining on the just and the unjust—a clear reference to Finney, I supposed. The difference between God's ways and our ways was once more emphasized, as though there might be some shred of hope for Finney in that irrefutable fact.

Terry B. shifted the pitch in his voice now, and I could tell he was winding down. "O Lord, you knew this boy better than we did, just as you know each and every one of us better than we know our own selves. Be merciful, Lord, just like you were with the thief on the cross. We are waiting for all mysteries to be revealed and all tears wiped away. Until the day breaks and the shadows flee away, through Jesus Christ our Lord."

We all said "Amen" to that, and I wished that Lois could have been there too. It might have done her some good. But then again, it might not have. Lois was about as much of a mystery to me right then as the ways of God were.

Terry B. picked a clod of red clay and walked over to the casket on the sawhorses. "The Lord giveth, and the Lord taketh away," he said, crumbling the big clod into a shower of smaller ones that rained down on the carnations. "Blessed be the name of the Lord." Then he turned and looked at Harva, who came and laid her hand on the casket for a moment before they started back down the hill to the Chrysler. The sister and brother followed at a distance, and I saw the guard glance at his watch and motion the trusty over toward the backhoe.

I followed the family down the hill too, threading my way among the concrete crosses. There wasn't any more to say, but I hugged both Terry B. and Harva and shook hands with the brother and sister.

"The ladies at the church have brought some sandwiches over, Beth Marie," Terry B. said. "You're welcome to join us for lunch."

"I appreciate the offer," I told him, "but I think I better get over to Holcombe's to see if there's anything I can do for Cecelia." I was grateful to have the excuse. I could imagine what a morose little group they would make, gathered around the sandwiches and Jell-O salad.

This time no attendant rushed out to escort me in when I pulled into the parking lot at Holcombe's a few minutes later in my newly reclaimed Toyota. But as I started up the wide front steps, the big double doors opened and out came Cecelia, shading her eyes against the noonday sun.

"I'm so glad you're here, Beth Marie," she called. "Guess what? I couldn't hardly wait to tell you the good news!" She beckoned me up the steps, smiling broadly.

"What is it?" I asked, hurrying up the steps. Maybe they'd found Lois some place safe and with a perfectly reasonable explanation for why she'd disappeared.

"The autopsy on Aunt Min," Cecelia whispered breathlessly. "It showed there wasn't anything wrong with her. I mean, she just died a natural death was all." Her face was beaming.

CHAPTER SIXTEEN

NOT UNTIL I WAS BACK HOME IN Point Blank did I have time to sort out my reactions to Cecelia's good news. For one thing, I hadn't reacted as though it was good news. I just stood there on the steps of the funeral home dumbfounded. Then I managed a silly smile and said something not only stupid but dishonest.

"See there, Cecelia. I knew everything would work out." But I hadn't known that at all. And for some reason, I didn't feel relieved either. Nevertheless, I asked if she needed me to help her with the rest of the funeral arrangements.

"No, honey, Evelyn's here, and she can talk to these people so—authoritatively." Cecelia took a deep breath after the word as though coming up with it had required not only mental but physical exertion. "They were hemming and hawing about whether they could do the funeral in the morning since they had so many scheduled just now, but Evelyn spoke right up and told them we were next in line and we'd been waiting to get this over with a terrible long time." Her hands fluttered up like fledgling birds. "I wish I could be like that."

Evelyn did have an undeniable knack for taking situations in hand and making them come out right. She was like my mother that way.

And Miss Mineola's autopsy report would surely convince even Norton there was nothing untoward about her death, I reflected as I drove home. That would be the end of his investigations in our part of the county.

To be honest, I guess that's why I hadn't been relieved to hear the news about the autopsy. I had liked sitting beside him on the back steps last night and talking. In a way I'd even liked him getting upset about me not locking the doors, although at the time I'd also been angry and embarrassed. Those little golden bristles on the back of his neck—would they feel like I imagined they would? And the freckles on the back of his hands and up his arms—well, there were some things I'd never know now.

I remembered Emily Dickinson's lines about her own heart and mind being population enough for a single continent. That might be so for her. At most, I felt like an island, not a continent. Besides, it might be fun to visit a foreign country every now and then. But I reminded myself again, a little wearily, that the last thing I wanted was to get that desperate look—like Muriel.

I had run into her in the parking lot as I was leaving Holcombe's. She'd driven up from Houston that morning when she heard her grandmother's body would be ready for viewing. After she'd seen Miss Mineola and was satisfied with the results, she had decided to run out to Point Blank to see her Uncle Larry. It occurred to me as the two of us stood talking for a while in the parking lot that Muriel's desire to see her ninety-year-old uncle might have something to do with reminding him of their kinship. Uncle Larry had no children; it wouldn't hurt to tighten the knot on the family ties.

She pulled out a cigarette and lit it as we stood in the blazing sun. Then she asked me, just as Max had the day before, only a little more tactfully, if I knew anything about her grandmother's plans to sell off her Watson County property.

"Heavens, no," I said. "There were a lot of people Miss Mineola would have confided in before me. Anyway, I don't believe she would do a thing like that—sell to a developer. She spent her whole life trying to buy up Watson County. Why would she want to sell it off?"

Muriel scanned the tops of the automobiles in the parking lot. "Well," she finally said, "she knew neither Max nor I were interested in farming or ranching. I mean, I've told her that myself. In fact, I suggested once that she would make it a lot easier on us if she just got rid of all this rural property and either invested in some Houston real estate or converted it to CDs."

Suggested, my foot, I thought. You've probably been harping at her for years about that.

"But she never seemed to like the idea," Muriel went on. "That's why I was so surprised when I got a call from some development company saying they'd made an offer on some of her property. And upset. I mean, Granny was simply in no condition to make those kinds of decisions alone. She could easily have been taken advantage of."

By someone besides yourself, I added silently.

"I don't guess it matters now," she said, dropping the cigarette on the asphalt and stepping on it with her shiny red patent pump, "but it sure got my brother upset when I told him about that call. I think he'd been trying to raise money off his expectations."

"His expectations?" I had just noticed she didn't have any stockings on with those high heels. It's one of those prejudices I picked up from my mother, I suppose, but I couldn't help feeling that wearing high heels with no stockings indicates some kind of moral flaw. It was hard for me not to connect such a failing with a certain grubby greediness in Muriel.

"Granny's will. You know how people in her family are about male children. Max will probably get the lion's share of everything. Just like he always has. He's been hard up for cash lately. Probably gambling debts. I know he must really need it since he even came to me—to me—for a loan a few weeks ago. I mean I work as a secretary, for heaven's sake. He said if I could get a loan through my credit union, he'd give me a guarantee against his inheritance for collateral. But then a few days later he told me to forget he'd ever mentioned it—he'd already gotten the money somewhere else."

I opened my car door to let the heat out before I got in. "Well, I guess it doesn't matter much now, does it? About the developer, I mean. Even if your grandmother had been thinking about selling, the deal wouldn't have had time to go through before she died." I dropped into the driver's seat, waiting for her to say good-bye so I could close the door.

"No, I guess not," she said, and started drumming on the roof of my car with her sculptured nails. I could feel her studying me closely behind her sunglasses. "I suppose we'll know all about it soon though. Max called Bartholomew. He's supposed to be here tomorrow for the funeral. Max wanted him to read the will tomorrow afternoon." She could scarcely keep the eagerness out of her voice.

I rolled down the car window and closed the door.

"By the way," she said, leaning in the window and lowering her voice as though someone might overhear us out there in the parking lot, "where's Lois anyway? Is she out at Point Blank? Evelyn said she hasn't seen her since Saturday. I didn't want to ask Cecelia. I know how really bizarre Lois can act sometimes." I could tell by the tone of her voice she smelled something fishy.

"I think she went back to her apartment in Houston," I said. "Since they weren't sure just when the funeral was going to be, you know." It was a lame excuse, but all I could come up with on the spur of the moment.

She straightened up and tapped her nails once sharply on the roof. I swear she could have used them for screwdrivers. "I see," she said, and smiled in a way that made me fearful that she really did. I smiled back, turned on the ignition, nodded, and got out of there as fast as I could.

At home I changed out of my funeral dress and hung it on the back of the closet door, ready to wear again the next day. Mother always said I should have a little black dress ("little" being an adjective she often used to mean something between insignificant and unobtrusive; she always referred to my friends as "little" too, even after I was grown) suitable for any number of occasions. She had in mind things like concerts and plays, but about the only place I ever wore my little black dress was funerals.

That was when I'd started thinking about why I hadn't been overjoyed to hear about the autopsy results. And Norton's freckles and the hair on the back of his neck.

Mother would have said that was "just physical attraction." I don't know. I've met lots of men handsomer than Norton, and while I admired their good looks, I wasn't curious about them the way I was about him. I didn't have the urge to explore them, like another continent. A lot of it was physical, I knew. But *just* physical? I wanted to know about his past, his family, his work. He was so different from me, too different maybe. But I knew that even my mother wouldn't have called him one of my "little" friends.

I put on the shorts and T-shirt I'd worn the evening before and went downstairs, determined to put thoughts of the deputy behind me. There are too many unavoidable disappointments in life to go around looking for more. I had the house I loved, I had my friends here, I didn't have to worry about money much. I had a lot better life than many people I knew, men or women. This was no time to start feeling sorry for myself. Look at Ila

Wanaker, I reminded myself, with her three little kids. Look at Lois.

I kept this internal lecture going while I made myself a peanut butter sandwich and poured a glass of milk. As I got a glass out of the hutch, I remembered the paper sack that had been sitting there the night before. I still hadn't asked Cecelia about that. She'd been so excited about getting Miss Mineola back for the funeral that I had forgotten to mention it. Well, it wasn't all that important.

After I finished my sandwich, I unlocked the front door and turned the plastic sign over to the side that said "Open." Since I didn't ordinarily open the office in the afternoon, business was pretty slow. I spent most of the afternoon getting the envelopes ready for next month's billing. I took a break once and went outside to turn on the sprinkler in the front yard. I was picking the dead leaves off the geraniums along the front walk when Cecelia drove by in her little blue station wagon and honked. A minute later I saw Evelyn's white Continental sail by. They must have finished all the arrangements for the funeral.

I finished the envelopes a few minutes after four and decided to walk down to the post office before it closed. Not that there'd be anything of consequence in my box. Grocery ads, catalogues, sweepstakes entries. But I put on my sandals and went anyway. No use feeling sorry for yourself, I reiterated. This is normal life, just like it was last week at this time. And it suited you fine then. What's so different now?

By the time I got there, Ora Lee, the postmistress, was getting ready to close for the day. Her husband C.T. had a stroke last year and she's always anxious to lock up and get home to him, so I took my mail out of the box, waved to her, and left. I walked home feeling more dejected than ever. I sat down on the front steps and sorted through the mail. Sure enough, it was just what I expected—junk mail, along with three or four Water Board checks from people who live in Houston now but like to keep the water on at the old homeplace.

As I stood up to go inside and put the checks away, a plain postcard fell out of one of the grocery store ads. A message was typed on one side: *Meet me at the top of the fire tower Tuesday night after dark. I need to talk to you. It's urgent. Don't tell anyone about this. Lois*

I turned the card over. My name and address were typed also. I flipped it over and read the message again. Then I took it into the kitchen with me and read it once more after I'd gotten ice out of the refrigerator and made some lemonade.

What was this all about? What was urgent enough to bring Lois back to Point Blank where she obviously didn't want to be seen? I sat at the table and looked at the card while I drank the lemonade. Why the fire tower? Did she think my house was being watched or something? And why didn't she just call? Where was she anyway? I picked up the card to check the cancellation stamp, but it was smeared and I couldn't make it out.

Of course Lois knew the fire tower would be a place I was familiar with and one where no one was likely to see us, but I didn't much relish the idea of climbing it after dark. Was she really in some kind of trouble that warranted such secrecy or had she just gone over the edge? Either way, I'd have to go.

I looked at the clock. Almost six. It wouldn't be dark for a good while yet. I puttered around the house, putting a load of clothes in the washer, changing the sheets, trying to put my restlessness to good use. When the sun began to lower, I went to the refrigerator to find something for supper. It's amazing how repulsive food can look sometimes. An old wrinkled hot dog. A plastic butter dish full of leftover spaghetti. Some guacamole with a black crust.

Finally I took out a ripe tomato and sprinkled salt on

it. I ate it standing over the sink so the juice wouldn't drip on the floor. Then I washed my hands and took a handful of goldfish crackers from the foil-lined sack in the bread box. Last of all, I drank a glass of milk. Emily Dickinson probably never ate supper like this, I thought to myself. But at least there were no dishes to wash. I ran some water into the glass I'd used and left it in the sink.

Then I did what I'd been putting off all that time. I dialed the number for the sheriff's department. When Lurline answered, I said, "Deputy Norton, please," trying to make my voice sound crisp, businesslike, and unidentifiable. While I waited for her to ring him, I tried to decide how best to put this.

"Norton here," he said brusquely.

"This is Beth Marie." There was a pause. "Cartwright."

"Oh."

"I just wanted to know where you found my car. I picked it up this morning."

"I noticed." Another pause. "In the Houston Impoundment Lot. It was towed in. Off the university campus. It didn't have a parking sticker."

"Oh," I said. Another long pause. "Then how could she get back here?" I said this aloud, but more to myself than to him.

"What are you talking about?"

"I just got this card, and I wondered where—" I suddenly remembered the last sentence on the card, the part about not telling anyone.

"A card? What about it?" From the change in his tone, I could sense him leaning forward insistently, on the edge of his chair, and I suddenly felt caught again between him and Lois.

"Never mind. It's not important. I was just checking on the car. That's all. I'm sorry. I shouldn't have bothered you." I stammered all this and hung up. Then I took the phone off the hook. I knew he'd try to call back again to find out about the card. He'd be angry. Well, I couldn't help that. Maybe he'd even think I was playing some stupid game with him. I couldn't help that either.

I looked at the clock and went upstairs to change into sneakers and jeans, knowing I'd have to wade through waist-high weeds. I went back downstairs to find a flashlight, checking to see if the batteries were still good by shining it into the dark stairwell. Lois hadn't said to bring anything with me. Nevertheless, I put some peanut butter and crackers into a plastic bag. For all I knew she might be starving. I decided to go on then while it was still light. Daddy always said that in hot weather the snakes begin to crawl in the evening.

I looked around at everything in the kitchen one last time before I went out the back door. The old candlewick tablecloth, the hutch with the apple blossom dishes, the aloe plant in the window sill over the sink— all looked suddenly homey and precious. Maybe I was just seeing it through Lois's eyes, someone who'd given up home. Or maybe you always felt like this when you were starting out on an adventure. I shook myself and pulled the door closed behind me.

The sun glowed like a new copper penny as it began to drop into the haze of dust and humidity hanging over the mown summer fields. There's a two-rut track that leads to the fire tower, but to reach it you have to go clear up to the cemetery on the north end of town, then double back through the woods that way. I decided to take the most direct route, which meant staying on the caliche road as long as I could, then striking out in a straight line across the pastures toward the tower. On the other side of the pasture I climbed through barbed wire and entered the pine woods. It was even hotter there where the trees cut off any breeze. Insects still droned in the heat, and cardinals flittered through the underbrush, surprised at a human intruder.

There was no sign of Lois when I reached the tower,

so I decided to climb up to the top to wait for her. It would be a while before she got there, and it was bound to be cooler higher up. The ladder zigzagged back and forth between the metal grid landings. The structure had grown rusty and rickety since the Forest Service stopped maintaining it. At the top I pulled myself up through the square opening in the wooden deck that surrounded an enclosed shelter with screened windows. I looked inside; the metal folding chair was still sitting in front of the built-in ledge that had served as a desk for the forest rangers. Nothing had changed. I walked all around the deck, testing the outer railing and looking at eastern Watson County spread out below me.

I loved that sight. I always have. At such a distance everything seems to be going about its business in a kind of sweet absorption. Pickups bumped over the roads that border the broad fields as though they were as much a part of the natural landscape as the cottontail I could just make out below, coming out to nibble grass stalks in the cool of the evening. Uneven lines of cows moved languidly toward someplace they vaguely thought of as home. Over in the clump of buildings that made up Point Blank proper, a car pulled up in front of one of the houses and a girl came out—I could just make out that it was a girl—and leaned on the door. I could even recognize Terry B.'s Chrysler edging slowly toward the church. Around me, a hundred or more feet up, purple martins were plunging through the ocean of air, diving for high-flying insects.

From such a distance you couldn't see all the complications, the anxieties or fears, the dissatisfactions. Life itself looked peaceful, for man and beast. It was all a matter of focus. Being up here had the same calming effect on me it always did.

I watched the edges of the clouds turning gold as the sun set and the martins darted for their invisible prey. Then I took out the peanut butter and crackers and ate half of them. I felt more like eating now that I wasn't so restless. I stretched out on the deck, gazing upwards into the sky which was growing steadily softer. Lois probably wouldn't be here for a while yet, I remember thinking. And then I didn't think anymore. I was asleep.

Later—I couldn't have been asleep long—something woke me with a start. Some kind of noise. I hadn't intended to fall asleep, but the past few nights of sleeplessness had finally caught up with me. The noise sounded like some kind of squeaking down below.

I inched over to the edge of the platform and peered down. It was dusk now, not completely dark, but there wasn't enough light to see clearly. The noise had stopped, and I decided it must have been made by a breeze moving the tower slightly and making it creak the way old houses do when they start cooling off at night.

Then I spotted a figure moving off away from the tower and into the trees, carrying something bulky, like a suitcase or box. It wasn't Lois, I was sure. In fact, it looked more like a man, but I couldn't see well enough to be certain.

I didn't like this at all. I felt for my flashlight. Fortunately I'd thought to set it down against the wall of the shelter so that I wouldn't forget and knock it off. Who had been down there? And what was he doing here? Was this some kind of trap to catch Lois?

I was still debating with myself about whether to stay or go down when I saw headlights approaching along the rutted track from the cemetery. They were moving very slowly, but then they'd have to. That road was hardly more than a cowpath. The Forest Service had used it when they maintained the tower, but since they'd abandoned the site, hardly anyone ever drove over it. Lois would know about the road though. The dark was thick by now, so I switched my flashlight on and off in the direction of the car to signal that I was there. Then I hooked it onto my belt and started down.

I climbed down the ladder slowly, feeling my way cautiously from one rung to the next in the dark. I decided that when I got to the last landing I'd wait there until Lois drove up. The person I'd seen disappear into the trees might still be around.

With relief I stepped off onto the last landing—and pitched headfirst into the darkness below.

CHAPTER • SEVENTEEN

LATER I COULDN'T REMEMBER falling at all. I guess there are certain memories your mind blanks out as simply too terrifying to deal with. But over the next few days parts of what had happened came back to me slowly, the way you sometimes remember a dream.

I do recall coming to with my mouth and nose full of damp dirt and matted weeds. Then something struck against my side, I heard someone swear softly in the dark, and a light shone in my face.

"Beth Marie? Good God! What's happened?"

"Lois?" I could barely get the name out.

"Lois?" It wasn't Lois. It was a man's voice.

I groaned. A hand brushed some of the caked dirt from my face. The light ran up and down my body and then slowly circled the darkness around us.

"Anybody there?" Norton. His face, lit from below by the flashlight, looked fierce. I closed my eyes and started to drift off. He shone the flashlight back in my face.

"Don't go to sleep, Beth Marie. Keep your eyes open. Tell me what happened." He aimed the beam directly in my eyes and pulled the lids back gently.

"I'm all right," I said. "I just fell." Anything to get that light out of my eyes.

"Fell? From where? Not the tower?"

"The ladder. From the landing. It gave way."

He played the beam over toward the tower. "Good Lord. That's over thirty feet." He muttered something else, but I couldn't make it out.

"Don't move," he said. "Not even a little, you understand? Not even to nod your head."

"I have no intention of moving." I had a strange desire to laugh.

He took his handkerchief and wiped my face some more. When it came away, I could see there was blood on it.

"I've got to go to the car and radio for help, Beth Marie," he said. "I'm afraid to move you by myself. Do you understand?"

"Sure," I said. I felt like I was floating along in the darkness. I didn't particularly hurt, but I didn't want to move either.

"As soon as I've called the ambulance I'll be back. It won't be long."

Why was his voice shaking so? "Don't worry. I'll be fine." I tried to smile.

"I'll leave the flashlight on here beside you. Don't try to move it or anything. And Beth Marie, try to stay awake. Try real hard."

"Okay." I didn't want to talk anymore. I heard his footsteps running away in the dark.

The next thing I knew there were lights all around me. And voices and faces floating overhead. I glimpsed Norton again briefly. His was one of the voices I heard, but the others seemed to be ignoring him. They were intent on strapping something around my neck and moving me onto a long board. I recognized some of the other faces, but somehow I couldn't put names to them right then. They were all Point Blank people though, and I felt peaceful and, more than that, overwhelmed with gratitude that they were there. I kept saying, "Thank you, thank you," until they finally told me it was better if I didn't try to talk.

It did hurt some when they lifted me into the ambulance, but once inside, I saw a face I knew instantly. Evelyn. "Don't worry, sweetheart," she said. "It's going to be all right." But she looked like she was about to cry herself.

"I know," I said languidly, trying to reassure her. Then my eyes closed again.

"Don't let her go to sleep," I heard Norton say. "Beth Marie, wake up!"

I wished he'd leave me alone.

"I'm coming too," I heard him say to Evelyn.

"But we're not supposed to let—" she started to protest.

"It's all right," he broke in sharply. "The county insurance covers me. And I'm the investigating officer." I felt the rear of the ambulance dip as he climbed aboard.

The ride to the hospital in Somerville didn't seem to take long at all. Norton took my left hand—I wasn't even sure where my right one was—and held it all the way, shaking it gently every time I closed my eyes. Even so, I must have drifted off from time to time since I could only remember a few details of the ride. They'd covered me with a blanket, but by the time they were wheeling me into the emergency room, I had begun to shake with cold.

I do remember Norton waving away the woman with the clipboard who came toward the gurney as soon as we'd made it inside and him holding the double doors into the emergency room open. "Who's on call?" I heard him shout at the woman.

Evelyn was still beside me too. I didn't know who she was most worried about, me or Norton. "It's all right," I heard her tell him. "The doctor will be here in a minute. Calm down."

"Where the hell is he now? That's what I want to know," he said loudly.

"If you want to leave," Evelyn said stiffly, "I'll be glad to stay with Beth Marie. She doesn't need to be upset right now."

"Okay, okay. No. I'm staying right here." I wished they'd both shut up and leave me in peace.

The doctor must have appeared eventually, because I have an even hazier memory of being pushed and prodded, turned and re-turned, x-rayed and exposed. I was beginning to get awfully tired. The euphoria I'd felt earlier was wearing off, and for the first time I could feel the pain. They cut off my clothes with scissors in order to avoid moving me, but even that hurt.

It must have been around midnight when they finally decided I wasn't in any imminent danger and took me to a regular room, with promises of more tests tomorrow. All they'd discovered so far was that I'd broken my right arm.

Evelyn finally went home, albeit reluctantly as though she wasn't sure it was safe to leave while Norton was still with me. After she left, he sat beside the bed, watching quietly now, his chin propped in his hands.

"In about half an hour you can go to sleep," he said encouragingly. "They just want to make sure your concussion's not dangerous."

I didn't make any reply. My mouth was beginning to hurt too. It seemed I'd bitten my tongue badly when I hit the ground.

He sat there in silence a while longer, his eyes never leaving my face. I started to make little involuntary groaning noises from time to time.

"They'll be able to give you something for the pain soon."

I didn't say anything to that either. I'd just discovered I couldn't move my head very well. Suddenly I felt tears brimming my eyes.

"Don't cry, Beth Marie," he said, smoothing my hair back. "Please don't cry. If you do you're going to have to blow your nose, and that's going to hurt a lot. Just try to hold back, okay? You can cry later when you're better."

At that I started to laugh, but as soon as my stomach muscles contracted, I knew I didn't want to do that either. "This is terrible. I can't laugh or cry."

"You're telling me. I was—I was really afraid." He stopped and took a deep breath. "I know you don't feel much like talking now, and I don't want you to, heaven knows. But there are some things I need to know tonight."

"Lois," I said.

"Lois was out there?"

"No. But I thought she was coming." For the first time it occurred to me to wonder why Lois hadn't showed up.

"No need to go into that right now," he said. "Just tell me what you remember about falling off the tower. Did you miss your footing in the dark?"

I forced my mind back to a few hours earlier. I had been coming down the ladder slowly and carefully, feeling for each rung and testing it before I lowered myself onto it. Then I'd stepped off onto the metal grid landing.

Suddenly my whole body jerked violently. It was the same reaction I would have for days afterward every time I tried to go to sleep. The sensation of falling would rush over me, and my muscles would contract as though to ward off the blow they knew was coming. I cried out, and Norton stood up and took my hand.

"No," I said weakly. "I didn't miss my footing. It gave way. The landing. Right beneath my feet. It just gave way and I fell." A series of dry, jerky moans shook me. My postponed emotions were catching up with me, and the moans were the closest thing to crying my body could tolerate.

Norton gripped my hand until it hurt too; then realizing what he was doing, he loosened his grasp and bent down and kissed it. "I'm so sorry," he said. "I acted like a jerk when you called. It was that, wasn't it? The card you called about?"

"Yes." I hung onto his hand.

He squeezed his eyes shut. "Why did I act so stupid? And why did—"

I think he was going to ask why I went out to the fire tower by myself, but he stopped himself. He took another deep breath, opened his eyes, and went on calmly.

"I got worried after you called. I figured there had to be something funny about that card for you to call. So I went out to your place. When I didn't get an answer at the front door, I went around to the back. Sure enough, it was open." He stopped, letting the reproach sink in silently this time.

"I found the card on the kitchen table. I knew you must have already gone. It made me uneasy, your being out there alone. So I found the cemetery and the road you'd told me about and followed you. I figured you might be angry, but I had to take that chance."

"Thank you," I said, with just about the last ounce of energy I had in my body. "I'm glad you did."

He smiled crookedly and kissed my hand again. "I was so afraid when I found you lying there."

I pulled his large, freckled hand toward me and held it in the crook of my chin. "Don't leave me, Norton. I'm still afraid."

The smile left his face, and he frowned slightly. "I've got to," he said. "I've got to go baßck out there right away."

"Why?"

"I've got to find out why that landing gave way. It's important."

My mind clouded over when he said that. I didn't want to ask any more questions then; I didn't want to know why. "All right," I said, and my voice sounded pitiful, even to me. "But hurry back."

After he left, I lay there with the pain gradually getting worse and my mind slowly beginning to admit the notion that I'd almost been killed. I finally pushed the call button for the nurse.

"You ready for a shot now, honey?" she asked sympathetically.

"Yes," I said, "but you've got to promise me something first."

"What's that?" she asked, as though she were humoring me.

"Don't let anyone in here, in my room. Not anyone except the deputy. No matter who it is."

She raised her eyebrows. "We don't get many visitors at two o'clock in the morning," she said wryly.

"I don't care," I said. "That's the only way I can sleep. If you promise. And tell the others out there too."

"You don't have to worry," she said. "The deputy already left the same order."

She came back with the injection in a few minutes, though the minutes had begun to seem like hours.

"You must be pretty popular out there at Point Blank," she said as she stuck the needle in. "Three people have already called and wanted to know how you are."

"Men or women?"

"One man, two women, best as I could make out."

"Be sure and tell the deputy when he comes back," I said.

And that really was the last thing I remember from that night.

CHAPTER • EIGHTEEN

WHEN I OPENED MY EYES again, a silvery grey light was coming through the window behind me. I couldn't turn over to see for myself, but it looked as if it might be raining outside. It took a moment for me to realize I wasn't in bed at home. I groaned. A figure standing at the window stirred and came around the foot of the bed.

"Good morning," Norton said.

"What happened?" My mouth was so dry I could scarcely speak, and my tongue was swollen. "Water."

He held a glass with a straw to my mouth and I took a couple of sips.

"You fell off the tower. Remember?"

I groaned again.

"You're going to be all right. You've got a broken arm and lots of contusions, but so far it doesn't appear you've got any internal injuries. They'll be doing some more tests on you this morning though. They want to keep you a while for observation and some physical therapy. You've got some torn ligaments too."

"Can I get up?"

"No. Not until they do some more x-rays and the doctor sees you again."

"Then call the nurse and go away. But not far and not long."

"Don't worry."

He left and an aide came and helped me wash my face, brush my teeth, and comb my hair. I was afraid to even look in a mirror. When they brought my breakfast tray, Norton came back.

"I'll help her now," he told the aide, waving her out of the room.

"Have you gotten any sleep?" I asked him.

"Don't worry about that. I'm in a lot better shape than you. Here. Try some cream of wheat."

We didn't talk any more until I'd eaten half the bowl of cereal and drunk some milk and he'd finished what was on the tray. Then he washed my face again and settled back in the chair with a fresh cup of coffee the aide brought him.

"Now then," I said, "before they give me something else that makes me groggy, or wheel me off to some new torture session, what did you find when you went back last night?" In the light of day I felt like I could face whatever facts I had to.

"It's what I didn't find that nearly killed you. The bolts were missing from three corners of the landing, and the other corner had been loosened. The landing gave way when you stepped on it."

"It didn't feel loose when I went up."

"Are you sure?"

"Certain. The whole thing's rusty and dilapidated. But if it had felt loose, I wouldn't have gone up."

"So someone must have taken the bolts out while you were up there. Did you see anyone? Hear anything?"

"I fell asleep for a while. Then I woke up when I heard some kind of noise down below. I couldn't make out what it was. But I did see someone moving across the clearing, away from the tower."

"Could you tell who it was?"

"No. It was already getting dark, and I could barely make him out. But I think it was a man—with dark hair."

"He must not have known you were already up there."

"The postcard said 'after dark.' But I went early. I wanted some time to think. And I didn't want to have to climb up in the dark."

"No. Well, it wouldn't have mattered whether you fell going up or coming down. The point was for you to fall. Still—" He stopped and ran his hand over his face. "Do you have any idea who it could have been down there?"

"No. I really couldn't see much—except the shape and the way he moved made me think it was a man."

He glanced at me sharply. "You're not just saying that to—"

"To protect Lois? No. Lois is small. You know that. This person looked a lot bigger. I know—the card was from her. But I don't think it was Lois I saw. She could have showed up while we were all still out there and been scared away. Or come even later and thought I'd deserted her."

"I'm not sure the card was from Lois," Norton said. He leaned back in the chair and closed his eyes. "I noticed it was hand-canceled. So that means it probably wasn't mailed from Houston. And the cancellation was smeared. Maybe deliberately."

"Besides," I said, relief showing in my voice, "Lois and I have been friends for years. She would never do anything like that. It's crazy."

"Just let me remind you," he said, his eyes still closed, "that your friend Lois has been known to act irrationally recently. We can't rule her out altogether. She does have dark hair. And from the top of a tower like that it's hard to judge the height of figures below."

"Archie has dark hair," I said.

"So we're back to Archie, are we?" He opened his eyes and grinned at me crookedly. "Just what motive would he have for trying to do away with you?"

"What possible reason could anyone have, for that matter?" I demanded.

"If we knew that, we'd know all, wouldn't we?" He sighed and leaned forward, studying the dusty toes of his boots. "It's got to be something you know, or what someone thinks you know. In the case of Lois, you know about her and Finney. But then so do I, and she knows that. With Archie, you saw him shoot Blalock. But then there's never been any question about that. Still, he was released yesterday. Bud Wylie came and picked him up. He said he'd keep Archie there at his house for the time being to see he stayed out of harm's way. Can you think of any reason Archie might want to harm you?"

"Not really," I had to admit. "He doesn't even know you've told me about the jewelry."

"True. You say he has a reputation for letting his temper get the best of him. But I can't see what he had to be angry with you about." He got up and went to the window. "I tried looking for footprints in the dark last night but I couldn't see any. Now this rain will have washed everything away." He sighed wearily. "I've got to say that at this point Lois still looks like the best candidate."

I tried to shake my head at that, but the motion was too painful. I lay there trying to think through the maze of people and places—who knew what about whom and when. "The irony of it is," I finally said, "that while Lois was so worried about her mother finding out about her and Finney, Cecelia knew all along."

"Really?" He turned away from the window at that.

"I guess I forgot to tell you. After I'd screwed up my courage to tell Cecelia about Lois and Finney, it turned out she'd known something was going on between them all along. A letter Lois had sent to him in prison got returned to Cecelia. She opened it by mistake."

"And she never let on? Not even when Blalock was killed?"

"No. So much happened there, all in one afternoon and evening. She had her hands full."

He pursed his lips, then let out a big sigh. "I know you're not going to like this, Beth Marie, seeing as how you admire this woman so much and all, but I think we've also got to consider Mrs. Ramsey."

"Cecelia?" I was dumbfounded. "What possible motive could she have for doing away with me?"

"One of the best in the world," he said. "Protecting her child."

I didn't—couldn't—respond to that, the idea was so overwhelming.

Norton went on quickly. "As you say, she thought you were the only one, other than herself, who knew about Lois's escapade."

"But Cecelia knew I'd never say anything about it. Not to anyone. She trusts me."

He shrugged. "Maybe. But when a child's future is involved, a mother will do anything, go to any lengths."

"Is this more of your female psychologizing?"

"We've got to consider all the angles," he said quietly.

I didn't reply at once. I was remembering again how Cecelia had asked me to tell Archie to meet her at the barn. And when I asked her why at the funeral home, she had refused to answer. Had she wanted to find out something from him about Lois and Finney? We had already heard about Finney's escape at that point. Did she suspect Lois might have helped with the escape, along with Archie? Mightn't she have wanted to find out what Archie knew? After Finney was shot, she didn't seem too concerned about talking to Archie anymore. Had she figured out he must not have known about Lois and Finney? Possibly.

But that was nonsense. Cecelia couldn't have taken the bolts out of the landing on the fire tower. Not only would it have been difficult for her physically, but she just couldn't do that kind of thing. Not and still be Cecelia. I couldn't believe it.

"Lois was her daughter, her only child." Norton spoke softly again, like the voice of the tempter.

"No. No, it's impossible. Besides, it was a man I saw. I'm almost certain."

He sat down again and started studying his boots in a way I didn't like.

"Max!"

He looked up. "What?"

"It's got to be Max," I said. "He's the most likely." I knew this would get his attention. "Physically, I mean."

"And just what do you suggest as a motive?"

I cast about in my mind wildly. "That mask," I said suddenly, surprising even myself. "It has something to do with that mask. The one that was stolen out my kitchen, remember?"

"I thought you'd decided Mrs. Ramsey came by and picked it up while you were in the shower. Didn't you ask her?"

"I never got a chance," I said, brushing over that omission quickly. "But maybe it was Max. After all, he knew I had it that afternoon he drove me out to Miss Mineola's place."

"But, Beth Marie, aren't you forgetting something? Remember the autopsy report? Mrs. Magillberry died a perfectly natural death. If she'd been gassed in some way, poisoned, that would have showed up."

"Maybe," I said stubbornly. "But Max is a diver. He knows about things like that—pressurized gasses. Maybe he knew some way to do it that wouldn't show up in the autopsy."

"Again, what would be his motive?" Norton came around to the side of the bed and kissed me lightly on the top of my head. "You're getting too excited. You'll be hallucinating next. I think I better go away for a while and let you get some rest."

I started to protest, but at that moment a new nurse,

one from the morning shift, came in to take me down to be x-rayed again. "Some rest," I grumbled.

"Will you be going down with her?" Norton asked the nurse.

"No. They send up their own aides from x-ray," she answered shortly. "We're understaffed as it is up here." She snapped the top sheet back under the mattress edge.

"You have been told that Miss Cartwright is not to have any visitors?" Norton's voice took on a steely professional tone.

"Yes, I have," she said. She looked at him, one side of her mouth tucked up in a smirk.

"And there are to be no exceptions made."

"We'll do our best," she said stiffly.

He frowned, but didn't press her.

"I'll be back in an hour," he said, turning to me. "I've got to run over to the office and check up on some things there."

"Then you'll probably be back before she is," the nurse said.

He glared at her and was gone before I could tell him good-bye.

CHAPTER • NINETEEN

S O THAT'S HOW I CAME TO MISS Miss Mineola's funeral. And Ila Wanaker got to write it up for the *Somerville Courier.* I couldn't do that with my right arm in a cast.

I did manage to get my name in the paper, though, and this time as a participant in the action, not just an observer. And on the front page too. My mother would have been mortified at the publicity. And to tell the truth, I didn't exactly enjoy it. People treat you differently after you've been involved in something like a murder, as if they aren't quite sure just what you might do next, even if you were only an innocent bystander who happened to get caught in the cross fire. I sometimes felt like I wasn't so sure myself just what I might do anymore.

As the x-ray attendant wheeled me down to the elevators that morning, I knew that all of Point Blank was gathering at Holcombe's Funeral Home, filing past Miss Mineola's casket with somber faces while scrutinizing the exposed parts of her body for signs of the autopsy.

I didn't begrudge them their curiosity. Far from it. Mineola Magillberry belonged to them. Maybe it had often seemed the other way around, especially for Loomis, her eighty-year-old handyman, or the tenants on her little forty-acre farms scattered around the county, or even for Cecelia. But now that the cat's eyes were closed, the mice could afford to come creeping up to inspect the woman who had ruled their lives for decades.

The reports I heard afterward said, as they always do, that she looked "real natural." She had left instructions with Bartholomew that she wanted to be buried in a red wool dress she'd bought especially for the occasion, figuring, I suppose, it might be cold six feet underground, even in Texas. She had little diamond studs in her ears and a square-cut emerald on her left hand. Watching the lid close on that jewelry must have cost some of her heirs a pang or two.

Miss Mineola never had liked the way Jackie Simpson played the little electric organ at the Point Blank Baptist Church, so they had taped music—"The Old Rugged Cross," "When They Ring Those Golden Bells," and of course "Amazing Grace." Then Terry B. read a few selected scriptures of the reassuring sort— nothing like what he'd read for his own son's funeral— but there was no sermon. She had been very specific about no sermon. Bartholomew read the eulogy, after which he announced that Miss Mineola had left "an appropriate sum" for a complete remodeling of the interior of the Point Blank Baptist Church, including new paneling, light fixtures, and carpet. There were oohs and aahs at that—the effect I'm sure she had aimed for.

After the service, the automobiles all wound their way through the wet Somerville streets out to the highway and back to Point Blank cemetery where there was a brief graveside service in the rain. Then the muddy mourners descended on the big white house out in the country where the briskets, cooked by Evelyn, waited for them, along with several tables loaded with food brought in by the ladies of the community.

I could have written the whole story without even being there. But no one except Norton and me knew that we hadn't yet reached the end of the story. Which was small consolation to me as the gurney I was on bumped out of the elevator and into the first-floor hall, where I was parked across from swinging doors marked X-RAY. An x-ray technician came out, handed a form to my attendant, who then went off to requisition another patient.

The technician patted my foot. "Won't be long now, honey. With all this rain, the door to the supply closet's swelled and I can't get it open. I sent for a maintenance man though. Just as soon as he gets it open, we'll be right with you." Then she disappeared through the swinging doors again.

I didn't care if it took all morning. Everything hurt now, all over my body, and it was going to hurt even more when they moved me. I closed my eyes and the sensation of falling rushed toward me again. I opened them and tried to concentrate on something else. Like who had taken the bolts out of that landing.

Norton was right. It had to be someone who thought I knew something I obviously didn't know—or at least wasn't aware that I knew. What would Max think I knew? Who the developer was that had called his sister? Or that he had tried to borrow money from her? According to Muriel, he had gotten the money he needed to pay off his gambling debts quite suddenly, and from someone else. But that was long before his grandmother died.

What about the ledger I had found behind the bed? It had mentioned something about Southwest Securities. Was that the development company? Had Miss Mineola really intended to sell the land after that domino game she'd lost to Bud? Maybe she'd decided she'd had it with all of them—relatives, friends, everyone. Maybe she intended to leave them one final surprise.

But what about the entry that Lois read? The one about talking to Archie and calling in a note? The figure

I had seen at the fire lookout had looked more like Archie than anyone else I knew. But why would he want to kill me? I had seen Archie shoot Finney, but then he'd never denied that. And he'd already confessed to helping Finney escape. Try as I might, I couldn't come up with any motive for Archie.

And Cecelia? I squirmed at that one. Other than Ora Lee, she was the only one in town who knew the combination to my post office box. When Mother had been dying, Cecelia used to pick up the mail for me and bring it by the house. She could easily have put that card in my box. Ora Lee let people come and go behind the counter all the time, mostly to rummage through free catalogues that no one claimed. It would be easy to pick up a cancellation stamp and smear a postmark across a card.

But that was ridiculous. Cecelia was the kindest person in the world, the one who always made excuses for other people's shortcomings. And she was painfully honest. She had been honest with me about Lois, in fact. She had sacrificed her whole life for others. Her husband. Her aging mother. Even the hardfisted old woman they were burying today who had been the nemesis of the entire family.

But there was nothing Cecelia could do for Lois this time, said a nagging little voice inside me. No sacrifice she could make to save her daughter's reputation. So maybe she had to sacrifice someone else instead. And Cecelia had refused to tell me what she wanted to talk to Archie about that night.

She must have wanted to find out if Archie knew about Lois's involvement with Finney. Later, when it was obvious he hadn't told either the sheriff or the TDC officials about the pair, Cecelia would have figured Archie knew nothing and that it was better for her just to keep quiet.

All the more reason, the voice whispered. Archie

didn't know. And you hadn't told Cecelia that Norton had found out about Lois's entanglement with the convict. Cecelia would think you were the only person besides herself who knew about her daughter's escapade. And even Cecelia could figure out that the promising professional career of her only child could be wrecked by a criminal record.

And where was Lois anyway? Had she sent that card? You thought you knew her. But then you would never have predicted her infatuation with Finney either.

I tried to shut out the voice. I don't understand all that frustrated passion, I told myself.

You don't? the voice persisted. Then why do you like Emily Dickinson so much? What about her slavish devotion to the Philadelphia preacher? She wrote about that in pretty violent terms. *My Life had stood—a Loaded Gun—.* She even said in one poem that she'd prefer Hell to Heaven without him. Once you've gone that far, you might do anything. Was that what Lois had felt?

And what about you, the voice went on. What might you do out of frustrated passion? When does it get to be dangerous?

This internal argument was suddenly interrupted by the sound of heavy boots coming from the direction of the Emergency Room. I tilted my head just enough to see a man in khakis with a leather toolbelt around his waist. He disappeared into the x-ray lab without a glance in my direction. The maintenance man. They should be out for me soon now, I thought. Getting a door unstuck shouldn't take long. We'd had such a long dry spell in August. The sudden rain would make my old doors at home swell too.

Doors. What was it about a door that kept nagging at me? Someone had said—when? Last Saturday? Or was it later? Something about a door sticking—the east porch door. *Be careful to close that door good.* Who had said that? And why did it seem important now?

It was just coming back to me when the double doors at the end of the corridor swung open and someone in surgical get-up—shower cap, mask, and gloves—came padding down the hall in little green footcovers. I closed my eyes. Dear God, please not surgery. I hadn't even thought of that possibility. I remembered the time I'd had my tonsils out when I was ten—.

Suddenly the gurney jerked and started rolling. I opened my eyes and saw I was moving away from the x-ray door, backwards. What were they doing to me now? Where were they taking me? Had I been mistaken for another patient? Stories came back to me of people being wheeled into surgery by mistake and waking up later minus an arm or leg or appendix. I struggled to turn over so I could tell this person it wasn't me they wanted.

But the gurney made a sudden sharp turn around a corner into an alcove by a large laundry hamper. Perhaps they were only clearing the halls so they could wheel someone out of the operating room. I wished they would at least tell patients what was going on instead of treating them like insensible slabs of meat.

Then I felt the sheet flicked back from my shoulder, and a gloved hand grasped my upper arm firmly above the cast.

"Just a minute," I said, batting weakly at the hand. "There's been a mistake. I'm only here for x-rays."

The glove gripped my arm tighter.

Despite the pain, I wrenched my head off the pillow, struggling to sit up.

"What are you doing?" I cried out, but my voice was shaky and breathless, from both pain and fear. For I saw not just the long spike of the needle, but, between the cap and the mask, the eyes I had trusted.

CHAPTER • TWENTY

JUST THEN ANOTHER DOOR BURST open and I heard the sound of shouts and running feet. A flurry of figures filled the alcove. Someone lunged across the gurney, falling on my broken arm. My own moan was drowned by a cry like a wounded animal's.

"No!" someone shouted. It was Norton. "Don't let—"

Everything froze, as though time had stopped on a single frame. The clustered faces looked beyond me, eyes widening. Then there was a collective intake of breath. An attendant shook his head with a shallow grunt and a nurse shut her eyes.

"Get away from me. It's too late now," the voice behind me said. My gurney was still barricading the corner of the alcove, keeping the others at bay.

"You don't want to hurt Beth Marie though," Norton said softly. Only his lips moved.

"I never intended for her to get hurt. But she found the mask."

"That's how you did it."

"I had to." The voice was getting weaker. "It wasn't for myself. And I did her a favor. She didn't linger. She went easier—"

"What was in that hypodermic?" His voice was still

quiet. He was speaking to the nurse beside him now, who only shook her head. He reached out and took hold of the gurney and pulled it slowly toward him.

The only sound behind me was the body slumping against the wall and sliding to the floor.

"All right!" Norton suddenly barked to the people around him. With one hand he spun my gurney out into the corridor and with the other he motioned forward the medical team that had assembled.

"Open the doors," another voice shouted. The shape in surgical green was dragged from the alcove, down the corridor, and through the double doors of the operating room.

Norton watched the doors swing to and then exhaled deeply. All the color had drained from his face, and he suddenly looked very tired.

I was beginning to shake all over. "What happened?"

He came over to the gurney and pulled the sheet up over me. "How's your arm?"

"It hurts. Someone fell on it. What's going on?" I couldn't stop shaking.

"I'll get a blanket," he said. "It may be a while before they get to you." He disappeared into a room down the hall.

Sheriff Dooley burst through the doors marked "Exit" at the far end of the corridor. "Where's Norton?" he demanded. "What's going on here?" He didn't even pause but disappeared through the swinging doors of surgery himself.

Norton came back with a blanket. "You're probably in shock. They'll need to give you something. I hope your arm's okay."

I had started to cry, and he took out a big white handkerchief and put it in my good hand. "Tell me something," I insisted. "Tell me what all that was."

He smoothed the damp hair back from my face. "Not now," he said. "Later."

At that moment the sheriff came crashing through the doors again. He stopped in his tracks when he saw Norton.

"The woman's dead," he said accusingly. "Couldn't you knock that needle out of her hand before she stuck it in her own arm? Insulin. A megadose, from what they say."

"She was trying to kill Miss Cartwright," Norton said. He looked dazed.

"A woman, Norton!" The sheriff spat the word out.

I started to cry again, sobbing this time. I couldn't stop.

The sheriff made a gesture with his arm as though he were pushing something flimsy away. "I gotta go get the coroner," he said and disappeared down the corridor.

Insulin. The word echoed in my head. If it had been injected into me, by the time they came to get me for x-ray they would have found me dead in the hallway.

"She needs some immediate attention," I heard Norton telling someone in white. "Shock. You need to do something."

I saw him glance over my shoulder, then relax a little. He bent over me closely, stroking my hair and whispering, "It's going to be all right now, Beth Marie. Everything's going to be all right." I didn't even see the needle coming this time.

• • •

I didn't see him again until the next afternoon, though a vase of pink rosebuds and a box of chocolate-covered cherries had arrived from him. The doctor thought they might have to take the cast off my arm and reset the bone, but in the end it wasn't necessary. It turned out that almost every ligament in my body had either been sprained or torn in the fall from the tower though, and they kept me in the hospital for a week, scheduling me for physical therapy several times a day.

Lying there, I had a lot of time to sort out what had happened.

When I saw Norton again I was anxious to tell him about the mask. One of the therapists had explained it all to me that morning. He had red curly hair and dropped by after his shift was over to see how I was doing. He even brought up an oxygen tank and equipment to demonstrate to me how it had worked.

Switching from the ordinary cannula, a tube with the little plastic prongs that fit in the nostrils, to another tube hooked up to a non-rebreather mask—the soft green plastic one I'd found wrapped in the towel—took only a few seconds. Of course Miss Mineola would have had to be convinced that this was an improved way of taking her oxygen so that she would cooperate and put the mask on. But if you already trust a person, it doesn't take much convincing.

After settling the mask gently over her nose and mouth, asking if she was comfortable, and pinching the soft metal noseclip closely to the bridge of her nose to make a good seal, then it would only take a readjustment of the dial on the oxygen tank to turn the gas flow up to eight, nine, or even ten liters a minute. At that point, Miss Mineola would have been breathing close to 100% pure oxygen. Small, thin rubber flaps would flutter away from the perforations in the mask by the nostrils each time she breathed out, allowing the exhaled air to escape. But they would be sucked in tight against the sides of the mask again each time she inhaled, making sure she breathed nothing but the gas from the tank, unmixed with the outside air.

"But can you die of too much oxygen?" I asked the redheaded therapist. I could sit with the head of my bed elevated now, and I had even managed to comb my hair. "I read that people in Japan actually carry around canisters of pure oxygen like hairspray and take a shot of it every now and then to clear their heads."

"Those are healthy people though," he said. "This old lady was in her nineties, wasn't she, and had emphysema besides?"

"Yes. We didn't see how she'd managed to hang on as long as she had."

"People with lung problems as severe as hers adapt to doing without much oxygen. Not just her lungs, but all her vital organs had learned to get along on very little. Then if they get a sudden jolt of the real stuff, especially if it's a high concentration, those organs go into respiratory depression. The liver and heart and kidneys send a message to the central nervous system that they've got more oxygen than they know what to do with. So the central nervous system gets confused as to what's going on and sends a message to the lungs and breathing muscles to relax and shut down for a while. An old lady like that—she just probably went to sleep and never woke up again."

"Especially with someone sitting there holding her hand and reassuring her that she was going to be better now."

"Yeah. Well." He shrugged, and I could tell he felt a lot more comfortable talking about the mechanics of the murder than the psychology of it.

"What about the insulin?" I asked. "Wouldn't my death have looked suspicious?"

"Not really. Your pancreas could have been damaged in the fall. The x-rays we took the night before wouldn't have shown that. A high level of insulin could very well have been the result of a ruptured pancreas."

I felt pretty smug about being able to explain to Norton that evening how the non-rebreather mask had been used as a murder weapon. He didn't seem all that interested though after he found out where I'd gotten my information.

"We've already got a technical deposition from a respiratory therapist in Houston," he said. "I don't imagine

I'll run into another case in my lifetime where a rebreather mask is used to kill someone."

"Non-rebreather mask," I corrected him.

"Whatever." He picked up a chocolate-covered cherry from the box he'd sent me and then looked at me sheepishly. "May I?"

I nodded and he popped it into his mouth.

"So how did the reading of the will go?" I asked. "What did Bartholomew look like? He's just a mythical figure in Point Blank. No one's ever actually met him, except Cecelia."

"Let's just say he's the first man I'd ever seen with a manicure," Norton said with his mouth full. "Muriel seemed glad to get half of the stocks and bonds, but Max was hopping mad about not getting the land too."

"And Archie?"

"He got the land—to be held in trust by Bud Wylie till Bud dies. And the jewelry. Sort of ironic, isn't it, Archie's own inheritance being used to blackmail him that way. He had no idea why he was being sent out there to the fire tower to take those bolts out. So there's not much point in charging him with that either. It'll save the county some money. No malicious intent."

"I still can't believe Bud Wylie could be so foolish though. Paying Max fifty thousand dollars for an option on his share of the land. Bud knew how often Miss Mineola changed her will. That was taking a terrible risk."

"Yes, but the terms of the sale, if Max had inherited, were awfully sweet. Bud would have come out way ahead."

"That's ironic too, isn't it?" I said. "He's lost the fifty thousand, but still ended up as trustee for the land."

"That's not all he's lost. Max had to have the money so quick—his gambling creditors were making it hot for him—that Bud had to take out a short-term loan using his own ranch for collateral. He obviously hadn't expected

Mrs. Magillberry to last much longer either. He won't be able to make the note now, so it looks like he'll lose his own ranch."

"Oh," I said. "I thought you might have been referring to another kind of loss."

He picked another chocolate-covered cherry from the box. "Aren't you going to eat any of these?"

"I only eat two a day. One in the morning and one in the evening. 'To make a prairie it takes a clover and one bee,'" I quoted Emily to him. "How did Bud take it?"

"Well, considering everything, I'd say he took it like a man."

"Like a man?" I repeated. "And how would that be?"

"You know. Hard. But he didn't break down or anything. Still, it's got to shake you up some, finding out your wife has killed your oldest friend for your sake. He said he hadn't known anything about what Evelyn had done and he was sorry for all the trouble it had caused."

"All the trouble? That's a rather mild way of putting it."

"Bud's a mild kind of guy. He doesn't trot out his emotions for everyone to see."

"Still, I think he could have managed something a little stronger under the circumstances."

He shrugged. "Everyone's not as articulate as you, Beth Marie. Just like not everyone would eat only two pieces of candy a day with a whole box sitting there."

"Evelyn must have put the card in my mailbox after she got back from the funeral home yesterday afternoon. I remember seeing her go by, right after Cecelia."

"I checked with the postmistress, and she said Mrs. Wylie came in that afternoon and asked to check a zip code in the book she keeps behind the counter. It would have been easy for Evelyn to pick up a cancellation stamp, smear it across the card, and stick it in your box while the other woman's back was turned."

"She must have known that might give her away."

"Only if her plan didn't come off. Otherwise, no one would ever be the wiser. And in case you didn't die in the fall from the tower, she made sure she was at home that evening, waiting for the emergency call for the ambulance crew to come in. I think she planned to finish you off in the ambulance. If I hadn't insisted on riding in with you, you never would have made it to the hospital alive." He propped his boots up on the footboard of the bed. "I think I deserve some credit for that."

The sight of Evelyn bending over me in the ambulance, on the verge of tears, had filled me with euphoric gratitude at the time. Now the memory made me shiver. Had she felt remorse about what she planned to do? She probably already had the insulin injection with her in the ambulance.

"If you just hadn't found that whatchamacallit mask and insisted on taking it back, none of this would have happened to you," he went on. "See what trying to be helpful gets you?"

"Even so, if she hadn't gotten scared and stolen it out of my kitchen, how would anyone have been the wiser?"

"Your unlocked kitchen."

"Are you watering the plants, Norton? In this hot weather they need a lot of water."

"No, no. Think about it," he said, taking his feet down off the bed and ignoring my last question. "If you'd shown the mask to Mrs. Ramsey, she wouldn't have recognized it. And if you'd taken it back to the medical supply place, they wouldn't either. I've checked with them, and they don't even carry those things. That might have roused people's suspicions. She got it from the ambulance. There's one missing from their inventory. They need them for trauma victims who sometimes need large concentrations of oxygen right away. But they're never used for daily therapy."

"And I spoiled it all. Right when she'd pulled off the

perfect murder, including the fact that she didn't have to feel too guilty about it, since Miss Mineola could have died any day. If only Bud hadn't told her about the option he'd bought from Max."

"Bud thinks she got the notion somewhere that Mrs. Magillberry was getting ready to sell her land. Which would have made Bud's option useless."

"The domino game," I interjected. "Bud beat Miss Mineola one night and made her mad. They had been talking about a lease; he wanted the Packard lease from her. But after she lost the domino game, she told him he'd never get it. She even threatened to sell all her land to a developer. I guess Evelyn must have taken her at her word."

"That's the part I don't understand," Norton confessed. "I mean a domino game? Surely Evelyn wouldn't have taken that kind of threat seriously."

"But the ledger, remember? There was a note about calling Southwest Securities."

"That's a big Houston company."

"Evelyn must have seen that note in the ledger and figured Miss Mineola was serious about selling her land. So she made a phone call to Muriel, pretending to be from Southwest Securities. She was trying to alert Muriel to what was going on. But it didn't work. Both Muriel and Max wanted Miss Mineola to sell the land. They'd rather have cold cash any day." I sighed and said, half to myself, "Poor Evelyn. So many things she didn't understand. Miss Mineola could never have brought herself to sell one square foot of Watson County."

"Now it's poor Evelyn, is it?" he asked, standing up and stretching.

"Well, Bud didn't tell her much about his business affairs. He and Miss Mineola went on about land deals all the time, but Evelyn was shut out of that. That must have been galling to her. Even so, she felt it was up to her to do something to avert what she thought would be a disaster for her husband. So actually, you see, if Bud had only told her—"

Just then there was a timid tap at the half-open door and Cecelia stuck her head in. "Are you two fussing again?" she said. I could tell from the pink flush of her face that she had good news.

"I made some pecan pralines and thought you might like some, Beth Marie." She was looking at Norton, though. "I don't know if they're any good or not. It's been so humid with all the rain, and my mother always said you ought never to make candy when the weather was wet."

"Cecelia makes the best pralines in Watson County—probably in the state," I said to Norton.

He moved the chair over by my bed for Cecelia. "Have a seat, Mrs. Ramsey."

"No, no. Thank you very much, but I can't stay." She fluttered her hands at Norton and the chair, turning even pinker, then sat down. "I just came by to let you know I heard from Lois. Actually, her faculty advisor—I think that's what he called himself—at the university. He's gotten her into a private clinic in Houston. He says she needs a good, long rest. I think she'd just been studying too hard. She wasn't in her right mind, you know?"

"Of course," I said.

Norton had wandered off a discrete distance and stood looking out the window. I saw his head shake slightly, and I knew what he was thinking. I was thinking the same thing.

Cecelia was hoping Lois's involvement with Finney's escape would never come out. But if it did, the hospital stay would certainly substantiate a plea of mental instability. Hospitals, however, don't come cheap. Cecelia would never mention it, but I was sure that the small trust she'd been left by Miss Mineola would go to pay for Lois's private clinic.

"Cecelia," I said slowly, "remember when you sent

me to tell Archie you wanted to talk to him in the barn—that night."

Her eyes went out of focus and she tilted her head to one side.

"What did you want to talk to him about? You never told me."

She frowned and glanced at Norton.

He turned from the window. "It's all right, Mrs. Ramsey. We know about the jewelry."

She put her plump hand on her bosom and let out a big sigh. "Why didn't you tell me? Oh, that takes a load off my mind. I've been so worried about that boy and what might become of him. You see, when I came home from the grocery store—remember I said I heard a thump?—well, I went in to check on Aunt Min and found her dead all right. But I also found her jewelry boxes all open and empty. As far as I knew, Archie was the only one around—and the only one who might have done such a thing. But like it says in the Bible, you're supposed to go to your brother first before you make any accusations to outsiders. That's what I intended to talk to him about. Then after they found the jewelry on Finney, I figured I didn't need to say anymore about it."

A shadow passed over her face, momentarily clouding her earlier exuberance. "I still don't know what's going to happen with that boy now that Aunt Min's gone," she said. Then, with another big sigh, she brushed her pink polyester knees as though dismissing the unpleasant thoughts intruding on her good news. "Well, I better leave you two alone. I've got to get to the bank before it closes."

Norton helped her out of the chair. She kept her grip on his arm after she got to her feet.

"I imagine," she said, looking up at him from under her cloud of pearly hair, "you all have a lot to talk about from the way you were carrying on when I came in."

With that she made her unsteady way from the room, waggling her fingers in a good-bye.

I reached for the box of pralines and looked at Norton.

"A very strange lady," he said, shaking his head.

"Only because she's so consistent," I said. "She goes by the book."

"No telling what Archie might have done if she'd confronted him alone there in the barn. He was already nervous about Finney."

I shrugged. "She didn't know that, but it would have made no difference to Cecelia." I paused a minute, thinking. "So Evelyn actually saw Archie rifling the jewelry boxes?"

"She must have. According to him, that's what she used against him. And it wasn't just theft she was threatening to expose. She said she'd swear she saw him smother the old lady. That's how she got him to go take the bolts out of the landing on the fire tower. Of course, he says he had no idea why."

"But didn't he wonder what Evelyn was doing at his aunt's house herself?"

"She told him she'd just stopped by for a visit and had stepped out to the east porch to find something for Mrs. Magillberry. Actually, she must have heard Archie coming while she was in the middle of removing that whatchamacallit mask and hid there."

"She would have seen Cecelia leave for town, knew that Archie was ordinarily asleep then, and thought the coast was clear. She had no idea that Lois and Finney were upstairs in Miss Mineola's attic. Lois thought that was the perfect hiding place for Finney. Miss Mineola was deaf, and no one else would ever think to look for him there." I watched as he took another praline from the box. "You're not going to believe this, but I had it all figured out—right before Evelyn almost did me in the second time."

He looked at me skeptically. "Isn't it time for you to walk some? I thought you were supposed to get up for ten minutes out of every hour." He picked up my robe—the floweredy silk kimono—and stuck out his arm for me to pull myself up by. Once we were out in the hall and past the nurses' station, he said, "All right. Come on. Tell me how you had it figured out. Or was it just female intuition?"

"Empirical evidence," I said breathlessly. "Can't we slow down?"

He looked at me with a mixture of pity and impatience, but I didn't continue with my explanation till we got to the end of the corridor. I leaned against the window and looked out at the world, steaming in the late August sun after the rain.

"All right," he said. "Let's have it."

"The thump," I said. "The thump Cecelia heard. And the door."

He frowned. "It couldn't have been Archie. He had already taken off for town."

"No. It was Evelyn. Cecelia came home earlier than expected, while Evelyn was still trying to get the oxygen equipment back to its normal state. In her hurry to reconnect the cannula, she knocked the tank over. She knew Cecelia would have heard the thump. She had to get out of there quick so she left by the east porch door. She must not have even had time to readjust the knobs on the tank and had to wait till she and Bud came back later for a chance to check the tank out. Remember? Cecelia couldn't find it that night for the j.p. I'm sure Evelyn had moved it. Then, of course, Evelyn volunteered Bud to return it Monday morning. No one else ever looked at it again."

Norton took me by the arm and started us back up the corridor. "And just how do you know that? That's all supposition."

"The next day I used the east porch door myself, to

avoid going through the kitchen, right after Uncle Larry and his wife had arrived. As I was leaving, Evelyn told me to make sure the door closed securely so it wouldn't bang in the wind. Yet only the night before when they were taking Miss Mineola's body away, Lois had said something about the door being stuck. Ordinarily it is hard to get open. But the long dry spell had shrunk the wood. It was Evelyn who told me to be careful that the latch caught. That's because she was the only one who had used it recently—the only one who knew it wasn't stuck."

I tried not to look smug. I really did. And he tried to sound magnanimous. But "Well!" was all he said.

"Why didn't I notice that earlier?" I said with a sigh as I collapsed onto the bed again.

"It might have saved us all a lot of trouble," he agreed. "And you might be feeling a lot spryer today."

I looked up at him. "Would you have noticed that remark about the door and put it all together?" I asked. "Be honest."

His little fawn mustache twitched a time or two. He opened his mouth and then shut it again.

"I wouldn't want to complicate things," he said.